"It's not hard to predict a brilliant future for this quirky new series!"
—Kari Lee Townsend, national bestselling author

DAWN EASTMAN

National Bestselling Author of *Be Careful What You Witch For*

BERKLEY
PRIME
CRIME
$7.99 U.S.
$9.99 CAN

S
EAN

ISBN 978-0-425-26448-5
9 780425 264485
50799

Praise for the Family Fortune Mysteries

Be Careful What You Witch For

"A delightful series with memorable characters, supernatural elements, and laugh-out-loud humor that will have you clamoring for more."
—*Books-n-Kisses*

"An entertaining cozy mystery with just the right amount of humor, paranormal woo-woo, and romance to shake things up. Enjoyable!"
—*Book of Secrets*

"The author shows no sign of a sophomore slump . . . and readers will find themselves experiencing moments of genuine sympathy and empathy for those very grounded and likable characters."
—*Kings River Life Magazine*

Pall in the Family

"A tightly plotted, character-driven triumph of a mystery, *Pall in the Family* had me laughing out loud while feverishly turning pages to try to figure out whodunit. This novel sparkles with charmingly peculiar characters and a fascinating heroine, Clyde Fortune, who effortlessly shuffles the reader into her world like a card in a tarot deck. Eastman is fabulous!"
—Jenn McKinlay, *New York Times* bestselling author of the Library Lover's Mysteries, the Cupcake Bakery Mysteries, and the Hat Shop Mysteries

continued . . .

"A kooky small town filled with eccentric characters, psychics, and murder make Eastman's Family Fortune Mystery series a stellar launch. Add a dog-walking ex-cop paired with her old-flame investigator, and it's not hard to predict a brilliant future for this quirky new series!"

—Kari Lee Townsend, national bestselling
author of the Fortune Teller Mysteries
and the Mind Reader Mysteries

"What emerges as most entertaining in this mystery by debut author Dawn Eastman is how well she slowly develops her characters and prevents them from being two-dimensional caricatures . . . The paranormal aspect is surprisingly realistic and matter-of-fact amongst the townspeople . . . Clyde proves to be a talented investigator herself with or without her 'extra' skills, and she is a very likable heroine with the humor to cope with her eccentric relatives." —*Kings River Life Magazine*

"[An] entertaining read . . . The cast of characters is a lovable bunch of kooky psychics." —*RT Book Reviews*

"Awesome new series alert! . . . I highly recommend picking up *Pall in the Family*." —*Cozy Mystery Book Reviews*

"I enjoyed this book from cover to cover . . . A must-read!"
—*My Book Addiction Reviews*

"A kooky read from start to finish . . . Eastman's character development is exceptional and the incorporation of animals made this book not only fun to figure out but also very entertaining. The psychic theme is thoroughly researched and adds another dimension to this charming whodunit."
—*Debbie's Book Bag*

Berkley Prime Crime titles by Dawn Eastman

PALL IN THE FAMILY
BE CAREFUL WHAT YOU WITCH FOR
A FRIGHT TO THE DEATH

A Fright to the Death

DAWN EASTMAN

BERKLEY PRIME CRIME, NEW YORK

THE BERKLEY PUBLISHING GROUP
Published by the Penguin Group
Penguin Group (USA) LLC
375 Hudson Street, New York, New York 10014

USA • Canada • UK • Ireland • Australia • New Zealand • India • South Africa • China

penguin.com

A Penguin Random House Company

A FRIGHT TO THE DEATH

A Berkley Prime Crime Book / published by arrangement with the author

For information, address: The Berkley Publishing Group,
a division of Penguin Group (USA) LLC,
375 Hudson Street, New York, New York 10014.

ISBN: 978-0-425-26448-5

PUBLISHING HISTORY
Berkley Prime Crime mass-market edition / April 2015

PRINTED IN THE UNITED STATES OF AMERICA

10 9 8 7 6 5 4 3 2 1

Cover illustration by Daniel Craig; design element © iStockphoto/Thinkstock.
Cover design by Judith Lagerman.

For Steve, my patron of the arts.

Acknowledgments

I am very fortunate to be able to work with the Berkley Prime Crime publishing team.

Many thanks go to my editors, Andie Avila and Katherine Pelz. Andie has nurtured these characters and this writer through three books. Nonc of us would be the same without her and I will always be grateful for her friendship. Katherine is new to Team Family Fortune—hcr cnthusiasm for these characters is awesome and I look forward to crafting more adventures with her.

A huge thank-you to Judith Lagerman and Daniel Craig for their work on the covers for the series. My favorite part of the production process is the cover reveal. Each time I think that they can't possibly create a cover as wonderful as the one before—and then they do.

I also want to thank Danielle Dill in publicity for getting the books into the right hands and helping to spread the word about the Family Fortune series.

Special thanks go to my writing group, Wendy Delsol, Kimberly Stuart, Kali Van Baale, and Carol Spaulding. Their encouragement, humor, and friendship help me to keep putting words on the page. A special shout-out to Murl Pace, self-appointed Baxter fan club president and early champion of the series.

Thank you to my street team, otherwise known as my family, Ann and Bob Eastman, Barb Laughlin, Brent and Nancy Eastman, Jim and Alyce Mooradian, and Kristin Morton. If you have been forced to accept a card touting the series, you have met one of them.

And, as always, I am grateful to Steve, Jake, and Ellie for tolerating a writer in their midst, and for making each day fun.

1

I knew Mac scoffed at all things psychic, but why must he taunt the fates?

"I can't believe we're finally getting away," he said with a boyish grin and took my hand. "This is going to be fantastic."

I smiled and hoped he would stop talking. The man had no sense of jinxes and self-preservation. We were barely twenty minutes down the snowy tree-lined highway away from Crystal Haven. Away from my parents, my aunt, his mother, my nephew, and two spoiled dogs. The back-patting phase of the trip sat happily in our future. Sometime after I had returned to my small Victorian, Mac had returned to his cottage, and we had shared the photos with our inquisitive families. We had decided to take my new Tahoe on the trip. Mac's pickup truck and my ancient Jeep seemed inappropriate for a potentially icy drive to Chicago. The unfamiliar vehicle made it feel like we were already far from home.

I looked out the window at the gray sky of a Michigan winter. It had snowed almost daily in January. Mac and I got through it by plotting our escape over a few chilly evenings as the white fluff had piled up outside.

I wasn't just excited to get away—I was desperate. Between Mac's job as a homicide detective, my live-in teenage nephew, and the rest of my interfering family that lived a stone's throw away and had no qualms about stopping by, we had little time to spend alone together. Plus, the pressure to either return to my own police career or find a new job that didn't involve walking dogs increased daily. I was more than ready to escape my everyday life and all I wanted was to step off that airplane in Mexico with Mac, alone. I craved it so badly that I felt certain I might hex it. What can I say? A life with psychics and tarot readers had instilled a strong superstitious streak. And the longer I stayed in Crystal Haven, the worse it got.

But, we were together. Finally. And we were about to jet away from winter for a week. Ignoring caution to join his reckless glee, I said, "What should we do first when we get there?"

Mac ticked an eyebrow upward in an exaggerated leer. His blue eyes sparkled and the lines around his eyes deepened. He spent so much of his life keeping every emotion in check that I cherished the moments he relaxed and allowed his humor to take center stage.

"Oh, nice. I walked into that one." I laughed, relaxing in my seat. I reached for my phone as it buzzed in my pocket. "*After* that," I said as I clicked the phone open.

My grin faded and my mood nosedived when I saw the message.

"Mac, pull over up here." I pointed to an exit just outside of Kalamazoo.

Mac turned away from the road long enough to see the concern on my face. He glanced at the phone in my hand and flicked the turn signal. "Was that Seth? Is something wrong?"

I shook my head. I *wished* it were from my nephew, Seth.

"The text was from the airline. Our flight got canceled. It says due to weather."

Mac pulled into a gas station parking lot and turned off the ignition. I looked out the windshield at the leaden gray sky releasing a few small snowflakes. Channel 8's weather guy hadn't said there was going to be a bad storm. Maybe we could take another flight. The high-pitched ping of the rapidly cooling engine broke the silence. I immediately tried to pull up the airline's website on my phone.

Mac leaned back and rubbed his jaw, staring out the window. "I was really looking forward to getting away from this." His gesture encompassed everything outside of the car. "And having a break from your family," he said quietly.

I looked away from my phone and put my hand on his shoulder. "I know. Me, too. I'm pretty sick of snow. And I know my family has been a handful. I'm tired of them, too."

Living in Crystal Haven, a town full of psychics, had its unique set of drawbacks. And so did growing up in a family that made its livelihood off of psychic messages and tarot cards.

"I'm checking to see if there are other flights. Hope is not lost." I waved my phone at him. I was waiting for the website to load when Mac opened the door and startled me.

"Let's go inside and regroup," he said.

I followed, thinking that it was typical of our luck that our vacation would consist of diet soda and popcorn in a roadside gas station. I thought I heard the fates giggling.

2

The balding, chubby proprietor smiled at us as we entered. Mac made a beeline for the cheddar popcorn, his go-to stress indulgence. I grabbed a diet soda and a package of almonds.

"Did it say when they might reschedule?" Mac asked. He put an arm around my shoulder, leaned down, and squinted at my phone as we walked to the counter.

I shook my head. "No, and I can't load the airline website."

We placed our items on the counter and the man began scanning them into the register.

"I hope you two are headed home before the storm hits," he said.

Mac and I exchanged a worried glance.

Mac handed over a twenty. "Storm?"

The man looked at us over his glasses. He turned his small TV to face us. The sound was muted, but we saw the news crawl along the bottom of the screen: BLIZZARD WARNING.

"They say Chicago's already socked in. Airport's closed and the roads are packed with people trying to get home. It should be here in a couple of hours." His voice held a note of excitement at being able to break the news.

I was leaning into Mac and felt him go very still. My own shoulders slumped as I saw our vacation dissolve.

The man smiled kindly at me. "You were headed to Chicago?" He slid Mac's change across the counter.

I nodded, and swallowed hard.

Mac pocketed his money, slung an arm across my shoulders, and steered me out of the store. As the door closed behind us, he leaned close to my ear and whispered, "I have a plan."

I stopped walking, which forced him to turn to look at me. "A plan?" I asked. Mac definitely had a romantic side, but I expected romance along the Mexican seashore, not along Route 131. When did he come up with a plan?

He moved his arm down to settle around my waist. "Just relax, I've got this."

He opened my door for me and swept his arm out to gesture me inside. He bowed slightly before swinging the door closed. I grinned and sat back in my seat, excited now by the new adventure.

I opened the weather app on my phone and scrolled through the many warnings and alerts caused by the snow currently pounding Chicago. A storm in Chicago would often head across Lake Michigan and slam into the west coast of Michigan. So while Chicago was digging out, we would be hunkering down to wait out the weather.

"They're saying we should start seeing serious snow by later this afternoon." I shut my phone off.

"We'll be safe and dry by then but *not* in Crystal Haven," Mac said.

I sat back and watched the white landscape scroll past my window. My attempts at questioning were met with off-key humming. Even though I'd grown up in Crystal Haven, I didn't know the Kalamazoo area very well and had no idea where he planned to take us.

Twenty minutes and miles of white fields and forests later we were nowhere near anything that looked like a city. We passed a sporting goods store touting the exciting sport of ice fishing and snowmobile rentals. Mac pulled down a dirt road that headed into dense woods. I hoped he wasn't planning to camp, even if a cozy cabin was involved. We routinely lost power during storms even in Crystal Haven; I could imagine what a cabin in the woods in February would be like.

"Mac . . . ," I said, and couldn't quite hide the nervous quaver.

He steered the car around a corner, the trees gave way to a wide clearing, and a beautiful snowcapped castle appeared. Its windows glowed gold in the afternoon gloom. Big wet snowflakes had begun to fall and added to the charm. It sat on a hill above us and as Mac followed the road that took us around to the back parking area, I leaned forward to get a better look out the front window.

It was big, but not enormous like some of the European castles I'd seen in books. It sported a large tower turret on the front and smaller turrets sticking off the side of the bigger one—with a wraparound porch and pointed roofline.

"What is this place?"

"*This* is Carlisle Castle," Mac said. "It was built by a furniture tycoon during the late 1800s. It's still owned by the same family and they converted it into a hotel about ten years ago. What do you think?"

Snow-covered and surrounded by tall pines, it looked like a storybook Christmas castle. Maybe I had misjudged Mac's planning-on-the-fly abilities. I smiled and squeezed his hand.

"Who needs Mexico?" I said. "This definitely makes up for the canceled flight. How did you know about it? Do you think they'll have a room?"

"I saw a brochure back at the gas station and remembered someone mentioning it," Mac said. "It didn't occur to me that it would be full. . . ."

The full parking lot ramped up my concern. Mac pulled in and found a spot as far from the entrance as possible.

We exited the car and looked up at the castle. Mac stood behind me with his arms around my waist. "It's not Mexico," he said, "but it's not Crystal Haven, either."

We headed toward the entrance holding hands. I glanced down the row of vehicles and saw an orange smart car. It looked just like my mom's. I shrugged off a brief flash of worry and followed Mac through the rapidly falling snow.

Inside, the entryway glowed from Victorian lamps reflecting off the dark wood of the front desk, tucked beneath a wide curving staircase. I imagined a cozy weekend with Mac, curled up by the fire—surely there was a fireplace somewhere—and *not* dealing with dogs, nephews, parents, aunts, or anyone but Mac. We shook the snow off our coats and stamped our feet.

At the desk, a young man smiled at us from behind a laptop and Tiffany lamp.

"Hello, welcome to Carlisle Castle," he said. His name tag read: WALLACE PRESCOTT. He wore round glasses, a bow tie, and a thatch of dark hair flopped over one eye. "Whoa, cool!" he said as I stopped in front of the desk. "Your eyes are two different colors!" Wallace pointed at my eyes and squinted his own as he examined me. He wasn't the first person to announce it to me as if I hadn't noticed in the past thirty years that one eye was bright blue, the other brown.

Mac cleared his throat and Wallace seemed to remember that staring at the customers was not in his job description. Mac asked about a room for the weekend.

Wallace's smile fled. "I'm sorry, we're completely booked. We have a group here this weekend and all the rooms are taken. . . ." Wallace clicked on his laptop but shook his head the whole time.

"Let me check some other nearby hotels for you. I looked at the weather channel before you came in and they say once the snow starts we'll get two inches an hour."

Just as Mac turned to me to discuss our predicament, we heard, "I knew it!"

I felt Mac stiffen next to me as my stomach dropped. We both turned in the direction of the voice and, as I had already surmised, there stood my Aunt Vi. At five foot two, she was shorter than me by several inches. She wore her gray hair in a long braid down her back and favored brightly colored skirts with layers of cardigans. Like my mother, she was in her seventies, but refused to acknowledge it.

"I just had a feeling your flight would be canceled," Vi said as she rushed toward us. "This is a great place, don't you think?" She waved her arms to encompass the entire castle. "I can't believe you came *here*! Are you staying for the whole weekend? This'll be a hoot! Wait 'til I tell your mom and Lucille."

"Lucille?" I squeaked.

Vi cocked her head at me. "Remember I said I was going to ask her to come with us since she's such a good knitter?"

Mac turned to me, his eyes a bit wild.

"My *mother* is here?" he said.

It came back to me in snippets. I'd been so excited about *my* escape from a snow-covered and frozen Crystal Haven that I hadn't paid much attention. I remembered talk about yarn and knitting classes and how my dad and my nephew, Seth, would have a boys' weekend . . .

"The knitting conference is . . . here?" I asked.

Vi nodded and grinned. "You should see this place, Clyde, it's so . . . *castle-y.* Wally here will give you a tour." She nodded toward Wallace.

"Ms. Greer, I don't have a room for them," Wallace said. "And it's Wallace." He pointed to his name tag. She looked him up and down and then turned away.

"Oh, don't worry," she said. "They can stay with us. Rose and I have double beds and Lucille has two twins in her room. Clyde can stay with us and Mac can stay with Lucille. It'll be great!"

Mac and I exchanged a terrified glance. Vi was unstoppable when she got an idea in her head and we both felt the tide of this vacation washing farther out to sea.

"We can't impose like that, Vi," I began. "Wallace was just checking some other hotels . . ."

Vi shook her head and crossed her arms. "Nonsense. Have you looked out there?" She gestured at the window. "You'll never get anywhere and then you'll be stuck in the woods in a blizzard." She pointed a knobby finger at me. "No. You can stay here at least until the weather clears. It's really no bother." She put her hand on Mac's arm.

Mac and I looked outside to see heavy flakes pouring down.

Wally cleared his throat and said, "Sometimes the road does become impassable in a bad storm."

"Let me just talk to Mac," I said and we walked a few steps away from the desk.

Vi crossed her arms and tapped her foot.

I put my hand on his back and turned away from our audience. "What do you think?"

Mac pressed his lips together and then let out a breath of air. "Well, it's the exact opposite of the way I thought I'd be spending the evening, but I'd hate to get stranded on the road somewhere."

I snuck a look at Vi over Mac's shoulder. "We can stand it for one night and we'll figure out where to go in the morning. How long can a snowstorm last, right?"

We walked back to the desk and I nodded to Vi and Wally.

"You make a good case for safety," Mac said. "We'll stay tonight."

Vi clapped her hands and grinned.

"How about that tour, Wally?" Vi asked. "I'll come along. I have a few questions. Plus I want to hear about the ghost again."

"Ghost?" Mac said.

Vi nodded. "It's a great story. I'm trying to talk the knitters into doing a séance. Come on, let's go!"

Wally hurried out from behind the desk in an attempt to take control of the tour. He smoothed his jacket, and smiled at us.

Mac took my hand and glanced longingly at the door. We heard it rattle on its hinges as a gust of wind struck it full force.

3

Our guide led us toward the back of the hotel and to the right, where we came to a restaurant surrounded by windows. It had the feel of a greenhouse except today everything was white outside. Small tables were scattered about the room. Black tablecloths topped with white squares lent a more cosmopolitan feel to the space than I had expected. The walls displayed black-and-white photos of Paris, and the large windows shared a view of the back of the property, which sloped down toward the woods. The snow was picking up and any lingering thoughts of escaping the knitters' convention fled as I watched it fall.

"This is our restaurant." Wally swept his arm in the direction of the dining room. "Complimentary breakfast is here from seven until ten. Usually we recommend reservations for dinner, but I don't think that will be a problem today." He chuckled and then turned it into a cough when no one joined him.

Wally led us out of the dining room and gestured toward a hallway outside the door and said that it led to the kitchen and offices. He took us to the back door, where a small area had been fitted with hooks for coats.

"Sometimes our guests prefer to leave coats and such here so they can grab them quickly if they want to enjoy the gardens." Wally pointed to the coats, scarves, and hats hanging on hooks—it looked like there were quite a few knitters here if the amount of outerwear was any indication.

I didn't imagine we would choose to enjoy the gardens on our brief stay during a blizzard, but we shrugged out of our jackets and found hooks for them. Mac took a slim envelope out of his inside coat pocket. I saw my name scrawled on the front. He folded it and stuffed it in his back jeans pocket without looking at me.

Mac felt more comfortable expressing himself in writing and I had been the recipient of a whole box full of notes over the years. I decided to pretend I hadn't seen it and let him give it to me when he felt the time was right. But I did wonder what could be so difficult to say that he had brought a letter with him on vacation.

We followed Wally back out toward the front and to the other side of the entry hall. This was the room I'd imagined when we'd first pulled up to the building. Rich mahogany wainscoting and subtly patterned wallpaper made the room feel cozy. Dark reds and greens accented the deep leather couches and chairs placed about the room in conversational arrangements. Worn Persian rugs anchored the seating areas. Heavy red velvet curtains looked as if they could insulate the room from any storm. An enormous fireplace with a bright and cheerful fire glowing within beckoned me toward the couch.

I sighed and squeezed Mac's hand, for the moment forgetting that we were leaving as soon as possible.

"Isn't this terrific?" Vi said in my ear.

I glanced upward in a reflex eye roll and saw something pink on the chandelier.

"What's that?" I pointed.

"You spotted it!" Vi said. She patted my back.

Wally rubbed the back of his neck and shook his head.

"Spotted what?" Mac craned his neck upward to see what we were looking at.

I noticed that it wasn't just something pink. It was also something purple and teal and lime green. Every arm of the beautiful crystal chandelier had a small tube of knitting attached.

"Yarn bombing," Vi said. She crossed her arms and nodded decisively.

"What bombing?" Mac said.

"It's a knitter thing," Vi said, and patted his arm in a reassuring way. I was pretty sure no one had patted Mac's arm in a reassuring way in many years. "When a bunch of knitters get together we just have to show off. There's a contest for the most interesting and difficult yarn bomb. It's supposed to be a secret until the last day when each knitter takes credit for her pieces. So you'll see lots of little knitted items all over the castle this weekend. This one wasn't easy to pull off. They must have gotten the maintenance guy involved. . . ." Vi walked in circles under the chandelier to get a better look at the knitting. "I would have liked to see that. He's a hottie."

"Are these normal knitters?" Mac whispered to me. I shrugged and moved a little closer to him. He moved his hand from the small of my back and put his arm around my shoulders.

Wally cleared his throat and gestured toward the door.

Mac and I followed quickly. I reconsidered the idea of braving the storm to go anywhere else.

We walked to the front of the hotel again and up the wide, dark wood staircase. Just as in the lounge, mahogany wainscoting gave way to Victorian-style wallpaper halfway up the wall. Torches had been placed along the hallway every ten feet or so. Fortunately, they were electric, but the effect was still one of walking into the past. We turned the corner at the top of the staircase and the sensation intensified. Tapestries hung from the walls and a large stained glass window loomed at the end of the hall. The weak outside light was unable to do it justice. I was no expert on antiques, but if any of the décor was as old as it looked, the furnishings alone must be worth a fortune.

Wally led us down the hall that ran along the front of the building. His description of the paintings, tapestries, and sculptures solidified the sense that we were in a uniquely preserved Victorian mansion.

"Here's your room, Ms. Fortune." He pointed to the left. "Mr. McKenzie, you'll be in here." He showed Mac the room two doors down. Wally pointed to the end of the hallway. "And that door leads to the turret room." His voice became quiet and his expression indicated we should know what he meant by "turret room."

"Tell them the ghost story," Vi said while bouncing on her toes like a six-year-old.

Wally lowered his voice. "Ms. Greer, I don't think I should have told you that story. I don't know if Ms. Carlisle wants to advertise the ghost."

"Oh, come on, Wally." Vi gave him a good slug in the arm. "Everyone in Kalamazoo has heard the story. There's no way she's going to get everyone to *un*-hear it."

He sighed and rubbed his arm. He glanced over his shoulder. "Okay, but not here, she might hear us."

Mac sighed.

"The ghost?" I whispered. I didn't believe in ghosts, per se, but in my anti-jinx state of mind decided to keep that to myself.

Wally shook his head. "Ms. Carlisle."

"Let's go in here," Vi said. She led us to her door. "All the rooms are decorated in a different theme. We got the red Victorian room—it's the best." She glanced at Mac. "Yours is good, too. Green, I think." She took her key and opened the door, gesturing us inside.

Mac hadn't said a word, which indicated his level of shock that his plans had fallen apart so completely. Wally sheepishly followed Vi inside before shutting the door behind us.

The room was larger than I'd expected, and definitely red. And Victorian. Dark, carved wooden headboards loomed over the two beds. Red and white floral bedspreads matched the curtains, swags, and tassels that framed the windows. I crossed to the small sitting area and a window that faced the back of the property. Snowcapped fir trees and white-outlined branches were just visible through the falling flakes. The tops of the cars had disappeared under a blanket of white.

"You can have that bed," Vi said. She pointed to the bed nearest the window. She stood next to me and looked out. "It's getting pretty bad out there." She turned and rubbed her hands together. "I'll have to empty one of the drawers. I brought a lot of yarn, but I can store it downstairs where we have the workshop."

Mom's tarot cards covered the coffee table in her standard pattern. I looked away, not wanting to know what dire predictions they held. Vi had evidently been using the pendulum and it sat waiting in the middle of its yes-no cross. Wally's eyes darted around the room.

"Okay, tell us." Vi sat in an armchair and gestured at the rest of us to sit.

"All right, but I have to make it quick," Wally said. "I'm supposed to be at the front desk."

Vi shook her head. "I don't think you'll get any more customers today." She waved her arm toward the window and the full-on winter storm that raged outside.

Wally's mouth tightened at the corners. He took a deep breath. "Alastair Carlisle built the castle in 1895, after a trip to Scotland. He and his wife, Ada, had fallen in love with the castles over there and wanted to build one of their own. Ada had inherited a large piece of forested land from her father, and the two of them designed the house together using her land and his money."

Vi waved her hand in a move-along gesture.

Wally grimaced and continued.

"During the five years it took to build the castle, Ada fell ill. By the time it was completed, she was essentially bedridden. The couple had two small boys and needed to hire a governess to watch them and begin their schooling. Alastair built a small cottage on the grounds for the governess and designed the turret bedroom for his wife."

"You can probably tell where this story is going," Vi broke in. "Mr. Carlisle and the governess had an affair and thought that his invalid wife would never be the wiser."

"I was getting to that." Wally cleared his throat. "And there's no proof . . ."

"Well, Ada was no dummy," Vi said, ignoring him. "Even though she was sick, it didn't mean she was stupid. She figured out what he was up to and she was *furious*."

Wally opened his mouth to continue the story.

Vi held up her hand. "She had nothing to do up in her turret room other than knit and contemplate her own death and feel betrayed by her husband," Vi said. "So, she hatched a plan."

"We don't know that, Ms. Greer," Wally said.

Vi crossed her arms, and narrowed her eyes at him. "The rumors say she told the nanny she had put a curse on her. The Victorians were very interested in spirits and many believed in ghosts. Mrs. Carlisle said if anything happened to her, she would return and curse the nanny and her husband." Vi nodded to Wally to tell his part of the tale.

Wally continued. "According to the story, by the time the castle was finished, Ada and Alastair were barely speaking. Her illness left her confined to her room, where she heard about the happenings in the castle from her trusted maid. The governess took over the care of the young boys and eventually," Wally said and paused with a severe look at Vi, "*rumors said*, Alastair fell in love with her."

Vi nodded to encourage him.

"One night, in the dead of winter, Ada drowned in her own bathtub," Wally said. "She had sent the maid to get some hot cocoa and by the time the servant returned, Ada was dead. Of course, there was an investigation, but they found no evidence of foul play. The police assumed she had passed out from her liberal use of narcotics and drowned by accident."

"Narcotics?" Mac asked.

Wally nodded, and began to speak when Vi interrupted again. "Calm down, Kojack. They all took laudanum back then." She waved her hand dismissively. "It wasn't like she was dealing drugs."

I placed a calming hand on Mac's arm. Not that I needed

to. There were many things I loved about Mac, but his restraint in dealing with Vi was definitely at the top of my list.

Wally raised his eyebrows at Vi.

Vi ignored him and took over the story. "Since then, rumors have flown and people say that Alastair or the nanny actually killed her off so they could be together. Her ghost looks out the upper window of the turret room and some people have seen it wandering the halls and climbing the stairs."

"Why would her ghost be walking the halls if she was bedbound?" I said.

Vi held my gaze. "You know as well as I do that ghosts can do anything they want—it's one of the perks of being a ghost."

"I hadn't realized there were perks . . . ," I said.

Mac cleared his throat and glowered at us both.

Vi resumed her tale. "Tragically, the nanny died about a year later. She had moved in to the main house and she fell down the stairs on a perfectly clear night. No one knows why she was out of bed, or what she was doing wandering the halls. The people in town said it was the ghost of Mrs. Carlisle who pushed her. Alastair never got over the double loss of his wife and his mistress."

"Alleged mistress," Wally said.

Vi narrowed her eyes at him.

"Alleged mistress," Vi said. "The boys grew up and had their own scandals. Prohibition was very lucrative—"

Wally stood, interrupting her. "I really need to get back to the desk. I'll let the chef know there will be two more for dinner."

"This is gonna be great!" Vi said.

4

After Wally left, Violet dragged Mac and me back downstairs to meet the knitters and to let Lucille know the "good news" that she and Mac would be sharing a room.

The knitters were ensconced in the library toward the back of the hotel. Vi led us to the doorway and swung her arm to usher us in. Mac stood motionless in the doorway and I bumped into him. I peeked over his shoulder to see what had stopped him.

The room held more yarn than I had ever seen in my life. I had been to many yarn stores as a child when Violet had dragged me along on her shopping trips, but this was overwhelming. Skeins and balls of yarn congregated in soft, fuzzy piles. Eight women sat scattered around the room, all holding a piece of knitting while a very attractive instructor spoke in that strange knitterly language. She said things like "keep your tension steady," "don't forget the yarnover in the middle of the fourth row," and "I have a great new cable needle to try, plus I'll show you how to cable without a needle—you'll love the freedom."

The library was smaller than the lounge, with a scaled-down fireplace and walls covered in bookshelves. Ornate Victorian wallpaper in bright green and blue covered whatever wall space was left. Two small couches and several chairs made a conversational arrangement in the center of the room. It still retained the masculine aura of pipe smoke, whiskey, and leather, and must have been Alastair's personal refuge. He likely would have been outraged by the invasion of fluffy balls of mohair. The knitters had dragged in some dining room chairs to accommodate their group. A wall of windows showed large flakes settling on the trees.

Mac seemed paralyzed and I pushed him to get him to move into the room. Either our tussling or Vi's loud "ahem" caught the interest of the knitters. They all turned in our direction.

Mom jumped up, letting her knitting fall to the floor.

"Clyde! Mac! What are you doing here?" Mom said as she approached. "Is something wrong? Is Seth okay? Is it your father?" She clutched my arm, and her forehead crinkled in dismay. "The cards warned me that something terrible would happen this weekend. . . ."

She and Vi shared similar delicate features but rather than a braid and brightly colored skirts, Mom pulled her hair back in a bun and favored either tracksuits (she had one in every color) or khakis and blouses.

"Mom, everyone is fine. Our flight was canceled and we came here to stay because of the storm."

Mom relaxed her grip on my arm, and a smile spread across her face. "Oh, how fun! You can finally learn to knit. Lucille was just saying how she thinks you're a natural." Mom leaned closer to me and lowered her voice. "I didn't want to burst her bubble and tell her you don't like knitting."

Lucille had joined us at the door by this time. She was my height, very thin, and wore her silver hair short and spiky. She turned to Mac and said, "Phillip, I'm so glad to see you. I was worried about you flying in the storm."

Mac's face turned a bit pink as it always did when his mother called him Phillip.

"Hi, Mom," he said.

Two of the other knitters, about the same age as Mom, Vi, and Lucille had joined us at the door. The younger ones showed a bit more decorum and remained in their seats. One of them had tattoos snaking up both arms, one sported hot pink spiky hair, and the other looked like a human Tinkerbell—tiny with a blond pixie cut.

"Oh, Lucille. Is this your son?" a short round woman with bright red lipstick on her lips and teeth asked. "He's much more handsome than you said." She batted her eyes at Mac.

Mac stepped back, onto my foot, and recovered by draping an arm over my shoulder. Lucille introduced the woman as Mavis Poulson and claimed Mac as her son. Mavis looked me over and returned to her seat without further comment. Her friend, Selma Stone, thin, tall, and entirely beige, shook my hand and then followed Mavis back to her seat.

The other knitters said hello and I quickly forgot their names in the sea of comments and yarn.

"Okay everyone, let's get back to our projects!" The instructor clapped her hands. "We only have a few more minutes to work on them before dinner."

She walked over to us and smiled. "Hello. I'm Isabel Keane." She was petite, with short dark hair and large, expressive eyes. She had tossed a multicolored scarf artfully around her neck.

She shook my hand briefly and then took Mac's hand and held on to it.

"It's lovely to meet you . . . both," she said.

Mom, Vi, and Lucille had returned to their chairs as instructed. Isabel asked us if we'd like to join them in a knitting lesson.

Mac shook his head. We smiled and backed out of the room.

"I don't know if I can do this for the whole weekend," Mac said. "My mother is here and that woman looked at me like I was dessert."

"I noticed. She's very pretty."

"Who?"

"Isabel."

"No, not her. Mavis—with the lipstick."

I smiled. "Oh, her. I don't think you have anything to worry about. I'm sure you can outrun her."

"Let's go talk to Wally and see when this storm is supposed to end. Maybe we can book another hotel and leave first thing in the morning."

He steered me back toward the front of the building. We stopped when we got to the turn in the hallway.

"Any idiot could do your job—I don't know why you can't!" a shrill voice announced from around the corner. "You must be a special kind of idiot."

I glanced at Mac. I didn't want to embarrass whoever was being yelled at by walking in on this scolding, but I wanted to stop it as well. Mac and I nodded at each other and swung around the corner. A young woman in a maid's uniform stood alone in the hall but I caught a glimpse of shiny black heels as they went up a nearby staircase.

The woman scrubbed at her eyes and turned away from us as we approached.

"Are you okay?" I said to her.

She nodded and sniffed. "I'm fine, ma'am. Thank you."

She smoothed her skirt and walked down the hallway away from the stairway.

Mac sighed and shook his head. "Let's go." He tugged on my arm as I watched the young woman turn the corner at the end of the hall.

Wally clacked away on his keyboard as we approached. He flipped it shut when he spotted us.

"How can I help you?"

"Do you have a weather report?" Mac asked.

"I just checked the radar." Wally shook his head. "It doesn't look good. High winds and more snow tonight. They say it will be blizzard conditions in another hour or so."

The wind rattled the windows to punctuate Wally's claim.

Mac slumped. "How long is it supposed to last?"

"They say it could blow through overnight, unless it meets another storm front they're watching from the south. If they meet, the whole thing could stall right over us and then they don't know how long it will last. The newspeople are saying everyone should check their supplies and stay off the roads."

I glanced at Mac and felt my shoulders droop.

Mac's grimace reflected my own emotions. When would we escape?

"We're having a cocktail party tonight to kick off the knitting conference and Isabel Keane's new book. I'm sure you'd both be welcome," Wally said. He tilted his head and gave a sympathetic smile.

Mac blew out air, but then pulled himself to his full height. "I'll go grab our suitcases before the weather gets even worse."

"I'll help you." Wally hurried from behind the desk.

"Thank you," I said. I followed them to the back door, where they donned coats and hats. The snow crunched underfoot as they stepped into the parking lot. A gust of wind almost pulled the door out of my grasp and I wrestled it closed as they made their way to my SUV.

Other than my toothbrush, there was very little in my Mexico suitcase that would be useful in a snowbound castle. I had the jeans I was wearing and one other long-sleeved T-shirt I had planned to wear on the plane ride home. The rest was swimsuits, shorts, and tank tops.

I opened the door again when I heard them approach. Stepping back, I barely avoided the spray of snow as they brushed it off while still outside.

"I'll set these in your rooms while you're in the lounge—unless you need something." Snapping open the pull handles on the suitcases, Wally nodded toward the stairs.

Mac echoed my thoughts and said, "I'm not sure I'll use any of it here—we were headed to warmer weather."

Wally dragged the wheeled suitcases down the hall. Mac pulled me into a side hug and dropped his voice. "I think I'm going to need a drink to get through the rest of the evening."

5

We approached the lounge and peeked inside. Women were scattered throughout the room with drinks and balls of yarn. Apparently the knitting wasn't limited to the workshop room.

Mac and I took a deep breath and squared our shoulders.

"There you are!" Mom said when she spotted us.

Mac nodded to her and planted a kiss on the top of my head before heading to the drinks table. I held onto his hand as he walked away, feeling that this was the last moment of any semblance of a vacation. I turned to my mom with a forced smile.

She leaned toward me and said, "Vi is going to tell you that she *knew* your flight would be canceled, but that's just because the tarot had indicated that something would happen to ruin your trip." She used her I'm-sorry-things-didn't-go-as-planned smile. She patted my shoulder. "I'm sure you and Mac can take another trip. And I'd rather you were safe. If I thought you were on an airplane in this kind of weather . . ." She put a hand to her chest in a dramatic display of distress.

A few months ago, Mom's constant worry would have irritated, but now I understood its roots. Neila Whittle, who was helping me understand my own psychic gifts, had once predicted that Mom would attend a funeral for one of her children. It was Neila's dubious talent to sense when a parent might lose a child.

I had yet to discuss Neila with my mother—unsure if she would be thrilled I was pursuing my gifts or furious I was spending time with Neila. As if proximity would make her prediction come true. But Neila had helped me and I felt I was finally gaining control of some of the premonitions that came unbidden in dreams or flashes of history when touching an object, and I was better able to find lost items. For whatever that was worth.

Mac caught my eye from across the room and held up a glass. I nodded gratefully and he turned to fix my drink.

Thoughts of Neila reminded me that I was supposed to practice whenever possible. A room full of strangers was a great opportunity to test my skills. My insights are enhanced through touch—mostly skin-to-skin contact. In my days with the police it was often difficult to maneuver that type of contact. Officers don't tend to shake hands with suspects. But the information, if it came, was invaluable and I trusted it.

I brought my thoughts back to my mom, who was looking at me expectantly.

"Sorry, Mom, what did you say?"

She grinned. "You can't keep your eyes off him, can you?"

"Pardon?"

"Mac. You're aware of every move he makes."

I felt my face growing hot. "I don't know what you mean." I studied her brightly colored scarf to avoid eye contact.

She put her hand on my arm. "It's lovely. I'm very happy for you."

"Thanks, Mom."

I glanced toward Mac again and saw that Mavis and Selma had ambushed him. Mom followed my gaze.

"I'll go rescue him in a moment," she said. "I want you to meet the rest of the knitters."

She steered me toward the fireplace, where a trio of young women were laughing and knitting. They turned and smiled when we interrupted.

"This is my daughter, Clytemnestra," Mom said.

I smiled while clenching my jaw—not easy to do, but I had a lot of practice.

"Call me Clyde," I said. I shot a look at Mom and said, "Everyone does."

Mom smiled at me and went to pry Mavis away from Mac.

Tinkerbell stood and introduced herself as Heather.

When we shook hands I focused my thoughts on that contact and opened my mind to any insights. A fizzy, bright tingling touched my face and I knew Heather was just as open and friendly as she appeared.

"I work as an ICU nurse, but only to support my yarn habit."

The other two chuckled.

"I'm Amy," the pink-haired woman said. "I own the local yarn store. And this is Tina." She gestured at her tattooed friend. "She's a fiber artist." Tina flicked a glance in my direction and grimaced a small smile. Both held a knitting project and didn't offer to shake hands.

"She's the mastermind behind the yarn-bombing competition," Heather said and hooked her thumb at Tina.

"Isabel even donated a cool set of knitting needles as the grand prize!"

"We were admiring the yarn bombing earlier," I said. "It's a very . . . unique competition."

"Knitting isn't just for grandmas anymore," Tina said. "I like to see so many new people embracing it and using knitting to make an artistic statement and bring awareness."

I wasn't sure what kind of awareness was related to colored tubes on chandeliers, but sensed this sentiment would not be met with warmth.

"It's a fun thing to do and since the owners are knitters—" Amy said.

Heather interrupted. "Not all of them. Clarissa has made her feelings pretty clear."

"Right, well Jessica and Linda don't mind having yarn draped everywhere," Amy said.

Heather turned brightly toward me. "Your mother told us you're a police officer on leave. Are you planning to go back to work?"

Amy elbowed her in the ribs. "She just met us—save the interrogation for later."

"Oh." Heather's smile slipped a bit but she recovered quickly. "Sorry, I'm so used to asking personal questions at work that sometimes I forget . . ."

"It's fine." I smiled to reassure her. But how do I answer a question I had been asking myself every day for the past couple of months?

My search for a new career was reaching a critical point. My sister, Grace, had a knack for investing in the stock market and she had parlayed my inheritance from last summer into a great nest egg. But I couldn't continue to use the money I had inherited for everyday expenses and I was getting bored. I didn't want to return to police work. I had to live in Crystal Haven for at least six more months before I could sell the house or move out—an odd and meddling stipulation of the will.

I chose the simplest route. "I doubt I'll move back to Ann Arbor, but I'm still figuring out what I'll do next."

"I understand that," Tina said. "I feel like I change careers almost as often as Amy changes her hair color."

The three of them laughed, and I grinned at them.

Heather tilted her head and looked into my eyes. "Your aunt was right: Your eyes are very striking. You know, people used to think that indicated psychic abilities."

I looked away. "Yes, I've heard that."

"Uh-oh." Amy tilted her pink head toward the refreshment area. "You might want to go rescue your boyfriend. Clarissa doesn't take no for an answer—ever."

I turned and saw Mac holding two drinks and leaning away from a stunning blonde who was invading his personal space. She wore a tight black pencil skirt with a leopard-print blouse and shiny five-inch black heels. A panther stalking its prey flashed into my mind. She didn't seem to be picking up on his signals, but I caught the SOS look he shot me.

"Excuse me," I said to the knitters.

I heard quiet giggles from the trio as I made my way across the room toward Mac.

"This is Clyde," Mac said, when I was still several feet away.

"Another surprise visitor! This weekend is getting more and more exciting." The blonde turned a brilliant smile in my direction. It rapidly fled when she saw me.

Mac handed me my drink and slung an arm over my shoulder.

"Ah, I see," Clarissa said. "Well, you can't blame a girl for trying."

Something caught her attention over my shoulder and her lips tightened.

"You must be the guests the storm blew in!" a woman with mousy blond curls said as she came from behind us to stand next to Clarissa. The two couldn't have dressed differently if they'd tried. Jessica wore comfortable flats, khakis, and a cozy-looking cardigan over a white T-shirt. "I'm Jessica Garrett, one of the owners. I see you've met Clarissa."

"We were just getting acquainted," Clarissa said. She finished her drink in one long swallow.

"I hope you'll enjoy your time here," Jessica said. "I heard you had planned a warmer vacation than this one."

"I'm sure it will be very relaxing," I said. "The hotel is beautiful."

"You'll have to return when we have the spa open," Clarissa said. "Have you ever had a spa treatment?" She looked me over and did not appear impressed.

"Once or twice," I said. "What I really like is the sense of stepping back in time. It feels like a different century here."

Jessica's smile appeared more triumphant than pleased. "See, Clarissa? People like the cozy feel of antiques and warm colors."

Clarissa's lip curled. "They'll like the new look even better, I'm sure. I can't wait to update this place." She swung an arm to encompass the whole lounge. "If we can convince your mother to part with even a few of her precious antiques, we can bring this . . . castle into the twenty-first century."

Jessica's triumphant smile slipped into a frozen, not-in-front-of-the-guests grimace. "Clarissa, could I speak to you in the hallway?" She turned to Mac and me. "Excuse us."

Clarissa beamed at Mac, set her glass down on the table, and stalked into the hallway after Jessica.

I was close enough to the door to hear heated whispers and then they faded down the hallway.

A glance at my watch told me we still had half an hour before dinner.

Vi had cornered Wally behind the drinks table and was interrogating him about the history of the castle.

Mom sat by the window with Mavis and Selma. She shuffled her tarot cards as they looked on.

I sighed.

Mac leaned toward me and whispered, "I guess this wasn't the best backup plan."

I shook my head. "No, but it's only for one night—we'll get out of here tomorrow. Maybe we can even get another flight to Mexico."

Isabel and Lucille walked into the room. Isabel zeroed in on the yarn in the room and went to sit with Tina, Heather, and Amy. Lucille zeroed in on Mac.

"What a wonderful surprise that we get to spend the evening with you two," she said as she approached.

We told her the story of our flight cancellation and Mac's alternate plan.

"I think Linda Garrett is planning to give us a tour of the hotel and tell us about all the antiques and artwork her family has collected over the years. She's very proud of this place."

"Is she the owner?" Mac asked. "I don't think we've met her yet."

"I thought she said she would be here. . . ." Lucille glanced around the room. "She and her daughter Jessica are co-owners with Clarissa Carlisle. Clarissa is Linda's brother's child. David Carlisle died recently and Clarissa moved here to help with the hotel."

"Yes, we met Clarissa and Jessica just before you came in," I said.

"They were together?"

"Well, no. They came in separately and then left . . . sort of together."

"I hope Linda is around," Lucille said. "She seems to be the only thing keeping the cousins from attacking each other."

6

I was about to ask Lucille to explain when Wally extricated himself from Vi and moved toward the doorway.

"Our chef, René, is from Paris and is an expert in French cuisine. He has a great dinner planned for tonight," Wally said. "You can go in anytime now."

The knitters noisily left the library and headed in to dinner.

I spotted a table for two by the window and quickly steered Mac toward it.

"Clyde! Mac! We got a big table for all of us," Vi shouted and waved from across the room.

I squeezed Mac's hand and trudged across the room to tell Vi we wanted to sit alone. Unfortunately, Mac followed me, and we found ourselves sitting with our families. I tamped down a flash of irritation and reminded myself it was only for one night.

Before the waiter arrived, Clarissa entered the room. She stopped at the table where Amy, Tina, and Heather sat. "I talked to Kirk, and he'll be happy to help you with your . . . competition," she said. They nodded their thanks and leaned toward one another, urgently whispering the moment she walked away.

She stopped at our table and Vi began to introduce Mac and me.

"Yes, we met earlier." Clarissa put her hand on Mac's shoulder. I felt him tense next to me. "Isn't this lovely! It's a family reunion," Clarissa exclaimed. "There's nothing like family, is there? Ever since I came back to help Aunt Linda and Cousin Jessica run the hotel, I keep asking myself why I stayed away so long. Of course, I had no idea there would be so much knitting." She shivered dramatically and leaned toward Mac and me. "It gives me hives just thinking about it."

Vi's face turned pink and her lips paled into a thin line. I hoped Clarissa would move on before a brawl broke out.

"I would love to stay and chat, but duty calls," she said. "You let me know if there's anything you need." She cocked her head at Mac and turned away.

She approached the table where Isabel, Mavis, and Selma sat. Mavis kept her head down and didn't speak to Clarissa. Isabel smiled politely but didn't encourage her.

After a moment or two of silence, Clarissa clicked her heels out of the dining room. And the three women sighed in relief.

Jessica approached our table before I could ask Vi and Mom why Clarissa had gotten such a cool reception.

She looked at the door and Clarissa's retreating back.

"Wallace just told me he didn't have a room for you. I might—"

"It's okay, Jessica, we worked it out," Vi said. "We're all sharing." She gestured around the table.

Jessica gave me a sympathetic smile and I liked her even more.

"Well, let us know if you need anything," she said. "Mother and I have always prided ourselves on making our guests feel at home." She glanced at the doorway. "Even before Clarissa joined us."

"Thank you, I'm sure we'll be fine," Mac said.

Jessica moved to the next table just as Wally came to announce he would act as our waiter and to describe the menu for the evening.

"Vi says you'll be sharing our room, Clyde," Mom said as she passed me the bread basket. "That will be so exciting—like a girls' weekend. We can't let Dad and Seth have all the fun."

"I haven't had a chance for some quality time with my son in years!" Lucille told the table.

Mac studied his plate and took deep breaths.

"I hope you and Mac can find something to do while we're in our workshops," Vi said to me. "Isabel has a very packed schedule for the weekend."

I thought about how we wouldn't be sipping cocktails and relaxing on the beach.

"Clyde, I'm sure you could join us," Lucille said, and looked at me hopefully. She was determined to make a knitter out of me. Vi and Mom had given up years ago to focus on pressuring me to use my psychic talents. Knitting was a distant second on their priority list.

"I should probably keep Mac company," I said.

"But Mac can knit," Lucille said.

The table fell silent as every eye was trained on Mac. He rested his elbow on the table and put his head in his hand.

"Didn't you tell her?" Lucille asked

"It never came up, Mom," Mac mumbled to his plate.

"I knew it!" Vi said.

"You knew that Mac could knit?" I said.

"No, I knew we'd figure out a way to get you to take a class. If Mac is there, too, it will be just like the vacation you planned."

"Not exactly, Vi," I said. *Not even close.*

Violet gave me a crooked smile. "Well, there aren't any beaches here, but you can still have some fun." She nodded once to end the discussion.

Fortunately, Wally arrived just at that moment with our meals. He apologized that the menu had been severely limited. The chef wanted to conserve supplies in case they couldn't get back out for a couple of days to replenish. I shuddered to consider that we could be stuck here for a couple of days.

My first bite of the coq au vin had me hoping we would never have to leave. The slightly salty, savory chicken and mushrooms was rapidly eclipsing all other favorite dishes. I'm not much of a foodie, and even less of a cook, but I recognized that this was something special.

"Wow," I said. "This is incredible."

Vi nodded. "They're pretty impressed with their chef."

"They should be," I said.

The room grew quiet as everyone focused on their meal. After a few minutes, the door swung open and the chef appeared. He made his way among the tables, accepting praise and chatting with the guests. He wore a white smock and a tall white hat. I was surprised to see he was about my age—probably early thirties.

He stopped to talk to Mavis and Selma. They both blushed furiously at something he said.

"Ah, our newest guests," he said when he reached our table. "I am René Sartin, head chef. I hope you are enjoying the dinner." He had a heavy French accent and I had a weird sense of watching a bit of dinner theater.

After graciously receiving compliments from our table, he gave a short bow and strode back into the kitchen.

I leaned toward Vi after René left.

"Vi, what's the deal with Clarissa and the knitters?" I tilted my head toward the table where Isabel and Mavis had been sitting. Only Selma remained.

Vi shifted in her seat to look. She shook her head as she turned back toward me.

"That's a very sad story," she said. "Mavis's daughter, Teresa, and Isabel were best friends in high school. Teresa was horribly bullied and eventually took her own life."

"Oh, that's terrible," I said.

"Mavis has always blamed Clarissa. She was the leader of a mean-girl pack and Isabel claimed that they targeted Teresa after an incident with a boy. It seems Teresa lured Clarissa's boyfriend away and she never let up after that."

"Why did Isabel have the conference here if she knew Clarissa would be here?"

Vi shook her head. "I don't think she knew. Isabel and Jessica had a bit of a dustup when we all arrived. Isabel said Jessica should have told her, and Jessica said she would keep Clarissa away from the knitters."

"What are you two whispering about?" Mom leaned over to look at us.

"Nothing, Rose. Just filling Clyde in on the situation with Mavis and Clarissa."

"Oh. Let's not ruin our dinner talking about that," Mom said. "When I think of what poor Mavis must have gone through . . ." Mom's eyes welled up. She grabbed her water and took a sip.

Silence fell over the table and we focused on our food. Lucille finally broke the tension.

"I wish Isabel had included a class on spinning yarn. I've

always thought it would be fun to spin my own yarn and then knit something wonderful with it." Her eyes held the kind of gleam Vi got when talking about the pendulum.

"That sounds fabulous," Mom exclaimed. I sensed she was just glad to change the subject.

"I wouldn't know the first thing about what kind of fleece to spin or how thick to make it," Vi said.

"That's why I wish there was a class." Lucille took a sip of wine. "I've been thinking about buying an alpaca from that farm outside of Crystal Haven."

Mac choked on his chicken and I pounded his back.

Lucille glanced at Mac and continued. "I could keep it in my garage in the winter and spin its fleece. I wonder if I need more than one—how many alpacas do you need for a sweater?"

Fortunately, Wally began clearing plates, and Mac was able to gain control of himself.

"I don't think I could eat another bite, but I heard the desserts are the chef's specialty," Mom said.

The hair on the back of my neck prickled, the lights flickered, and the room plunged into darkness.

Someone screamed. A plate shattered on the floor.

"Everyone stay calm," Wally announced. "I'll go get some flashlights." He crashed through the dining room, bumping into tables on his way out.

I heard muffled whispers and the shifting of chairs.

Mac raised his voice to be heard over the mutterings around the room. "Let your eyes adjust to the dark," he said. "I'm sure Wally will be back in a moment."

As if on cue, Wally clicked on a large flashlight that he shone in everyone's eyes before realizing he had blinded us all with its brightness.

"Oh, sorry everyone. I have some flashlights here," he

said as he pointed his light at the ground and made his way to the tables, passing out the lights.

"We only have a few of these, but Jessica went to get some candles," Wally said. "Unfortunately, we do lose power occasionally during severe storms. We have a backup generator and it should be working momentarily."

Murmurs spread as people clicked on their lights and checked to be sure their friends were okay.

"Why don't we all move into the lounge?" Wally swung his light toward the door. "The fire is warm and bright, and we can have coffee while we wait for maintenance to get the power up and running again."

The flashlights and promise of coffee had improved the mood of the room. Scraping chairs, giggles, and exclamations of "just like camping!" and "delightfully spooky" accompanied the group out of the room. We trooped down the dark hallway, following Wally's light, and settled by the fire.

I was grateful for the shadows in the corners as Mac and I separated from the group for a moment of privacy.

"I would think that this was the most romantic place ever, if we didn't have most of our families along for the weekend," I said.

"This hasn't worked out quite the way I planned, but we should be able to find another place tomorrow," he said quietly. He leaned toward me and kissed my neck just below my ear. I slid my arm around his waist and was enjoying the moment when Wally's light shone right in my eyes again. Mac jerked away. And Wally swung the light back toward the group.

"Sorry! Just doing a head count," Wally said.

Mac and I stepped closer to the group sitting by the fire. Vi looked like a kid on Christmas morning.

"Isn't this exciting?" she said. "A blizzard, a power outage, and a haunted castle! What could be more fun?"

"Haunted?" Mac's lipsticked admirer asked with a quavery voice.

"Oh, definitely," Vi said. "The original owner died on a night just like this. Drowned in her bathtub up in the turret room."

Wally was standing close enough that I heard him sigh.

7

Vi had grabbed everyone's attention.

"What?"

"Drowned?"

"Who?"

Vi launched into her tale of treachery and deceit.

I'd assumed that the ghost story was part of the hotel's offerings. Like a "George Washington slept here" kind of thing. But, apparently, Vi had pried the information out of Wally and he seemed to be regretting it.

". . . found her dead in the bathtub when she returned with the cocoa," Vi concluded. "Her ghost walks the halls and stands at the turret window on nights like this." The flashlight she held cast spooky shadows on her face.

The lounge was silent as the group digested Vi's story. Jessica rushed into the room at that moment carrying a box of candles and a lighter. "I'm sorry it took me so long to get back." Her hair stood out in excited springs and she stopped to catch her breath. "I see you're all settled comfortably here." She glanced around at the pale, shocked faces. "What?"

"I was just telling them the story of your ghost," Vi said. "It's a doozy."

"Our . . . ghost?" Jessica's eyes grew wide and she glanced at Wally. "We're trying to leave that in the past." Jessica passed out the candles. "Clarissa doesn't think it represents our new direction. She's even living in the turret room in order to prove to the staff that it's just a story."

"What do *you* think?" Lucille asked. Several heads turned at this question.

"Well, I did grow up hearing the stories," Jessica said. "And certainly had some fun with my friends at sleepovers scaring one another." She glanced at Isabel, who smiled. "But I've never seen anything out of the ordinary in that room or any other room in the castle."

Wally coughed quietly next to me.

"Now, maybe we should talk about something else," Jessica said. "The castle has a very interesting history besides the tragic story of Ada Carlisle."

"I heard that rumrunners used to hide alcohol here during Prohibition," Vi volunteered. "I heard there was a speakeasy in the basement."

"I don't think that's the kind of history Ms. Garrett means," Wally said.

Jessica smiled gratefully at him and nodded.

"No, I was talking about the architecture and some of the furnishings and paintings," Jessica said.

Vi yawned in my ear.

"The castle has been in my family since it was built in 1895, and every generation puts its own stamp on the building. We have an extensive art collection as well as authentic period furniture. My mother has spent much of her career curating the collection. I often tease her that the castle is her favorite child. Clarissa is working to make this a destination spa and hotel. And our chef, René, is close to having our restaurant Michelin rated."

"Do you do other conferences here?" Mom asked.

"We try to schedule something once a month. We don't like to do too many because we are small enough that a conference can easily fill all the rooms and then there aren't any for regular guests." She glanced at me and tilted her head. "My mother could tell you so much more about the history of some of our artwork. It's really her obsession, right after running the hotel. I wonder where—"

A muffled shriek cut across Jessica's words.

Everyone turned toward the door, candle flames dancing with the movement.

We heard it again, but louder.

I rushed toward the exit, and Mac followed right behind.

"Everyone stay where you are," Jessica said. "We'll be right back."

I assumed no one followed directions, based on the stampede of feet that trailed Mac and me into the hallway. We heard someone running on the floor above and headed for the stairs. As we reached the top, a well-dressed older woman approached carrying a kerosene lamp. She wore a navy suit and low heels, its conservative feel contrasting with her huge, wild eyes. She put her hand to her mouth when she spotted us.

"Oh, she's . . . where's?" the woman said.

Jessica quickly introduced the woman as her mother, Linda Garrett.

"Mom, what's wrong?" Jessica stepped forward and hugged her.

"It's Clarissa." Linda took a shaky breath. "She's dead."

Her hands shook and caused the flame to bounce and flicker. Jessica gasped.

An uproar of shocked dismay rose from the stairs where the rest of the guests congregated.

"Let me take that, Mrs. Garrett," Mac said. "I'm a police officer. Can I help?"

"Police?" She scanned Mac's face and handed him the lantern. "Yes, please. I . . . can't believe it." She stared, open-mouthed, at Mac and swayed a bit. Jessica put an arm out to steady her.

Mac turned to Wally. "Take everyone back downstairs to the lounge, please. Then gather the rest of the staff and wait for us there."

Wally nodded and turned toward the group to begin his crowd control.

"What happened?" Jessica said. She sniffled and rubbed her eyes.

"I went up to check on Clarissa and to bring her a lamp." Linda pointed to the lamp Mac held. "She didn't answer the door, but it was unlocked, so I went in." She took a shaky breath. "I know she likes to take a bath in the evening and thought she might be in the bathtub and couldn't hear me."

We waited while Linda gulped air and dabbed at her eyes with the hem of her sweater. She took a steadying breath and continued. "It was pitch dark in her room and I had to walk carefully." She turned to Jessica. "You know how she is with her shoes. A person could turn an ankle walking through her minefield of shoes."

Jessica nodded and gave her a small, encouraging, if watery, smile.

"I knocked on the bathroom door, and it swung open. I could see she wasn't in the tub." Linda looked at Mac. "It's a large claw-foot tub and takes up most of the room. Then

I saw her on the floor. She was still dressed—she must have slipped and hit her head."

Linda stopped and stared past us, back in the moment.

"She wasn't breathing." She turned and buried her face on Jessica's shoulder.

Mac placed a hand gently on Linda's arm. "I need to go secure the scene."

"I'll come with you," I said. I felt a rush of adrenaline at the thought of investigating a mysterious death. A sharp moment of guilt stabbed at my conscience. A young woman was dead. I was getting worse than Aunt Vi.

Mac started to say something and then nodded.

"Mrs. Garrett? Are you able to come back to her room and show us?" Mac asked.

She nodded and clutched Jessica's hand as we walked to the end of the hall. The lantern cast grotesque bouncing shadows on the walls. The climb up was steep and winding and reminded me of the previous November, when I had climbed a different twisting staircase while investigating a murder, not knowing what I would find at the top. That remembered sense of dread sobered any Vi-like excitement I had been feeling.

We reached a small landing at the top of the stairs. Mrs. Garrett pushed the door open and a white streak tore out of the opening. I flashed onto Vi's ghost story just as the streak let out a very feline yowl. I watched it race down the staircase and out of sight.

"Oh! That cat is always jumping out when you least expect it," Linda said, her hand clutching her chest.

We stepped into the room. Weak light from the lantern cast flickering shadows on the furniture. My shoulders felt tight and my ears strained for any sound. Mac clicked on the large flashlight he'd taken from Wally and the spooky feeling began to dissipate.

When we got to the bathroom door, Jessica hesitated, took a deep breath, and then nodded to us to proceed.

Inside, it was just as Mrs. Garrett had described. The claw-foot tub stood in the middle of a partly circular room that would have been lovely on a sunny day. The old-fashioned cabinet and pedestal sink lined up along the wall, and a toilet hid behind a half wall in the corner.

Clarissa lay on the floor between the tub and the sink. Her right leg was bent at an awkward angle and her eyes were closed. In the weak light from the flashlight and lamp, a dark glistening stain spread from underneath her head. She was completely still. I knelt down next to her and shone the flashlight on her face. Mrs. Garrett gasped and I heard her move into the other room. Jessica followed.

"Mac," I said quietly, "look." I pointed to Clarissa's neck. The faint bruises barely showed in the flashlight's glow, but they were there. I put a thumb on her eyelid and lifted. The whites of her eyes were pink.

"I don't think this was an accident," I said.

Mac let out a gust of air.

"Strangled," he said. "Whoever hit her in the head made sure they finished the job."

I cleared my mind, as Neila had instructed, reached out, and touched Clarissa's shoulder. I hoped I would get a sense of who might have harmed her, but all I felt was a surge of rage and fear. A wave of nausea spread and I felt dizzy. I pulled my hand away and took a deep breath.

Mac knelt down next to me, his arm over my shoulders. "Are you okay?"

I didn't want to tell him I was experimenting with psychic solutions. "I'm fine . . . it's just . . . she looks like she's sleeping."

I put a finger under Clarissa's jaw along her neck to check for a pulse, but we both knew I wouldn't find one.

8

We regrouped in the bedroom. Mac asked Jessica when she thought the power would be back on.

"It should have come on by now." Jessica held her hands out and shrugged. "The generator works very well and can usually supply power for a couple of days. I don't know why it hasn't kicked in." She put a shaky hand to her lips. "I had planned to go find our maintenance man after I dropped off the candles in the lounge."

Mac paced in front of the bathroom door. "Okay, we'll need to call the local police and see what they want us to do."

"I thought *you* were a police officer," Linda said.

Mac stopped moving.

"Yes, we both are," he said, and gestured toward me. "But Clyde is on leave and I'm out of my jurisdiction. If the local police can get here, they'll be in charge."

"I doubt anyone can get through tonight," Jessica said.

"The snow is still coming down and when René arrived this afternoon just before dinner, he said he almost didn't make it."

"Surely we don't need to call in more police," Linda said. "We can make arrangements with a funeral home. . . ."

Mac held up his hand. "I'm afraid it's more complicated than that."

"Because it was an accidental death?" Jessica said.

Mac and I exchanged a glance and I could tell he thought it would be best not to upset Mrs. Garrett further.

"Police need to be notified whenever someone unexpectedly dies," I said.

Mac pulled out his cell phone and dialed. He looked at it again, and sighed.

"I don't have service. Clyde, is yours working?"

Mine was the same—no service.

"There's only one cell tower near here and reception can be spotty," Jessica said. "We have a landline tucked under the front desk."

"Let's go try the landline," Mac said.

We trooped down the circular stairs. Mrs. Garrett had begun crying again, but it was more of a slow leak than a flood.

"Maybe you can take your mom to her room and get her some tea or . . . something?" I said to Jessica.

She nodded. "I'll meet you downstairs." She put an arm around Linda. "C'mon, Mom, let's go."

Jessica took the lamp and led her mother off a side hallway that I assumed led to the family's living area. Mac and I went to the front desk and found the phone. Mac dialed 911 and listened. He clicked the button on the phone and tried again. He groaned.

"The landline is out as well?" I asked.

"I'm not sure what to do." He shook his head. "I don't like the idea of leaving her body up there."

"We don't want to disturb any potential evidence," I said.

Mac nodded and rubbed the back of his neck.

He took a deep breath and blew it out. "Leave it to us to stumble onto a murder."

"Murder?" said a voice from behind us. "I knew it!"

I turned, but it had to be Vi and her selectively tuned hearing.

She hurried over to us, her candle flickering wildly. "She's been murdered? Poor Clarissa!" She paused and lowered her voice. "Of course, she didn't have many fans around here." She looked from me to Mac.

Neither of us spoke.

"Unless . . . it was the ghost seeking her revenge!" Vi announced.

"Ms. Greer, that's ridiculous," Mac said. "And dangerous. Don't get everyone all worked up about a ghost story."

Violet was silent for a moment. "You're probably right." She nodded. "We've got to figure this out—there's a murderer among us!" She turned to go back into the lounge.

I grabbed her arm. "Vi, you can't tell anyone. Let us handle it. We know what we're doing." I glanced at Mac for backup.

"We wouldn't want to let the murderer know we're onto him, or her," Mac said.

"Oh, of course. But I can tell Rose, right?" she said to Mac and then turned to me, her finger already pointing in a menacing fashion. "You can't suspect your own mother of murder?"

"Shhh! No, I don't suspect Mom," I said. "But let's just keep this between us until we can figure out what's going on."

"Okay, got it." Vi nodded, and then winked.

I looked at the ceiling and hoped it was too dark for her to notice.

"What's going on?" Wally emerged out of the shadowy hallway.

"Ms. Carlisle is definitely deceased," Mac said.

"Oh, no." Wally put his hand up to his neck. "How did she die?"

"We think she hit her head," Mac said, "but we'll have to wait until the police get here to examine the evidence."

"That could be a while," Wally said. "The emergency weather radio says the snowstorm has stalled over Southwestern Michigan. If the phones are already out, it's not likely we'll get a call out anytime soon."

"How did you know the phones were out?" I asked.

"I tried to call our head of maintenance earlier when you were upstairs. His assistant is down in the basement working on the generator, but I thought if we could call Gus, he could tell us how to fix it." Wally leaned closer to me and whispered, "The new guy is not that good."

"Wally, maybe you and Vi can go back in the lounge and try to keep everyone calm," Mac said. "I need to talk to Jessica and figure out what we're going to do."

"Sure, okay." Wally held his arm out for Violet and escorted her down the hall as if they were heading to dinner in an English country house.

"We can't leave a body sitting up there all night," I said to Mac.

He nodded. "I know. And I don't know how to keep everyone out of there. I'd post a guard, but I don't know whom to trust besides you, our mothers, and maybe your aunt. They can't stand guard through the night."

"No, Vi is likely to see the ghost and send up an alarm . . . if she doesn't fall asleep on duty."

"This sounds awful, but I'm tempted to wrap the body and put it out in the snow to preserve it. We know the general time of death is between the time we saw her before dinner and an hour later when the body was discovered."

I suddenly felt queasy and leaned my back against the wall. No matter how many times I had dealt with violent death, there was always a moment when it snuck up on me. Mac pulled me toward him and we stood, leaning against one another more than embracing, for a long moment.

I took a deep breath and pushed away from him. "We should find Jessica and see if they have any large sheets of plastic—like a new shower curtain. Maybe there's an outbuilding that we can put the body in that will keep it cold."

"Good idea," Mac said. He grabbed my hand and squeezed gently.

I followed Mac up the stairs, and back in the direction of the side hall where Jessica had led her mother. She turned the corner just as we got to the turret stairs doorway.

"Oh, there you are," she said. "I just got Mom calmed down. She's resting in her room. Did you get in touch with the police?"

"The phone lines are down," I said.

"Oh, I thought . . ." She put her hand to her head. "This is all so awful. Are the guests okay?"

"We sent Wally and Violet in to keep everyone calm," Mac said.

"I don't know what to do," Jessica said.

I stepped forward to touch her arm. "We're so sorry, Jessica."

"Jessica?" The chef strode up to us down the dark hallway. "I just heard about Clarissa. What's going on?"

"She . . . she's dead." Jessica threw herself into René's arms and sobbed.

Mac shifted his weight and I could see him sizing up the situation.

"How can she be dead?" René asked. "I just saw her at dinner."

Jessica said something unintelligible into his shoulder. His brow wrinkled and he rubbed her back.

"Mr. Sartin, we need to secure the room and the body for when the police arrive."

Jessica winced when Mac said "the body."

"Police? I doubt anyone will get through tonight," he said. "I'm so sorry, Jess."

"Is there an outbuilding or someplace we can store the . . . Clarissa . . . to keep her cold?" Mac asked.

Jessica pulled herself together and nodded. "The garden shed would work. We just built it this past spring to store equipment. There's plenty of room and it has a dead bolt."

"I'm sorry, but we think it would be best to put her out there," I said.

Jessica's voice shook as she said, "Okay."

"We need to keep people out of her room so no one can interfere with evidence," Mac said.

"Evidence?" René said.

"We didn't want to further alarm Mrs. Garrett, but we think she was murdered," Mac said.

Jessica gasped and René's mouth dropped open. Jessica leaned toward him and he slipped an arm around her shaking shoulders.

•

We sent the knitters off to bed with promises of more information in the morning. Wally, René, Jessica, Mac, and I went back up to Clarissa's room with a new shower curtain and the largest flashlights Wally could find.

The room felt still and silent when we entered, as if it held its breath. I had sensed this in other sudden-death cases. The vacuum left behind was palpable. Mac and I got to work quickly. We had both been trained in crime scene protocol but Mac had far more experience. He took the lead and photographed the body as best he could in the poor lighting conditions. René had provided us with plastic kitchen gloves and paper bags. We examined the area around her body carefully and bagged anything lying nearby. We found an earring that matched the one in her left ear not far from the body, a used bandage under the front foot of the large tub, and a few stray hairs that appeared to match Clarissa's length and color.

The lack of electric light hampered our efforts. Mac and I did the best we could to collect items near the body with the idea that we would return during the daytime to better examine the rest of the room.

We laid the curtain on the floor next to Clarissa, and Mac and René carefully lifted her onto one edge. They gently rolled her in the shower curtain to protect any evidence that might remain on her body, under her fingernails, or anywhere else on her person. As they shifted her over, a metallic clang sounded just underneath her. Wally shined the light on the ground and a reflective glint winked at us. I bent down to examine the piece of metal.

I knew immediately what it was and fought the urge to touch it to get more information. It was an elongated U-shape with one end longer than the other. I had seen Vi use something like it to do her knitted cables.

"Jessica, was Clarissa a knitter?" I asked.

Jessica had been standing just outside the bathroom while we worked and she stepped inside. "No, not a chance. She mocked Isabel any chance she got."

I pointed to the metal U without touching it. "Isn't that a cable needle?"

Jessica bent down and looked. She took in a sharp breath. "Yes, it's . . . it's a cable needle." She stood back quickly as if to put some distance between herself and the needle.

"Do you know who it belongs to?" Mac asked.

Jessica shook her head quickly and stepped back out into the bedroom.

Mac slid it carefully into a small paper bag and put it with the rest of our evidence bags. He directed Wally and René to lift Clarissa and we all trooped out of the bathroom and down the stairs after them.

I took up the rear and after we got down the stairway the guys moved ahead to bring the body out to the shed. I found Vi lurking in the shadows around the corner from the staircase.

"Vi, what are you doing here?" I hissed and hoped Mac was too busy to notice.

"I just wanted to see if I could help," she said. "Where's that cat? I saw her race out of the stairway when you guys went upstairs the first time. She might be able to tell us something about what happened."

Vi had been known to interview dogs, cats, and even woodland creatures to try to solve a mystery.

"I didn't see the cat upstairs," I said. "Let's get to bed and we can look for her in the morning." I steered her back toward "our" room and pushed her through the doorway.

I told her I would be right back and used my own wag-gling finger to threaten. Mom began her interrogation of Vi as I swung the door closed.

I got to the back door just as the guys stepped outside with Clarissa's plastic-wrapped corpse. Jessica stood in the doorway shivering. Her hands shook as she pulled her car-digan more tightly across her shoulders.

"They said we could wait here," she said. "Kirk, our maintenance guy, has the keys and I didn't want to . . . see her there. In a shed." She scrubbed at her eyes, smearing her mascara into a raccoon mask.

"I'm so sorry, Jessica."

She sniffled. "It's not like we were close. Just the opposite, in fact." She turned to me. "Who could have done this?"

"We'll do our best to figure it out and the police will investigate as soon as we can get in touch with them." I didn't want to point out to her that as long as the storm continued, we would all be stuck in the hotel with a murderer; she had probably already concluded as much. I thought that Mac and I would have just as much work keeping everyone calm as we would investigating the murder.

9

After an uncomfortable night listening to the howling wind, snow lashing the windows, and Vi's snoring, by Friday morning I felt cranky and tired. The frigid air chilled me through my thin sleep shirt as I climbed out of bed in the dark. A quick flick of the light switch confirmed that the power had not been restored.

I fumbled with a pack of matches and lit a candle.

Vi sat up in her bed as I shivered and hopelessly examined my suitcase full of shorts and T-shirts. I had planned for a Mexican vacation, not a blizzard in Michigan.

"Look in the closet, Clyde," Vi said through a yawn. "I brought lots of sweaters. Knitters get pretty competitive so we all bring our best stuff."

"Thanks, Vi," I said.

I slid the closet door open. The candle flickered as I held it up to better examine the sweaters. Assaulted by the bright, multihued choices, I flipped through the hangers until I found a muted purple cardigan that looked soft and warm.

"That color will be perfect for you," Mom said from the bed. "It will show off both colors of your eyes and complement your dark hair."

"I'm just interested in being warm, Mom."

"It never hurts to look nice while you're getting comfortable," Mom sniffed.

I tossed the sweater on over a T-shirt and my one pair of jeans, told the ladies I'd see them later, and slipped out into the hallway.

The candle cast jumping shadows on the walls as I walked down the staircase. I got a tingly feeling along my spine remembering Vi's ghost story. I'm embarrassed to admit how many times I glanced over my shoulder. I wanted to run down the hall toward the lounge, but didn't want the candle to blow out.

Mac and I had planned to meet in the lounge at seven a.m. to avoid the knitters, but we hadn't planned on it being so dark. Their first workshop wasn't until nine and they were meeting at eight for breakfast. At least the sun would be up by then.

After my spooky trek from upstairs, I found Mac huddled by the fire with a pot of tea all ready for me. His small notebook was open and he flipped it shut when I approached. He was wearing a thick, dark blue cardigan with no buttons and loose strings hanging off of it. When I got closer I saw the smiling snow couple that had been knitted into the front. Neither of us had packed for winter in a cold, drafty castle. I assumed one of the knitters had taken pity on him.

I sat next to him and kissed him in spite of the snowman.

"Nice sweater." I tried to swallow the giggle.

"I think it brings out my eyes." He wiggled his eyebrows to demonstrate.

"Oh, it's definitely *you*," I said. "I assume it's a loan from Mavis?"

"How did you know?" He pretended to be shocked.

"A hunch." I smiled. "Plus, I'm psychic."

Mac's slow grin spread. "So I hear."

"I'll have to keep my eye on her."

"Now that I have this sweater, you might have to keep an eye on all of them."

I laughed and kissed him again.

"How did you get this?" I asked as I lifted the pot of tea and poured a cup.

"I have connections." He smiled. "The gas stove still works if you light it with a match."

I sipped the tea and pulled Aunt Vi's sweater closer around my shoulders.

"What's the plan for the day?"

His smile faded and was replaced by his cop face. "Ideally, the power comes back on, the phones are reconnected, and the police arrive to take over. But I'm not holding out much hope."

I could tell there was more, and waited.

"I don't see how we can leave now," he said. "Even if the power comes back on and the roads are miraculously cleared, we're witnesses. *I* wouldn't let us leave if I was in charge of the investigation, and right now I guess we are in charge."

I felt another little thrill at the thought of investigating a case with Mac, even though we'd miss our time alone in Mexico. Crystal Haven had unfortunately seen several murders in the last nine months and Mac and I had found ourselves, if not on *opposite* sides, at least on different teams. He viewed me as a civilian until I returned to the police force, but both situations had been too close to home for me to sit back and wait for the murderer to be caught. Now, we were *both* unofficial investigators.

"So, we start building a timeline and questioning people about their whereabouts?" I asked.

He nodded. "Maybe not everyone. I'd rather not start a

panic by telling them we think it's murder, but we might not be able to avoid it. I made a list of the people that weren't with us in the dining room. Remember, Clarissa came in, talked to a few people and left. That was the last we saw of her. Lots of people stayed in that room."

I stared into the fire, and pictured the dining room. "Isabel left shortly after Clarissa. Jessica was in and out of the room. René and his assistant weren't in the dining room the whole time. The maintenance guy and the housekeeper were presumably doing their work elsewhere."

Mac poured more tea into my cup. "The only staff member in the clear is Wally. He was in the dining room the entire time we were, and then he stayed with the group when the power went out."

"He left to get flashlights," I said. "But that wasn't long enough to get upstairs and kill Clarissa."

He opened his notebook and read from his list. "We need to talk to Isabel, Jessica, Linda, the chef and his assistant, maintenance, and housekeeping. There's only one entrance to that turret room, maybe one of them saw something if they were in the hallway."

"I think your friend with the lipstick left for a little while."

He glanced up at me. "She did?"

"I saw her get up and go into the kitchen, but I didn't notice when she came back."

He rubbed the back of his neck. "Maybe I shouldn't make assumptions about who was there."

"We know *our* table stayed in the dining room."

I sat back and wrapped my fingers around my teacup.

"Yes, but I didn't suspect our mothers or your aunt."

I raised an eyebrow. "Aunt Vi should never be assumed innocent."

"Innocent of what?" Vi said from the doorway.

"Of murder, Vi," I said to my tea.

"Oh, very funny." She hustled to where we sat and pulled up a chair to get closer to the fire. "Are you making a list of suspects? I think that maintenance guy is kind of sketchy."

She leaned over to look at Mac's list.

"Nice sweater," she said.

Mac held her gaze. He was even better at a stare-off than she was.

"We were just talking about who was in the dining room the whole time and then also in the lounge after the power went out," I said to break up the tension.

Vi nodded. "Wally was there the whole time. He hovered with that water pitcher all through dinner. I've never been so well hydrated in my life!" She took Mac's notebook and examined his list. "The only guests I saw leave were Isabel and Mavis. But I can't believe one of the workshop gals would have done it. Frankly, knitting is what *keeps* us from killing anyone. It's like therapy." Vi shook her head. "It had to be the maintenance guy. Maybe that's why the power went out in the first place. He was busy killing Clarissa and wasn't dealing with the generator the way he should have."

"That's a huge leap, Ms. Greer," Mac said. "The last thing we need is for everyone to jump to conclusions."

"We need more information then," Vi said. She flipped pages in Mac's notebook. Mac's fingers clenched. I took it from her and handed it back to Mac.

"It wouldn't hurt to start asking people what they saw," I said. "The longer we wait, the more likely they'll forget, or talk about it enough that no one will remember what they actually saw that night."

"You can start during breakfast," Vi said. "You should talk to Isabel before she gets involved with her workshop."

10

The knitters straggled into the dining room looking somewhat unraveled. With no hot water for showers, no electricity for curling irons or hair dryers, and a distinct chill in the air, it looked like we were in for a very long weekend. I noticed, however, that every one of them was wearing a warm, cozy-looking sweater or shawl. Fortunately, René had managed to create a lovely breakfast without electricity. At least the gas stove allowed for a hot meal. He told us he and Emmett had moved all of the perishables out into the snow until the power came back on for the refrigerator.

The gang piled their plates with eggs, toast, potatoes, and fresh fruit. Only orange juice and tea were offered since the coffeemaker was electric. I saw Mac approach Isabel across the room. She wore a different stunning scarf and apparently needed no electricity to make her hair look perfect. Her smile was dazzling until he spoke and gestured in my direction. She nodded and followed him to our table.

"Hello again, Clyde." She touched my shoulder as she passed to sit across the small table from me.

"Isabel." I sipped my tea. I was still annoyed at the way she kept looking at Mac.

"We're asking everyone about their movements last night during dinner and after the power went out," Mac began.

"I feel like I need an alibi," she said and laughed.

"It's just routine in a case like this," I said.

Isabel pursed her lips. "Routine to question people in an accidental death?"

I let out a gust of air and glanced at Mac. He nodded and tilted his head toward Isabel. There was no way we were going to be able to keep this a secret.

"We think that Clarissa was killed," I said quietly.

Isabel sat back in her chair and held my gaze. "I'm surprised it's taken this long."

"We heard you had a history . . ."

Isabel made a hissing noise that sounded like an irritated cat. "That's an understatement—but before you jump to any conclusions, Clarissa plowed through her life leaving decimation in her wake. It would be harder to find someone who *didn't* want to kill her."

"We've heard that as well," Mac said. "So, last night?"

She sat up straight and clasped her hands on the table. "I went to my room with a headache just after dinner started. I wanted to be sure everyone was settled and then I went to take some medicine and lie down for a few minutes." She stopped and took a deep breath. "The next thing I knew, I woke up and the lights were out in my room. I felt a bit disoriented, but was sure I'd left the lights on after I took the medicine and lay down."

"What time was it when you woke up?" Mac asked.

"I don't know." She pointed to her wrist. "It was so dark I couldn't make out the hands on my watch. But I went out into the hall and sort of stumbled along until I found the stairs. I heard voices coming from the lounge and saw lights at the end of the hallway, so I went there." She shrugged. "It must have been just after everyone had arrived, because Wally was explaining that the power would be back on soon. I waited with everyone else until Jessica entered with the candles and then we heard Linda screaming and went upstairs to see what was wrong."

"Did you see anyone in the hallway on your way to your room?" I asked.

She thought for a moment and then slowly shook her head. She didn't look at either of us. "I don't think so. Only the maid. She was finishing in my room just as I arrived."

"Did you see where she went after your room?" Mac asked.

Isabel shook her head and her earrings swung gently. "I was so focused on getting to my medicine, I didn't pay any attention."

Mac thanked her and she walked to the group of workshoppers that had gathered by the door.

Isabel led the knitters into the lounge where the fire was lit, and we stopped Mavis on her way out of the dining room.

Mac explained what we needed and her face lit up.

"Oh, I'd be honored to help you, Detective McKenzie. Your mother has told us all about you." She batted her eyelashes at him. "That sweater looks wonderful on you." She tugged on a loose string. "Maybe I'll finish it this weekend and you can keep it."

Mac gave her a tight smile and gestured toward the table. We sat and Mavis gazed at Mac while producing tiny scissors to snip the loose strings. I worried she planned to finish the sweater with Mac still in it. He cast a pleading glance in my direction.

"I noticed that you went into the kitchen during dinner last night," I said.

Mavis tore her gaze from Mac to look at me. She nodded. "Yes, I went to find that handsome chef fellow. His food was just divine and I wanted to compliment him and find out what else was on the menu for the weekend."

Mavis rummaged in her voluminous purse and pulled out a large sewing needle. She began weaving the loose ends into the sweater. "But I couldn't find him. His assistant was there, looking rather sullen at having to do all the desserts on his own. I went through the back door of the kitchen to see if the chef was there, but *still* didn't find him. Then I remembered my blood pressure medication and went up to my room to get it. I had just come back into the dining room when the lights went out."

"Did you see anyone on your way to your room?"

"No." Mavis slowly shook her head. "I didn't *see* a soul. But I thought I heard someone in Violet's room. I'm right between Violet and Lucille."

Mac and I looked at each other and I raised an eyebrow. Who would have been in that room?

"What, exactly, did you hear?" I said.

"Just a couple of thumps. I guess it could have been anything—even that white cat that keeps jumping out at people."

Mavis's mouth pulled downward into a frown. "I can't say I liked Clarissa at all. We had a bit of . . . history, but it always makes me very sad when a young life is wasted." She dabbed at a tear in the corner of her eye. Before I had a chance to react to what she had said, she spotted another loose string and went after it. Mac held up his hand to stop her.

"Okay, thank you," Mac said. "We appreciate your help. Let us know if you think of anything else." He stood up and backed away from her.

I thought it was one of his fastest interviews on record and suspected he regretted accepting her offer of a warm sweater.

"I wish I could have been more helpful," Mavis said. She lunged for another string, but I stepped between them and walked her to the door.

11

Mavis reluctantly left, casting an adoring glance toward Mac on her way out of the dining room. Mac kept his eyes on his notebook. Once the room was empty, we decided to try to catch the kitchen staff while they were still cleaning up from breakfast.

Mac walked into the kitchen and came out with the chef. René wore white from head to toe including one of those tall hats—not quite Chef Boyardee, but not subtle, either.

He sat and nodded at us. “I’m sorry your vacation has been ruined. I heard you were on your way out of this winter weather,” he said. “But from a selfish standpoint, I’m glad you’re here. I don’t know what we would have done if you hadn’t taken charge.”

His accent was less pronounced than it had been the day before, or maybe I was getting used to it.

I grimaced and nodded. “We’ll do our best to figure out what happened.”

"How can I help?" He spread his hands out, palms up.

"Can you remember what you were doing last evening during dinner and afterward when the lights went out?" I asked.

René took a deep breath. "Of course. Obviously, I was short staffed due to the weather." He waved his arm in the direction of the windows, which showed a bright white sky and piles of snow. "Jessica sent most of the staff home yesterday when the weather started to get bad. They all have families to get home to, so she took volunteers."

"And you volunteered?" Mac asked.

René turned pink. "Actually, I live here. Jessica and I are engaged. First, she fell in love with my cooking, then she fell in love with me." He grinned. "The family quarters are fairly spacious, so I stay with her most nights. I have a small apartment in town, but I haven't seen it in a week."

Mac sat back in his chair. "So, who volunteered to stay?"

"Well, Emmett is a single guy and he practically lives here anyway," René said. "He's a good worker and he wants his own restaurant someday. Kirk is also single and his boss had to get home to his wife. We had one housekeeper stay—there are only three of them and I think they drew straws."

"Where does the staff sleep in a situation like this?" I asked, thinking of my own rooming situation.

"We have a couple of small rooms in the basement that we use for emergencies. They were originally for the servants when the house was built. Staying there for a night or two is one thing. I can't imagine living there." He wrinkled his nose.

"Back to last night," Mac said. "Can you tell us where you were?"

"Right, sorry. Emmett and I made dinner. Fortunately, with this knitter convention, I knew ahead of time how many people I would be feeding for the weekend, so I'd purchased enough food to last. But, as you know, we still decided to limit choices to be sure the food would stretch and we wouldn't end up serving grilled cheese sandwiches by the end of the weekend."

He shuddered dramatically at the thought of grilled cheese. We waited for him to continue.

"I helped serve the meal, and then went down to the freezer to get the ice cream to go with the tarte tatin. I had just returned to the kitchen when the lights went out."

"We have a witness who went looking for you during that time. She couldn't find you and said that Emmett didn't know where you were."

René shrugged. "I don't know why he would have said that. He knew where I went."

"Did you see anyone while you were in the basement?" I asked.

René shook his head no. "I just went to get the ice cream and came back. I didn't see anyone."

"What did you do when the lights went out?" I asked.

"Unfortunately, it happens more than we would like so we have a protocol in place. Emmett and I checked the thermometers in the fridges and freezers and recorded it in the log. Sometimes it takes a little while to get the generator working so I keep track of the temp to be sure things aren't defrosting and refreezing. Emmett grumbles, but I like to be safe. The health inspector is a stickler and having everything documented shows that I run a tight ship." He sat back and his accent got a bit thicker. "Plus, I am attempting to have the restaurant rated by Michelin. I don't want anything to interfere."

"So you and Emmett were together the whole time that the lights were out?" Mac asked.

René nodded. "We were busy trying to stack dishes and get organized in the dark—we had a couple of portable lanterns. We heard noise in the hall and Wallace came to tell us about Clarissa—I went to find Jess and that's when I met you in the hall."

Mac reached out to shake his hand.

"Thanks for your time. Will you ask Emmett to come talk to us?"

After René had gone through the kitchen door, Mac said, "What do you think?"

"It seems reasonable, but he doesn't have an alibi for the time of the murder. We'll have to see what Emmett says about how long he was gone."

Emmett greeted us with a wide smile and a wave from the door. He was tall and lanky with short brown hair. He also wore kitchen whites but had left the hat in the kitchen. He sat in the chair that had been vacated by René.

"René told me you're talking to people about last night. I'm happy to help." He sat back in his chair and crossed his arms.

"As you probably know, we're treating Clarissa's death as suspicious. We're just trying to get a picture of what happened," Mac said. "Can you tell us what you were doing during dinner and after the power went out?"

Emmett sat forward and rested his elbows on his knees. "First, René and I served the dinner. It got pretty hectic since Wally was our substitute server and he had never been a waiter before."

Mac and I grimaced.

"We hardly noticed," Mac said.

Emmett chuckled and lifted one shoulder and let it drop. "He tried his best, but it's not an easy job. Fortunately, he seems to have charmed all the knitters and no one complained."

I waited for him to continue.

"Then, once everyone seemed settled out here I went back into the kitchen to start preparing the dessert. It was going to be tarte tatin and ice cream. René went downstairs to get the ice cream and then just as he got back, the power went out. He has a list of things we need to do in the kitchen if the power goes, so we turned on our lanterns and got to work." He sat back and laced his fingers over his knee.

"Did you see anyone else in the halls or the kitchen?"

"One of the guests came through looking for René but I told her he was gone and she went out through the hallway door. I didn't see her again until this morning at breakfast."

"That must have been Mavis," I said.

Emmett shrugged. "I don't know her name, but it's not unusual for us to have visitors wandering into the kitchen to talk to the chef." He smiled. "Some of the guests act like he's Wolfgang Puck or something."

Emmett echoed René's story about working in the kitchen until they heard noises in the hall. We thanked him and watched him lope back to the kitchen.

12

Mac limped slightly as we followed the signs to the front desk. He had suffered a shooting injury to his left leg a year ago while working narcotics in Saginaw. He almost never mentioned the event and only limped when he was stressed, tired, or both. I figured this morning it was both. I slipped my hand into his and felt his reassuring squeeze. We'd decided that even though Wally had been in the dining room with us during the pertinent time period, he would be a good source of information about the staff and the running of the hotel. He was nowhere to be found so we followed the hum of voices down the hall.

The knitters had commandeered the lounge and set up their equipment by the big bay windows, which gave plenty of light off the reflected snow. They all wore some variation of shawls, fingerless gloves, scarves, or sweaters. Someone had set up two silver samovars with Sterno burners underneath.

Wally sat in the midst of the knitters holding a fuchsia skein of yarn around his hands and chatting with the ladies. He had a navy and gray houndstooth scarf thrown jauntily around his neck. Isabel turned a crank on a yarn winder while Wally fed the strand to her.

The lively conversation abruptly halted when they noticed us standing in the doorway.

Mavis hopped up and rushed toward us.

"Oh, Detective. We're so glad you're here with us this weekend. What would we have done if poor Clarissa had died and there was no one to take charge?" She lowered her voice. "I think Violet is under the impression that she is helping with the investigation. Certainly, you don't need *her* help?" She clutched his arm and steered him toward the group. I followed.

"Mavis has been telling us that you're questioning all the witnesses," Vi said. "You didn't question me. Maybe I saw something and don't even realize it and then you will be able to figure out the whole mystery by my one comment."

I dropped my head to cover my smile.

"You're right, Ms. Greer," Mac said and my head popped up. It wasn't a sentence I expected to hear, *ever*. "We'll want to talk to each one of you this morning."

A babble of voices began and Mac held up his hands.

"It would be very helpful if you would refrain from discussing your theories. I need to speak to everyone and if you have already discussed it among yourselves, it could cloud your memories."

"The horse is already out of the barn on that one, Phillip," Lucille said as her needles bobbed rapidly.

"If you could all just stop talking about it now and wait until I have a chance to meet with everyone, that would be very helpful. We need to speak with anyone who left the dining room during dinner, or anyone who thinks they might have information about Clarissa's death."

Tina, of the tattoos and art awareness, said, "Aren't you out of your jurisdiction? Why are you two questioning everyone?"

The room got quiet.

"If the Kalamazoo Police were available, I wouldn't have to take charge, but they aren't, so Clyde and I are the best chance we have of figuring out what happened to Clarissa." He gave her one of his squinty-eyed stares and she looked away.

"What are you doing to protect the rest of us?" Selma asked. "There's a murderer loose and we're all stuck here!"

She wore beige again and I hadn't noticed her until she spoke. She sat between Mavis, with her bright red lipstick, and Amy, with her pink hair, and seemed to fade into the couch.

Mavis shushed her and gave Mac an apologetic smile.

"It *is* a good question," Amy said.

A few nervous nods made their way around the group.

Mac tightened his jaw. "I take it you all know Clarissa's death was not an accident?"

More nods.

He shifted his weight to his good leg.

"It's extremely unlikely that anyone is in any danger," Mac said. "The best way to keep everyone safe is for you to all cooperate while Clyde and I try to piece together what happened last night."

Vi's hand shot up. "I'll go first! Where have you set up your headquarters?"

Mac passed a hand over his face and pulled his mouth into a frown.

"We don't have a 'headquarters,' Ms. Greer."

"We really need to speak to Wally first," I said.

Vi slumped in her chair and sighed.

Wally stood importantly and smoothed his cardigan. He followed us back to the front desk.

"Your mom is going to read my cards later," he said to me. He had that wild gleam I had seen in others before—he thought all his questions would be answered through the cards.

"That's . . . nice," I said. I never knew how to deal with the truly fervent fans of the tarot. I opted for politely noncommittal.

"Violet says she's the best. She can tell my whole future." He spread his hands wide and moved his arms in a semicircle as if envisioning his entire life.

Mac snorted and tried to make it sound like a cough.

Wally turned to him with a questioning expression.

"Wally," I said, "we need you to help us figure out where everyone was supposed to be last night from the time Clarissa left the dining room until Mrs. Garrett found her."

Wally put his hands in his pockets and looked down at his shoes. "I think Mrs. Garrett or Jessica would be better able to tell you that, but I'll do my best."

We sat in the room near the reception desk. It served as a smaller lounge and looked toward the front of the property. The blinding landscape made my eyes water. I had sensed an edgier note among the knitters today. Not just because one of them had questioned Mac, but it was starting to sink in to all of us that we were stranded here. And now they knew one of us was capable of murder. A worried group was more frightening than a single murderer.

Mac took out his notebook and gestured at Wally to begin.

"The kitchen staff obviously would have been in the kitchen or the dining room. The only ones who stayed yesterday were René and Emmett. We let all nonessential staff go home around three o'clock, when it was clear that the snow was starting to pile up."

Mac and I nodded.

"Kirk Barstow, our maintenance guy, also stayed. You met him last night. He's new and works with Gus, who has been here for years. I don't know if Kirk's ever worked on an old house like this before because he doesn't seem to know how to fix *anything*. He mostly follows Gus around and assists. But Gus wanted to get home yesterday—his wife has been ill and he didn't want to be stuck here. Once the phones are back on, maybe he can tell Kirk how to fix the generator."

"The building doesn't have a backup for the backup?" I asked. "If you lose power as often as you say, don't you need to be extra careful?"

Wally tilted his head. "I don't know much about that. Usually, it just kicks back on after a few minutes. You'll have to talk to Kirk."

"Who else was working last evening?" Mac readied his pen and notebook.

"Holly Raeburn. She's in charge of the housekeeping department, which consists of her and two other women. I was surprised she decided to stay. I know she has a young daughter at home, but she said the daughter was staying with her grandmother and she let the other women go home."

"All of the staff members are staying in the basement?" I asked.

"Yes. There are some small rooms down there that used to be servant quarters. Mrs. Garrett remodeled them a few years back after a blizzard that had the staff living four or five to a room and the guests doubling up during a three-day snow-in."

Three days! I hoped we'd be done with this case and onto another hotel well before that.

"Other than you and the four staff members, it was just Linda and Jessica Garrett?" Mac asked. "Is that enough people to handle all these guests?"

"Jessica didn't expect it to be very long. We didn't anticipate the storm to be as bad as it's been." He gave a small shrug. "Plus there was Clarissa. She would have pitched in if we needed her. She's only been here for about six months but she knows everyone's job. She spent time with each department when she started so she could get a feel for how things worked."

"Sounds like she was really dedicated to her job," Mac said.

Wally snorted and then slapped his hand over his mouth. He stared at us with wide eyes.

Mac tilted his head and gave Wally an "out with it" look.

"Shortly after she finished 'learning' the departments"—he made quotation marks in the air and narrowed his eyes—"she cut staff by twenty-five percent. She said everyone could be much more efficient and we didn't need so many people working here."

Mac glanced at me and raised an eyebrow.

"That can't have gone over very well with the staff," I said.

Wally shook his head, and crossed his arms. "Mrs. Garrett was against it. She feels like the hotel is part of the community and didn't want to let those people go. She knew that they all had families to support." Wally's voice got louder as he spoke. "But Ms. Carlisle inundated her with charts and numbers and told her the place couldn't support such a large staff. She wanted to expand the spa services and thought the other departments needed to be more efficient."

Wally glanced from Mac to me.

He lowered his voice. "I probably shouldn't talk about

this anymore. Mrs. Garrett knows a lot more about it. She can tell you what happened."

"Anything you've seen or heard could help us, Wally," I said.

"That's it." He held his hand up to ward off any more questions. "I don't know anything else." He sat back and glanced at his watch. "I should go see whether Kirk has made any progress on the generator."

He hopped up and made a hasty exit.

"That was strange," I said. "It's like he suddenly realized what he was saying. It doesn't sound like things were running smoothly here between Clarissa and her family."

Mac shook his head. "I think we need to talk to the Garretts as well as the knitters."

We found Jessica in the kitchen talking to René. The room was bright and clean with stainless steel appliances and white countertops. It looked more like a high-end New York kitchen than a Victorian castle kitchen. Their voices were low and urgent and stopped abruptly when we approached.

Jessica's smile stopped short of her eyes. "I hear you're looking for me."

Mac glanced at me as if to say, "Wally was quick."

"We're talking to everyone who might have seen what happened last evening," he said.

She nodded and gestured toward the dining room, which was empty.

I led them to a table away from the windows and we sat.

"You don't think one of the knitters could have harmed her, do you?" Jessica said.

Mac took a deep breath. "Someone murdered your cousin, Ms. Garrett. If it wasn't one of the knitters, it was one of your staff. Given the blizzard last night, we can hardly assume this was the work of a stranger."

Jessica rubbed her arms and shivered. "I just . . . I can't imagine any of the knitters doing this."

"But you *can* imagine your staff doing this?" I asked.

She shook her head. "I didn't mean that. It's just that the cable needle kind of points to a knitter, doesn't it?"

"Maybe," I said. "There must be a bunch of those needles lying around and the workshop room wasn't locked."

Jessica shook her head. "The needle was Isabel's."

"How could you tell?" Mac said.

"It's one of the needles she had made for the class," Jessica said. "It's designed by a very exclusive knitting needle company. They use airplane-grade metals and hand-tool their needles. Isabel has raved about them on her review blog enough that they send her samples all the time."

"You could tell just by looking at it that it's one of hers?" I asked. I remembered her hesitation when I asked her about it the night before.

Jessica nodded. "She had them make purple ones and most people here have plastic cable needles that aren't curved like that."

"You said she had them made for the workshop?" Mac said. "So, does everyone have one?"

"No, she hasn't passed them out yet. In fact, I don't think anyone knows that there is more than one. She used it to demonstrate during class yesterday and she planned to give them all their own as part of the goody bag at the end of the workshop."

"Why didn't you say anything last night when you saw the needle?" I asked. "Do you think Isabel could have killed your cousin?"

Jessica was already shaking her head. "No, I don't think that. That's what I'm trying to say. But I was worried that it would look bad for Isabel."

Jessica took a deep breath and looked at us.

"Clarissa was not a nice person," she began. "Frankly, I couldn't stand her. She spent most of our childhood trying to one-up me and criticized everything I did. By the time we got to high school, she was the classic mean girl with a posse of supporters."

Jessica closed her eyes and rubbed her forehead. "Isabel and I were good friends in high school. That's why she has this workshop every year here. At first, we were doing *her* a favor, but now that she's famous through her blog and her designs, she actually brings us business throughout the year." She looked at the tablecloth and traced the pattern in the fabric. "She's still one of my closest friends. She knew that Clarissa was back in town and we talked about canceling the workshop. Isabel and Clarissa never got along."

She looked up to meet our eyes. "But Isabel isn't a killer. She's one of the nicest people I've ever known. And she's a successful businesswoman now. There is nothing Clarissa could do to hurt her." Her voice broke on the last words and her eyes filled with tears.

She took a shaky breath and continued. "Truly, if Isabel was going to kill Clarissa, she would have done it years ago. She said to me just before she came that the best revenge is to lead a happy life. There's no way she would throw it all away over an old grudge."

Mac leaned forward.

"What old grudge?" he asked. "What happened between them?"

Jessica shook her head. "She'll tell you if you ask. She doesn't have anything to hide, but she's my friend and I'm not going to share her story with you."

"Is it about Mavis's daughter, Teresa?" I asked.

Jessica drew in a quick breath. "How do you know about that?"

I shrugged. "People talk."

Jessica sat back and crossed her arms. "*I*'d rather *not* talk about it."

I looked at Mac, wondering how he would handle this. In his normal life, he probably wouldn't let Jessica slide. But this was an unusual situation. He only had the authority that he had given himself. We expected to be able to get the police involved shortly, and no one was leaving the hotel anytime soon.

I saw the struggle pass quickly over his face and then he relaxed.

I let out a breath of air and sat back in my chair.

"Okay, Ms. Garrett. We'll talk to Isabel," Mac said. "Do you have anything else you'd like to add?"

Jessica shook her head and dabbed at her eyes with a tissue.

13

I wanted to talk to Mac about his impression of Jessica's story, but we still needed to talk to Linda. I couldn't tell whether Jessica was trying to protect Isabel or make sure we focused on her.

We asked Jessica to help us find her mother. She led the way through the dining room and up the stairs to a back hallway that had not been part of Wally's tour. It was dark without the wall sconces, and the weak light filtering in from the windows in the guest hallway barely penetrated. I was wishing they were real torches when she opened another door and brightness spilled out.

Jessica had led us into the family quarters, which were small but comfortable and had a beautiful view over the back garden, where the winter white blinded us. It would be a lovely room in the summer when the flowers were in full bloom. The walls were a soft sage color and the neutral couches and chairs were the perfect backdrop for the brightly colored knit pillows and throws. Obviously knitters lived there. On that day, it looked out onto a wonderland of snow-covered trees and a rolling white lawn that ended in a wooded area at the back of the property.

Several doors led off of this common room and Jessica tapped lightly on one of them.

"Mom? Can I come in? The detectives are here and want to talk to you."

It felt strange to be called a detective again. Like putting on old clothes that had gone out of style and didn't fit anymore.

Jessica must have heard a reply because she opened the door and Mrs. Garrett stepped out. Her eyes were red and swollen and she looked as if she hadn't slept all night. She shuffled into the living room wearing slippers, jeans, and pulling an oversized cardigan more tightly around her shoulders.

Jessica gestured to the small couch and chairs and we all sat.

"I can't thank you enough, Detective McKenzie, for helping us like this," Mrs. Garrett said. "I don't know what we would have done if you hadn't stopped here yesterday. We wouldn't have known what to do."

I wasn't surprised that she had singled out Mac. It was a constant battle to be taken seriously as a woman in a "man's" job. I bristled reflexively. Then I reminded myself that I wasn't planning to return to the police force and that this sort of thing would not be my job anymore.

"No need for thanks, we're just doing our job," Mac said, and put a hand on my shoulder.

Mrs. Garrett ignored the subtle correction.

"But it's not your job, is it?" she said. "You're here on vacation. In fact, when this is all cleared up you two should come back and stay with us—my treat."

"That would be really nice, Mrs. Garrett," I said. After being stuck here with a gang of knitters and chasing a murderer, I wasn't sure I'd ever want to return, but it was a nice offer.

"Please call me Linda," she said. "And I mean it—I want to see you two back here for a relaxing weekend."

Just then, a white blur streaked into the room, directly at Linda.

"Oh, my!" she said. She put up her hands to protect herself and the white blur slowed and landed on her lap. Linda smiled down at the cat. "This is Duchess." The cat purred and blinked its golden eyes.

Mac shifted in his seat to put some distance between himself and the cat. Ever since I told him that Vi uses them as spies, even though he didn't believe Vi could converse with animals, he had been wary around them.

"We just wanted to ask you a few questions about what you may have seen last night," Mac said. "Did you see anyone in the hallways during dinner? Where would your staff have been?"

Linda sighed. "Jessica, you know more than I do about the staffing. But, I did see Isabel go up to her room partway through dinner. I had stepped out of my office to be sure Holly, our housekeeper, would be able to do the turndown service all by herself. She was on the second floor working on those rooms and I saw Isabel go into her room."

Duchess jumped down and sauntered in Mac's direction. She had clearly picked up on his aversion and in a classic feline move had locked on to him as her favorite person.

Jessica leaned forward to get the cat's attention, but Duchess scooted away from her. She smiled an apology at Mac, and said, "Emmett and René would have been in the kitchen and Kirk was probably still working on plowing the front walk. He had said he wanted to snow-blow the first several inches so that when the rest of it came down, it would be less of a job."

"Would he have been out there in the dark?" I asked.

"I guess you're right." She bit her lower lip. "I'm not sure where he would have been during dinner. Maybe in the basement? I don't remember seeing him until I went to check with him about the generator after . . . Clarissa was found."

"We heard Kirk is new here. Since he wasn't in the dining room, we'll need to talk to him soon," Mac said. "Has he been hired since Clarissa started, or has he been here longer?" Mac tried to extricate his ankles from the weaving feline.

Linda glanced at Jessica. "I think he started about four months ago. Is that right, Jess?"

Jessica nodded. "Uncle Dave died in July and Clarissa came here in August. I think Kirk started just before Christmas, so about three months. I'd have to look at his file to be sure."

Mac marked the date in his notebook. "I just wondered. It sounded like he was the newest employee."

They both nodded. "He's a very nice guy, but I don't know if he'll work out," Jessica said. "Gus says he doesn't really know how to fix anything and he can't believe he ever worked as a maintenance person before. He's had to teach him everything, which is why we're still out of power today. Gus would have had the generator running again in no time."

"Mrs. Garrett—Linda—do you know of anyone who would want to hurt your niece?" Mac asked. Duchess gave up on Mac and jumped on the couch next to Linda.

Linda's eyes welled with tears and she shook her head. She dabbed at her face and sniffled. "She wasn't always the easiest person to get along with," Linda said.

Jessica slowly closed her eyes at her mother's words.

"But she meant well and I don't think anyone in this hotel would want to hurt her," Linda concluded.

"I should really get back to work." Jessica stood.

I was surprised at Jessica's abrupt end to the interview. Mac shook his head once in my direction and I let it pass.

"Thank you for your time," Mac said. He shook Linda's hand and stood.

I thanked them as well and bent to pet Duchess, who ran behind the couch.

We left the Garretts' apartment, and Mac said he wanted to look at Clarissa's room again in the daylight. I felt a cold chill and rubbed my arms but nodded. We had barely been able to evaluate the scene with the room full of people and only a couple of flashlights for illumination.

Mac had his cop face on, but I slid my hand into his anyway. He relaxed, smiled, and squeezed.

"What did you think of the Garrett ladies?" Mac asked.

"There wasn't a lot of affection between the cousins. The aunt seems pretty torn up though," I said.

"I agree, her aunt seems to be the only one upset about her death."

Mac led the way down the hall, past the unlit sconces and up the spiral staircase. The stone was rough in the stairwell and we felt our way upward with only a small flashlight for illumination. I had the sense of winding my way into the past. I thought about Violet's story of the invalid wife who had drowned in her bath. She must have been very isolated back then if these twisting steps were the only way out of her room. I imagined the flickering light of candles on the uneven stones and almost believed a ghost might inhabit the room at the top.

We reached the landing outside Clarissa's room and my hand was on the doorknob when we heard a distinct thump from inside. I knew it wasn't the cat this time. Mac and I exchanged a wide-eyed look and I hesitated before opening the door. We leaned closer to the door and heard swishing noises and a footstep. Vi would claim it was the ghost if she were there.

"I think there's someone in there," I whispered.

Mac put himself between the door and me. "Stay back," he said and held his arm out.

"*You* stay back," I hissed and grabbed for the doorknob.

We were leaning into one another, jockeying for position in front of the door.

"Can't you just be my girlfriend?" Mac whispered. "I don't want you to get hurt."

"I can take care of myself." I felt like a fourteen-year-old arguing for a later curfew.

Mac's face softened. "I know that, but that doesn't stop me from wanting to protect you."

"It's probably just the wind." I released the doorknob and let Mac take the lead.

Mac put his finger to his lips and slowly, quietly turned the knob. We both peeked through the crack. I couldn't see much with Mac blocking most of the opening. It was dim inside because the curtains were still closed, but enough light leaked in that I could see the room was empty. I pressed Mac's shoulder to let him know that we should go ahead.

He slowly pushed the door open and we stepped inside. I went to the window and opened the heavy curtains. They scraped loudly along the rod, and light flooded the room.

I jumped when I heard, "Oh, it's you."

Vi walked out of the bathroom with her hand to her chest.

"You two scared me to death," she said. Her finger pointed threateningly.

"*We* scared *you*?" I said. "What are you doing here?"

Mac crossed his arms and glowered but let me deal with my aunt.

"Looking for clues, of course." Vi matched Mac's stance.

"What are you talking about? We'll examine the room." My voice rose to that shrill tone I hated. "We're trained professionals."

Mac waded into the conflict. "Ms. Greer, you can't be in here. You're interfering with a crime scene," Mac said, in a much calmer tone than I was using.

Vi sniffed. "It's not like there was any crime scene tape across the door. How was I to know . . ." She stopped when she saw the double glare we sent.

"Okay, okay." She held her hands up. "Wally said you were talking to the Garrett ladies and I decided I'd come take a look." She crossed her arms again. "I might be able to help. I might be able to sense something you two miss."

Mac shook his head, and took a deep breath.

"Vi, you really need to leave, *now*," I said and edged closer to Mac in case he wasn't as calm as he looked. Vi could infuriate even a meditating monk.

"It's fine, Clyde," Mac said. "Let her look." He waved an arm to encompass the room.

Violet grinned and my mouth must have dropped open because he looked at me and shrugged. "It's too late now to protect any evidence, we already collected what we could, and we don't have a crime scene team on the way. Maybe she'll find something."

This was so unlike Mac, I wondered if he'd been possessed by a friendly ghost.

"No touching." Mac pointed his finger at her and tilted his head until she nodded.

"I'll just look," she said and rubbed her hands together.

I opened the rest of the curtains and the chamber brightened. Cheery yellow walls with blue toile accents on the bed and upholstery made for a bright and feminine space. A small couch and a comfy-looking chair sat near the window, a low white dresser with a mirror sat across from the window, and the reflected light made the area warm and friendly. I wondered if this was Clarissa's touch or if it had been decorated when she moved in. I thought Wally had said that the turret hadn't been used in years due to the ghost story.

The three of us looked around the room, which *was* in a bit of disarray. Did Clarissa always leave it this way? Or had her murderer been looking for something? As Linda had said the night before, shoes were tossed everywhere, and clothing was draped over the couch and chair. The bed had not been made—maybe Clarissa didn't allow housekeeping to come up here and was too busy firing people to make it herself. I went into the bathroom to see if there was anything we had missed the night before. I stopped at the doorway and swallowed. There was still blood on the floor.

I stepped around the stain and went to the sink. Clarissa had left a huge array of makeup spread out on the counter. Eye shadow and foundation shared space with about ten pairs of false eyelashes stacked in a corner and a small basket of lipsticks. In contrast to her clothing, it seemed she kept her makeup well organized.

I opened the mirror over the sink and found birth control pills, acetaminophen, toothpaste, bandages, and a bottle of Valium. It didn't seem like she'd been taking *that* on the couple of occasions I saw her.

It all appeared ordinary and I wasn't really surprised. I doubted we would find the answer to her death among her belongings. I thought that the quickest way to find the killer would be to trace everyone's movements from the evening before. There was only one way into this room—hopefully someone saw who came up here besides Clarissa.

Mac and Vi were still looking around in the main

bedroom when I came out. They turned toward me and I shook my head.

"I'm not finding anything useful here," Mac said. "She certainly wasn't a very neat person."

"Unless the killer did this to make it look like she was a slob," Vi said.

She was examining a tall bookcase that sat on the wall opposite the door. It was built in and a different style from the white bed and dresser. Its dark wood and intricate scrollwork made me think it was probably original to the room.

Vi ran her hand over the carvings, while Mac's lips pressed into a white line. She was ignoring the "no touching" rule.

"Hey," Vi said. She pushed her finger against one of the scrolls and the bookcase swung away from her like a door.

"What did you do?" Mac said and took three strides over to where she stood gaping at the dark passage that had appeared out of nowhere.

I hung back, half expecting a mummy to lurch out at us, shredded linen dragging.

"I just pushed this little button thingy," she said. "It looked different from the other ones." She pointed to a small round carving in the center of a scroll. It looked the same to me, except it stuck out just a touch more.

We peeked into the opening and saw only darkness.

"Is it storage? Or another closet?" I said. "Didn't women have huge dresses back then? Maybe this is some kind of cedar closet."

Mac turned the flashlight on and shone it into the void. A few feet from the opening, the floor dropped off. He stepped forward and his light bounced off the walls, finally resting on a set of steep steps.

Vi said, "What are we waiting for? Let's go!"

14

Of *course*, the castle has a secret passageway. And, of course, Vi would be the one to find it. I peered into the dark. After the first five steps, there was only inky black. I took the flashlight and shone it up toward the ceiling, where heavy cobwebs hung in the corners as if the stairs had not been used in decades.

Vi charged ahead and motioned for Mac to follow.

"Wait, Vi," I said and grabbed her arm. "We don't know where it leads and there's no light."

She shrugged off my hand and turned toward me. "How are we going to know where it leads unless we go down those steps?" She put her hands on her hips and looked at Mac for backup. "The flashlight is bright enough to show us the stairs."

I knew she was right. We'd been assuming the killer could only come in through the one door, but if this stairway led to another room, then maybe more people had access than we thought.

I felt my shoulders slump. "Okay, but let Mac go first, Vi. I don't want you breaking a hip."

Vi gestured for Mac to lead the way.

We carefully descended the staircase following Mac's flashlight beam. It only illuminated as far as the next few steps. For all we knew, the stairs could dead-end or drop off into a crumbling pit. I kept one hand on the stone wall for balance and one hand on Vi's elbow. It was slow going and the skittering of creatures in the dark didn't add to the enjoyment. I sent up a request to the universe that Mac's light wouldn't fail.

Finally, we came to a wooden door. I was certain it would be locked and we'd have to turn around and make our way back up in the gloom. Mac tried the handle and it turned. He gave the door a gentle shove and we peeked out into the hallway that Wally had said contained offices and the back entrance to the kitchen. It was empty, but we heard René and Emmett in the kitchen. The three of us looked at one another in various states of surprise. The door was one of several in the hallway. There was a sign affixed to it on the hallway side: STORAGE—STAFF ONLY. This opened up a whole new avenue of investigation.

"I knew it!" Vi said. "It's the chef. He did it."

I chose not to mention her last suspect had been the maintenance guy and we hadn't even interviewed him yet.

"Why would René want to kill Clarissa?" I said.

"I don't know yet, but he has a back entrance to her room. That's pretty suspicious."

"It *is* pretty suspicious," Mac said. "Mostly it's suspicious because the staff and the family must have known this staircase is here, but none of them chose to tell us."

"Staff and any curious guests might be aware of the staircase," I said. "It's not locked on either side."

Mac nodded. "Let's get out of here and go somewhere we can talk in private."

Vi insisted we return to "our" room. Mac's look of dismay made it clear he had meant that he wanted to talk to *me* in private, not Vi.

"Should I get Rose and Lucille?" Vi asked. "Wally might be helpful, too."

Mac opened his mouth to speak, but Vi held up her hand.

"He knows lots of stuff about this place, you just have to ask the right questions with him," Vi said in a lecture-y tone. "There's no way he could be the killer because he was with us from the time Clarissa left until Linda found her." Vi rummaged in her purse and pulled out a small black notebook that looked remarkably similar to the one Mac carries. She flipped it open and began writing a note while we walked along the back hallway toward the stairs.

"What's that you're writing, Vi?" I said.

"I just don't want to forget anything. You never know what will be important to an investigation."

"Ms. Greer, you aren't investigating anything. Clyde and I will figure this out."

Vi's mouth turned down. I could tell by the softening of his expression that Mac interpreted this as sadness. *I* knew it was her stubborn streak expressing itself.

"I'm sorry, I didn't mean to offend you—" Mac began.

Vi cut him off by saying, "I understand. You haven't worked with us before so you probably don't know what a great team we make. But Clyde and I have done some good work in the past when we had murders to solve." She elbowed me in the ribs. "Tell him, Clyde."

Mac turned his incredulous face in my direction.

I couldn't look him in the eye, so I addressed his snowman.

"Actually, Mac, they do sometimes have some good ideas, and they have helped me in the past."

"In the past? You mean the times you took it upon yourself to solve a murder and almost got yourself killed, not once, but twice? *Those* times?" Mac's face had turned stony and red. It was as if he didn't know whether to be outraged or terrified.

I lowered my voice and leaned closer to Mac.

"It's easier than fighting it."

Mac took a deep breath and let it out.

"Okay, go get Wally and Rose," Mac said to Vi. "But leave my mother out of it."

Mac took my hand and stormed up the stairs toward my room.

"I'll be right there! Don't say anything until I get back," Vi said, and scurried off toward the front desk.

Mac dragged me to the room and waited while I pulled out my key. He closed the door quietly behind us and took a moment before he turned around.

"I don't like the idea of getting civilians involved in a murder investigation," he said to the door.

"I know, Mac, but honestly, we can't stop them from talking about it and throwing around ideas. I think it's better if they think they're part of the action. Otherwise, they'll go around talking to everyone and we won't be able to keep any information to ourselves." I put my hand on his shoulder to turn him around. "This way we have some control over them. Plus, technically, we're *all* civilians in this case."

Mac nodded. "I get it. Wally might actually be helpful anyway. He's in a unique position—we know he's not guilty and he knows all the suspects better than we do."

"Besides, if we hadn't come here, Vi would probably be in charge of the investigation all by herself," I said.

Mac shuddered and held his hands up. "Okay, okay. You're always looking on the bright side, aren't you?"

I smiled at him, glad he wasn't going to fight Vi on this. Arguing with Vi was always a losing proposition.

He put his arm around my shoulder and pulled me into an embrace. "This is not the way I planned on spending our first full day of vacation," he said into my hair.

"Oh, what did you have planned?" I asked and moved a little closer.

"First, breakfast on a balcony looking out over the ocean." He tightened his hold and kissed me. "Then, maybe a stroll on the beach. Followed by—"

The doorknob rattled and we sprung apart.

"Here we are!" Vi announced as the door opened.

Mom came in first, followed by a nervous-looking Wally and then Vi.

Vi was breathing heavily. "They weren't in the lounge, so I had to track them down in the library. Good thing Rose was looking at the door when I cracked it open," Vi said. "Lucille was focused on her cables so I gave Rose the special signal and she snuck out without anyone noticing." Vi turned to Wally and said, "Detective McKenzie doesn't want his mother mucking around in the investigation. She doesn't have any experience in this sort of thing."

Mom cleared her cards off the coffee table and we sat by the window.

"Rose, you won't believe what we just found!" Vi said.

Mac cleared his throat to interrupt her. She glanced at him and miraculously fell silent.

"Wally, do you know anything about a back staircase that leads to the kitchen from the turret room?" Mac asked.

Everyone looked at Wally, who turned bright red.

He nodded. "Yes, I know of it. I've never used that staircase. It was put in when the house was built. Ada Carlisle liked to cook even though in those days, everyone had servants and it was considered unladylike to be involved in the household duties."

Wally stopped and looked at us.

Vi crossed her arms and raised her eyebrows at him.

"Once they moved in and she was so sick, her maid used it to get her meals and tea from the kitchen without going all the way through the house," Wally said. "I think it had been closed up for a while after she died. But the family knew about it. I only found out when Ms. Carlisle moved into the turret room because she said she wanted Gus, the maintenance guy, to check it out and be sure the staircase was still safe."

I watched Vi carefully. Her gaze kept straying to the velvet bag that held her pendulum. Mom gripped her tarot deck and I could tell it was all she could do to refrain from laying them on the table. My family liked to get a small amount of information from humans and then consult the oracles. I shook my head at both of them. If they started pulling out their psychic solutions, Mac would never confide in them again.

"Do you know if anyone has been using it?" Mac asked.

Wally's face went blank and he wouldn't meet Mac's eyes. He shook his head. "Not that I know of, no."

"Who do you think was using it, Mac?" Mom asked.

"I don't know, but it opens up a new avenue of discussion if there was another way into that room."

Wally adjusted his tie and looked at his lap.

"Okay, well, thanks for the information, Wally. You can go," Mac said.

Wally jumped up and banged his leg on the table on his way out.

"He's hiding something," Vi said. In the absence of her pendulum, she had begun knitting. She claimed it helped her think.

"I agree," Mac said.

"Then why did you let him go?" I said.

"I'll follow up with him when he has a smaller audience. He might talk then."

"I feel like I'm out of the loop," Mom said. "How did you find the staircase?"

"I found it when we were searching Clarissa's room," Vi said. She sat up straight and puffed out her chest—her demeanor and wildly colored clothing brought a peacock sharply to mind.

"You searched her room without me?" Mom looked at us as if we had just told her we had gone to Disney World and left her at home.

"Not exactly, Mom. Mac and I went to check on a few things, and Vi was snooping around in there," I said.

"It's a good thing I was, or you never would have found the secret staircase." Vi's knitting project fell, forgotten, to the floor. "This castle is so amazing! Secret staircases, a ghost, a blizzard—the knitting is like the icing on the cake!"

Mac sighed.

Mom had grown quiet while Vi exulted over the castle. "There was a murder, Vi. I'm not feeling very cozy knowing there's a killer lurking in the shadows."

Vi's smile faded and she adopted a more somber countenance. She quietly picked up her needles again.

"We should head back to the workshop," Mom said. "I told Wally I'd read his cards later today. Maybe I can get a sense of what he might be hiding. . . ."

Mac took a deep breath and was about to say something, but I interrupted.

"I think Mac and I are going to go sit in the lounge for a while before lunch," I said. I stood up and headed for the door, pulling Mac along with me.

15

"Tarot cards?!?" Mac said as I closed the door behind us.

"Mac, you know how they feel about that sort of thing. They think it helps. And how can it hurt, really?" I pulled him farther away from the room in order to have this conversation somewhere away from my mother's ears.

His bristling calmed a bit. "Look, it can't really hurt, but you know how I feel about all that mumbo-jumbo. Charging people money to tell their future is dangerous."

Mac's father had died when he was twelve and his mother had spent a lot of money over the years trying to contact her dead husband. Mac didn't have a benign relationship to all things psychic.

"I doubt Mom is charging Wally for a reading, she just really likes to read cards and in this case, she thinks she's helping."

Mac sighed. "I'll try to keep an open mind. But I'm not

going to start investigating based on tarot cards and ghost stories."

We had reached the lounge while talking and I peeked in. It was empty. We sat on the couch closest to the fireplace, where Mac took off his ridiculous sweater. I glanced around the room, soaking in the atmosphere and enjoying a moment of quiet with Mac when I noticed it.

All the legs of the couches were wearing socks. Pink and yellow and neon green. I don't know why I didn't see it immediately. I started giggling and Mac turned to look at me.

"What? I know the sweater is silly, but it's drafty in this place . . . ," he began.

I shook my head and pointed to the sofa feet.

He put his head in his hands, but I could see he was smiling. "I thought I had seen all the crazy I was going to see."

We got up and looked around the room. It was like an Easter egg hunt and now that we were looking for it, we saw little flashes of woolly color all over the room.

Tiny hats adorned the bishops of the chess set. The statue of a rider on his horse sported a striped scarf and the fire poker had a knitted cover on its handle.

"These people really need to get out more," Mac said.

"I think it's funny."

We were returning to the couch when a ladder carried by a rugged Marlboro man entered the room. The man and the ladder stopped abruptly and Wally bumped into them.

"Kirk! Why did you stop, you have to put this up on that portrait."

Wally held a long piece of rainbow-colored knitting that looked like triangular banners. He followed Kirk's gaze and froze.

"Hi, Wally," I said. "Are you the yarn bomber?"

He turned pink and shook his head. "No, but I was

volunteered to assist. Ms. Garrett said I should put this up over the portrait of Alastair Carlisle." He gestured toward the fireplace where Alastair glared imperiously at the room.

Kirk shuffled his feet and looked at Wally.

"You remember Kirk." Wally gestured at his partner in crime.

Mac stuck out his hand. "Thanks for your help last night."

Kirk shook hands and nodded.

"Kirk, this is Clyde Fortune," Wally said. "She's working with Detective McKenzie to figure out what happened to Clarissa."

Kirk stuck out his hand and bestowed a dazzling smile. I noticed how clean his hands and nails were—my stereotype of a maintenance guy tended toward a balding, potbellied, older man with a cigar clamped in his teeth. In my imagination, his nails are always filthy with grease and dirt from all the repair work he does. This guy was nothing like that. He was in great shape, with longish dark hair that fell forward over his dark eyes. He sported a day-old beard and looked more like my idea of a sexy pirate than a maintenance man.

"Actually, Kirk, we were hoping to talk to you about Ms. Carlisle's death," Mac said.

"I don't think I can help—I didn't see her yesterday." He set one end of the ladder down and gave us a look of careful patience.

"Anything you can add about your whereabouts and the location of any of the other staff would help," Mac said. He cocked his head and narrowed his eyes at Kirk, who studied the floor.

Wally looked at his watch. "Can we get this knitting up on the picture first? Ms. Garrett really wanted it up before the knitters take a break." He lowered his voice. "They're getting agitated over Clarissa's death and Jessica wants to keep their minds off the . . . murder."

Kirk took the ladder to the painting and climbed up. Wally handed him the multicolored banner of wool and Kirk draped it along the top.

"No, I don't think that looks right," Wally said. "Can you make it drape a little more? Just there on the right?"

Kirk adjusted the knitting.

Wally stood back and nodded.

"You know, that's not as subtle as the rest of them," Mac said. "It's hanging right over his face."

My head swiveled rapidly in Mac's direction—who knew he cared about the yarn bombing?

I definitely saw Kirk's eyes roll toward the ceiling. He pulled the banner up so it just ran along the top of the frame. Not exactly subtle, but not as obvious.

Wally nodded and Kirk climbed down.

"Do you have a minute right now?" Mac asked Kirk.

"Sure. Let me go put this away." Kirk gestured to the ladder as he clicked it closed.

He took the ladder out of the room. Wally checked his watch and rushed out as well.

Mac and I resumed our seats on the couch and admired the new yarn installation. I wondered if there were other little yarn-y things hidden around the castle. I'd have to ask Vi what the rules were. I hoped there was a prize for the most things spotted. I didn't care about knitting needles, but the hidden-object part of the contest was fun. Maybe it would entertain the knitters and keep them from whipping themselves into an anxiety-fueled frenzy.

We heard the door open down the hall and voices made their way in our direction.

"We better get out of here before the knitters come in," Mac said and jumped to his feet.

"Are you afraid of them?" I asked jokingly.

"No. I would just rather not get sucked into another conversation about tarot cards and yarnovers."

I grabbed his snowman sweater off the back of the couch and followed him out of the room.

We waited for Kirk in the front reception area. Wally went to herd the knitters into the lounge for their break and the big reveal of more yarn bombing.

Mac and I sat on one of the comfy couches that graced the entryway. I looked out at the white landscape, the trees outlined in snow, and the drifts that had piled up outside. It would have been a perfect romantic getaway—if only we were somewhere else, or the knitters were, and no one had died.

Surprisingly, even though the weekend had been altered, I wasn't upset. I liked working a case with Mac, and even Vi had been helpful. I filed this feeling away to examine later. As I sat with Mac, I realized I didn't want to move on. I needed to find a way to stay in Crystal Haven that didn't involve rejoining the police force, or setting up shop as a fortune teller.

"Mac, what do you think—" I was interrupted by Kirk, who strode toward us, apologizing for taking so long.

"Sorry, I got delayed talking to Mrs. Garrett. I keep hoping the power will come back on because I really don't know how to fix the generator." He sat across from us and leaned forward, elbows on knees.

"I'm sure you've heard that we suspect foul play in Ms. Carlisle's death," Mac began.

Kirk nodded.

"We're hoping you can help us piece together the movements of staff and guests that evening," Mac said.

Kirk sat back. "Like I said, I don't think I'll be much help because I didn't see many people yesterday. I was outside trying to keep the walk clear for an hour or so during the afternoon. I think I finished around five thirty. Then I stopped in the kitchen to grab some dinner—Ms. Garrett said any employees that stayed could help themselves in the kitchen. After I ate, I went down to the staff rooms and took a shower. Just as I finished, the lights went out."

"You didn't see anyone, then, before the lights went out?"

Kirk shook his head, but then stopped. "I did see René come down to the freezer to take something out, and then I saw Emmett a little while later, but that's pretty routine. They had moved things to the downstairs freezer earlier in the day when the storm started to pick up. The freezer has its own generator—apparently René insisted last year when the power went out and he lost all the food for a wedding reception."

"So, that generator is still working?" Mac asked.

"Yup, the frozen food is safe, even if the rest of us are shivering and using flashlights. The upstairs refrigerator does not have its own generator, so I think they've been storing some things in the snow."

"Do you think you can fix the generator?" I asked.

"I don't know." Kirk leaned back and crossed his arms. "Gus is the head of maintenance and he has all the manuals tossed into a filing cabinet. I've been trying to sort through them with my flashlight and checking the landline every ten minutes in the hope I can call him and get some advice." His mouth quirked up on one side. "This is my first gig in a maintenance department and I don't have a lot of experience with generators. If Gus's wife hadn't been sick, he would have stayed this weekend instead of me. I'd probably be further along if the knitters would quit with the yarn bombing. I have one or another of them finding me every half hour needing help with something."

I suspected I knew the reason for the exuberant yarn bombing and it had nothing to do with yarn, or the contest. It was all about Kirk.

"We won't keep you," Mac said. "Let us know if you think of anything else. Anything you saw out of the ordinary or anyone in a place they didn't belong."

Kirk nodded and stood.

"Yeah, I'll let you know if I think of anything." He shook my hand and then Mac's. The two men looked at each other longer than was necessary and I wondered why Mac was using his stare-down technique on Kirk.

After Kirk turned the corner, I said, "What do you think? Is he telling the truth?"

Mac nodded. "I think so. You don't believe him?"

"Yes, I believe him. You just looked at him weird."

"No, I didn't. I looked at him in the normal way."

"Looked at who in the normal way?" Vi came toward us from the lounge.

"Nothing, Vi. We were just talking to Kirk," I said.

"Mavis can't stop talking about him. She says he's a hunk."

I turned to Mac. "Looks like you've got some competition."

Mac grunted and said, "Thank God."

Vi had been watching this exchange like a tennis match. "Have you been in the lounge today? There's more bombing and it's fantastic! You should come and see it. I don't know how they're sneaking out and getting it done. I've been keeping track of all of the knitters—even if they're using the hunk as an accomplice, they have to meet with him at some point. . . ."

"We saw it, Vi," I said.

"The little hats for the chess people? The banner on Alastair's portrait?" she asked.

I nodded.

"Hey, you two aren't helping, are you? That would be really sneaky."

We shook our heads, Mac much more vigorously than me.

Vi cocked her head. "Do you hear that?"

Mac and I stood still and listened. Then I heard it. It sounded like a motorcycle. Or maybe two motorcycles.

16

I looked out the window.

"It's coming from out there," I said, pointing toward the woods.

Mac cocked his head. "Sounds like dirt bikes."

"It must be snowmobiles," Vi said.

We squinted and peered out the window in the direction of the woods. Wally had come back in and joined us at the window.

"Did you hear that weird noise?" he asked.

Then I caught sight of them. Two snowmobiles broke into the clearing from the trees. They were still pretty far away, but approaching quickly. It looked like a bear drove one of them.

As they drew nearer, I saw that one of the riders wore a backpack strapped across his chest like a baby carrier. The one with the bear also had a person riding just behind. The riders wore ski masks and goggles, and the fluffy layer of snow sprayed around them as they approached.

Mac and I stared at each other, mouths open.

The knitters thundered out of the lounge. Mavis and Selma led the charge, moving rapidly toward the back door. "We're saved!" Selma announced as she hurried past the reception hallway.

The rest of the knitters followed in her wake. They acted like castaways spotting a cruise ship.

I trailed the crowd down the hall toward the back door. I heard the engines rev and then cut out.

The gang poured out the back door, no one bothering to put on coats.

I felt my breath catch when I saw the riders dismount. The bear bounded off the snowmobile and let out a very canine woof. His huge doggy face smiled up at his copilot—Dad.

He pulled off his ski mask and his shock of white hair stood up even more than usual. I viciously suppressed the comparison to a cockatoo. Mom immediately greeted him with a big hug. His face was red from the cold but he looked delighted at his hero's welcome. Baxter leaped and barked in his joy at seeing Mom again and when he spotted me, he barreled toward me and jumped, knocking me into a snowbank. My beloved mastiff weighs almost as much as I do.

The other rider was my nephew, Seth. Taller than me now at fourteen, his lanky frame and blond hair reminded me of his mother, my sister, Grace. He came to my rescue and pulled Baxter away while Vi helped me up. Vi walked over to Dad to get the scoop from him.

Seth threw a snowball for Baxter to chase and he bounded off into the garden.

"What are you doing here?" I said to Seth.

"What are *you* doing here?" he said. Tuffy's head popped out of the backpack, his nose twitching as he assessed the situation. Tuffy was Seth's shih tzu and they had been inseparable since they met last summer.

"Our flight was canceled and we had to find a place to stay, then we got snowed in," I said.

Seth nodded. "I knew your flight got canceled—the airline called the house. But how did you end up here . . . with them?" He tilted his head toward the ladies.

"We didn't know they were here," I said quietly.

"Great. I bet Mac was really happy to see them." Seth had been privy to Mac's exuberance at getting away from the psychic dream team.

"You get more sarcastic every day."

Seth grinned and bent down to let Tuffy out of the bag.

Tuffy sniffed the ground and minced his way over to a mound of snow that looked like it used to be a bush. He lifted his leg and left a yellow stain before kicking up the snow with his back legs. He trotted back to Seth and sat on his foot.

By this time all of the knitters had come outside to see the snowmobiles, the dogs, and the newcomers. Vi introduced everyone.

"So, tell us!" Vi said to Dad.

"Yes, Frank. What are you doing here—not that we aren't thrilled to see you . . . ," Mom said.

"We got a call from the airline that Clyde's flight was canceled and we couldn't get through on her cell. We couldn't reach either of your phones or the hotel. I saw on the news that a lot of this area was without power and we got worried." Dad shrugged and smiled when he got another hug from mom.

"We hoped you had heard from Clyde and would know where she was staying, but didn't expect that you'd all be here," Seth added. He succumbed to a hug from Mom. When she released him, he continued his story.

"Papa's police scanner told us the police and emergency crews were working to clear accidents off the road." Seth lowered his voice and said to me, "I had to keep my eyes on the ditches all the way here."

"How did you get here so fast?" I asked.

"We left when it was still dark out," Seth said. "Papa wanted to get on the road right away." Seth bent down to pick up Tuffy, who had begun shivering.

"We tried to get through by car, but there's a big tree blocking the road to the hotel," Dad said.

Gasps and tsks went through the crowd. Mavis mumbled that we were stuck here until spring. Tina, Heather, and Amy stepped aside and whispered.

"I saw a snowmobile rental place," Seth said. And out of the corner of his mouth to me, "While I was watching the ditches for your crumpled car." He raised his voice and said, "They told us there was a path through the woods we could use if we went slow."

"How did you get Baxter to ride on it?" I asked while rubbing Baxter's ears. He looked up at me, tongue lolling with a huge doggy smile.

Dad shrugged. "Seth just told him to hop on and he did."

Seth and I exchanged a look. His ability to communicate with animals was still our secret, but they'd figure it out soon if he kept convincing the dogs to do crazy things.

"You two are quite the heroes," Mac said from the doorway.

Everyone turned to see Mac smiling and Wally looking at Baxter with a mixture of fear and fascination.

Vi announced she was freezing and gestured everyone

inside. "You two won't believe what's been going on around here," Vi said. "There's been a *murder*."

"Oh, Frank, I'm so glad you're here," Mom said and hooked her arm through Dad's.

Mac and Wally grabbed two duffel bags and the bag we used to tote dog food off the back of the snowmobiles and brought them inside.

Vi launched into her story of ghosts, murders, and yarn bombing as she shepherded the gang back to the hotel.

Seth hesitated outside with the dogs.

"Do you think it's okay to bring them in?" he asked. "We couldn't leave them alone at home but we didn't think about where they would stay."

"Why don't you clip their leashes on and we'll just keep them close until we figure out what to do. It's too cold to leave them outside," I said.

The general hubbub in the back hallway drew Jessica out of her office.

"Oh, my. What's going on?" she said.

Vi explained about our rescuers.

"Rose says the generator isn't working?" Dad said. "I can take a look at it if you like."

"If you think you can get it working, I'm sure we'd all appreciate it," Jessica said. "It's not getting any warmer."

Dad nodded and rubbed his hands together. There was nothing he liked better than to fix things.

Vi leaned over toward me. "I hope he doesn't blow the place up."

"It'll be fine, Vi. He knows about generators, he's been dealing with the one at your house for years." Vi crossed her arms and watched him walk away with Wally.

"Jessica, the guys brought the dogs with them," I said.

"Do you mind if they stay, or should they try to find a hotel that will take them and is within snowmobile distance?"

Jessica looked at Tuffy, who was shivering in Seth's arms. "How cute. No, it's fine. He doesn't look much bigger than Duchess." Baxter had been by the back door sniffing the bag with his food and he took this moment to amble forward through the crowd.

"Oh. This one is a bit bigger." Jessica's face had gone a shade whiter. "I think maybe we should put them out in the cottage."

"Cottage?" Mac said.

Jessica nodded. "It's for families and small groups. It sleeps six and has a small kitchen. The dogs can get outside easily."

"Wally never mentioned a cottage when we were checking in," I said.

"Well, we haven't been using it this winter. But it will only take Holly a little while to open it up and get it ready. It's not as convenient in the winter because it's away from the main hotel. He probably didn't even think of it with the storm coming on Thursday."

A cottage would have been the perfect place for Mac and I to stay. I would have to have a word with Wally later.

"Oh, Frank, Seth and I can stay out there with the dogs," Mom said.

Vi nudged me in the ribs. "It's just you and me now."

The knitters dispersed to the lounge to continue their projects.

"Nice sweater, dude," Seth said and couldn't hide his smirk.

"If you're jealous, I'm sure one of the ladies could make you one," Mac said.

"Um, no." Seth shivered dramatically. "So, do they have any food around here?"

17

Mom went to pack her bag and we left the dogs with Vi. The knitters dispersed to put their things away before their break. Seth, Mac, and I wandered to the kitchen to check on timing for lunch—I figured they'd be getting ready to serve it soon.

Emmett stood at the long worktable arranging sandwich supplies for the buffet. René entered through the other door, lugging a large pot of red soup. He and Emmett had loaded coolers with all the perishables and they kept them outside in the snow. Based on their muttering I deduced it wasn't going very well.

"Hi, René," I said. "We have a hungry newcomer—any chance he could get an early sandwich from the lunch buffet?" I asked.

René turned and looked Seth over. "Sure, anyone who arrives on a snowmobile should at least get a sandwich."

Emmett pulled the rest of the things out of the cooler to

show Seth the choices. Seth stepped forward to help and the two of them began discussing sandwich fixings.

René had set the large pot on the floor when he closed the door. He bent down and started to lift it onto the stove. Mac stepped forward to help and they carried it across the kitchen.

I heard a crash from the other side of the door and Vi's voice raised in alarm.

Jessica cracked the door open and said, "Help!" and just as I turned to see what was wrong, a white streak flew into the room straight at René.

The cat jumped up onto his chest and climbed up to his shoulders, where she sat hissing in the direction of the door. René tried to get a better grip on the pot with a cat stuck to his neck. Just as I started toward René to help with the cat, the door flew open and Baxter charged in with a deep bark. He ran at the chef and the cat. René backed up until he hit the table. He dropped the pot, and Mac's grip slipped as well. They sprayed a good amount of bouillabaisse all over the kitchen and themselves. The cat continued to hiss and must have been digging in its claws if René's shouts were any indication.

A stream of angry French ensued and I was glad that I didn't understand a word he said.

Baxter slipped in the mess on the floor and then began sampling it. Mac stood looking shocked as the red liquid soaked into his jeans.

At that moment, Wally entered the kitchen through the swinging door from the dining room. He carried a large, several-tiered cake and was backing into the room with it.

Duchess hissed again. Baxter looked up from his soup and narrowed his eyes. Duchess launched herself at Wally and Baxter followed. Wally was caught off guard and threw his hands up to protect himself from Baxter. The cake went flying. Wally ended up covered in frosting and Baxter began gulping down bites of cake.

"Not Isabel's cake!" Jessica cried. She hurried forward but stopped when she started to slip in the frosting.

Duchess ran toward Seth and attached herself to his neck. Baxter gave chase again and I stepped in front of him to stop his progress. I grabbed his collar.

"Baxter!" I scolded. "Sit!"

Baxter looked at me mutinously, but sat.

"Look at what you did," I said. Baxter hung his head and refused to look at me.

René, Mac, and Wally were covered in either bouillabaisse or frosting.

Tuffy had wandered in as well and hid behind Seth's legs, growling.

"We must get these animals out of the kitchen!" René said, his face almost as red as the soup.

I dragged Baxter to the door. Vi was there and took the dog. I handed her some paper towels to wipe the soup and frosting off his feet. Tuffy followed Baxter and cast a menacing glance backward at Duchess.

René stood with his arms out, surveying the damage to his chef's whites.

"I don't know how that cat always finds me. It's like she knows I don't like cats and does it to spite me."

"You're covered in soup," Jessica said. She dabbed ineffectually at the red spots.

René was already stripping his chef's smock off. He wore a sleeveless T-shirt underneath and I spotted a fleur-de-lis tattoo on his upper arm.

"Cool," Seth said. He pointed to the tattoo. "Are you from Quebec?"

René tilted his head at Seth as if trying to figure out how

he had come to that conclusion. He glanced at his arm and shrugged a new smock over his head.

"No, I am from France," René said.

Jessica pried Duchess off of Seth. The cat had begun purring and clung to the boy like she had found a long-lost friend. "I'm going to take Duchess back upstairs—I don't know how she keeps getting out," Jessica said and went out the door that led to the dining room to avoid the dogs.

"Let's get your sandwich finished up so I can move these coolers outside, and clean up this mess," Emmett said. He cast a concerned glance at René who was still muttering under his breath.

Seth shrugged. "I can finish it." He picked up a knife and spread mustard on the bread.

Mac and I grabbed paper towels from the sink area and began wiping up the mess on the floor and the walls. We dabbed at his jeans, but they would need to be thrown in the wash—if they survived at all. I handed Wally a roll of paper towels and he began wiping up the cake and frosting.

"The cake was for Isabel—to celebrate her new book," Wally said as he dumped the remains in the trash.

"I can make another one," Emmett sighed. "Why did you bring it back in here?"

Wally held his hands out. "I was trying to help. The title was spelled wrong—I wanted to have you fix it before anyone saw it."

After most of the mess was under control, I left Seth to his food prep and ducked back out into the hall to see how Vi was doing with the dogs. Mac followed and went upstairs to change.

"What happened?" I said to her.

"Baxter just went nuts when he saw that cat. I don't know why—he's never had a problem with cats before. . . ."

I wondered where she got her information since he had been known to chase the neighbor cats up a tree. I knew he wouldn't have hurt Duchess—it was more of a game to him than anything else. I had seen him slow down while pursuing an older cat. It seemed the chase was the goal, not actually catching the feline.

"You're going to get yourself kicked out of here and then what will you do?" I said to him.

He had the decency to lower his ears and look at the floor, but I wasn't fooled.

"We better check on the cottage and get these guys out of here before they cause any more trouble," I said to Vi.

She nodded and headed off toward the front desk to talk to Wally.

I sat and petted Baxter and Tuffy while waiting for Seth. He eventually appeared, munching on a muffin that was left over from breakfast.

"Did you leave any food for the rest of us?" I asked. "We have to get through another day or two, you know."

Seth broke off a piece and shared it with the dogs. "There's plenty," he said through a mouthful of muffin.

As I pointed out some crumbs Baxter had missed, the lights clicked on. And I heard the whirring of a fan blowing in the heating vents.

Seth and I heard a round of applause and cheering start up in the lounge.

"Papa's a genius with the generators," Seth said.

I nodded and thought I had underestimated my dad's skills. If he could fix something that the maintenance guy had been unable to repair, either Dad was way better than I thought, or Kirk was a terrible mechanic.

"Let's get the boys outside after all the cat excitement," I said.

We grabbed our coats from the hooks by the back door and stepped outside with the dogs.

The crunch of snow underfoot was the only sound in the softly padded yard. We took the dogs through the garden toward the cottage, which I had assumed was some sort of outbuilding, but now saw was a small house. The walkway became more snow covered as we moved farther from the parking lot.

I smelled snow on the air and knew that we were in for more of it later that day. I started thinking about winters as a kid when we had lost power and schools had shut down. It only happened a couple of times, but it had been fun then. In Crystal Haven, we lived close enough to town to at least walk to buy food and I had had access to all of my things. And there wasn't a murderer on the loose.

"So what's the deal with that chef guy?" Seth interrupted my thoughts.

"He's engaged to the owner's daughter and I guess he's trying to make the restaurant some sort of destination dining. Why?"

"In New York, I took French in school and we had this teacher from Quebec." He threw a snowball for Baxter who chased after it with glee. "He was really cool and taught us all the swear words."

"I'm sure your parents are thrilled that their tuition money was well spent."

Seth grinned. "Did you hear what he said when the cat jumped on him?"

"Something angry in French," I said.

"He said, '*Tabarnak.*' "

"So?" I said. Baxter returned and bounded around Seth until he made another ball to throw.

"It's a swear word, but only in Quebec. Someone from France wouldn't use it."

"So, you think he's not French, but Canadian?"

Seth nodded. "I don't know if it matters. Who cares where he's from? But why would he lie about it?"

It was a truth in police work, and probably many other fields, that people lied. Sometimes it was a big lie and sometimes a small one. The trick was figuring out which it was and how it related to the case.

Baxter loped back to us without the snowball and waited for Seth to make him another one. Tuffy barely cleared the snowdrifts and after finishing his business, pawed at Seth to pick him up.

"He's covered in snow," I said. "We better get him inside and dried off."

We turned and made our way back to the hotel. Holly came out of the cottage as we passed and said it was ready.

"I'll ask Kirk to clear a path from here to the back door so your parents can get in and out easily," she said as we walked back together.

"It feels like we're all going to be stuck here for a while. Unless we use the snowmobiles to shuttle everyone out of here."

"Well, now that the power is back on, it won't be too difficult to tolerate."

She held the door for us and we went just inside the door with the dogs.

"Do you have any old towels we could use to dry off the dogs?"

She nodded, went down the hall toward the kitchen, and came back with a pile of fluffy white towels that looked anything but old.

"You can use these. Maybe you can put one on the floor there so they don't drip too much."

She patted Baxter and he leaned into her hand. Tuffy stretched his head forward to sniff her leg while Baxter distracted her. Tuffy seemed satisfied she wasn't dangerous because he stepped closer and wagged his tail. Holly bent down and rubbed his ear. Tuffy sat and looked at her adoringly.

"Wow, he doesn't usually like strangers," Seth said.

Holly shrugged. "Dogs typically like me. It's cats that I have a hard time winning over."

"If you're talking about the white cat, she seems to be nothing but trouble," I said.

"She's not so bad," Seth said. "She just got scared of Baxter."

"Duchess? She's been in a snit since Ms. Carlisle moved here," Holly said. "I used to find her up in the turret room sleeping in the sunshine in the window. I think when she had to share her room, she got mad."

"She didn't belong to Clarissa?"

Holly snorted. "Hardly. They barely tolerated each other." She lowered her voice. "They were too much alike. Predatory and entitled." Her eyes grew large and she put her hand over her mouth. "I'm so sorry. I shouldn't have said that."

I was surprised by how easily she had criticized her dead boss, but remembering the way Clarissa had berated her, I couldn't really blame her.

I held up my hand. "Don't worry about it. Already forgotten," I said. But I did file it away to mention to Mac later.

18

Vi strode into the hall just as we were finishing with the dogs. They were still damp and filled the hall with that distinct wet dog odor.

"Here you are! We've been looking for you. Lunch is set up in the dining room."

"Oh good, I'm starving," Seth said.

"You just ate!" I said.

"That was just a snack. What's for lunch?"

Vi waved her arm in the direction of the dining area and Seth disappeared down the hall.

I stood there holding the leashes and wondering what to do with the guys.

"I just had something to eat—you go ahead and I'll guard the dogs. As long as that cat doesn't show up again, I should be fine."

"Thanks, Vi. I'll be quick and then we can get them out to the cottage. Holly said it's ready."

She nodded and knelt to talk to Baxter and Tuffy.

Everyone crowded around Dad in the dining room, congratulating him and thanking him for fixing the generator. He glowed with all the attention.

I filled a plate with pasta salad and half of a sandwich and sat at an empty table. Mac came to the door and scanned the room—his face lit up when he saw me. He wore the blue snowman sweater and pink plaid Bermuda shorts. As he walked toward me, conversations dwindled.

I tried to control the smile that spread across my face, but couldn't.

He twirled for the knitters and took a bow. Everyone clapped and went back to their discussions.

"I asked Holly to put my jeans in the wash, but it'll be a little while," he said.

"If anyone can pull off that look—and I'm not saying it's possible—you can." I laughed when I noticed his white socks and boots.

"Baxter isn't getting any treats from me for a while. I'm just glad the soup was cold."

"Go get some food," I said. "Maybe not the bouillabaisse . . ."

He nodded and returned a few minutes later with a loaded plate.

"Your dad is the hero of the hour, I see." He tilted his head toward Dad, who stood in the center of the young-knitter contingent. He moved on from talk of generators to teaching them his ten-code vocabulary gleaned through his police scanner hobby.

I nodded. "He doesn't usually get so many accolades for his repair work. Now I know why Vi volunteered to stay with the dogs—she probably couldn't stand it." I scanned the room. "Where's your mom?"

"She had some secret knitting project to work on. She's still upstairs." He spread mustard on his sandwich from the little pots of condiments. "I'm thinking about taking one of the snowmobiles out to the road and calling the police. I don't like the idea of Clarissa out there in the shed," Mac said.

I shivered.

Mom and Seth came to our table, and Mom sat next to Mac.

Seth glanced at Mac's shorts and blinked. He wisely stayed mute.

"We don't have another workshop until three. Your father wants to check out the cottage to be sure everything is working before it starts getting dark." She narrowed her eyes at the fawning knitters. She lowered her voice. "He doesn't trust that everything will be in working order."

"I'll come and help Seth with the dogs," I said.

"Do you need help with your suitcase, Mrs. Fortune?" Mac asked.

Mom smiled and put her hand on his arm. "I keep telling you, you need to call me Rose. And yes, I could use some help—it's slippery out there. Thank you."

After lunch, Mom and Mac went to get the suitcase and we met them in the hall where Vi was waiting with the dogs.

Tuffy began vibrating when he saw Seth walking toward him. Baxter stood and wagged his tail. He pushed his head against my leg when I approached. They sensed that something was happening and Tuffy began a little tap dance on the tile.

Baxter's ears drooped when he saw Mac walking toward him. Either he was a fashion critic, or he was picking up on Mac's irritation.

Seth grabbed his backpack from the floor. Tuffy dropped his ears and curled his tail downward. He brightened and hopped straight into the air when Seth pulled out the leash.

I grabbed Baxter's short lead and we all ventured out into the cold. I ruefully noted that now that the heat was back on I seemed to be spending a lot of time outside.

The path had been cleared as promised. Dad opened the door with the key Jessica had given him. Inside we found a cozy living room and small kitchen. Holly had started a fire in the fireplace and the whole room glowed. I sighed.

Wally had some explaining to do. Mac and I could have stayed here all this time and it would have been almost as wonderful as Mexico. Except for the murder.

The dogs ran ahead into the bedrooms, sniffing every inch. Baxter's deep bark sounded from the bedroom on the right. I went to investigate with Seth close on my heels.

The room was decorated in deep blues and greens. Baxter sat in the middle of the small Persian rug and looked at us expectantly. When we didn't respond, he barked again, turned a circle and lay down.

"Do you think he likes the room?"

Seth shrugged. "I'm not sure what he's trying to say."

Tuffy joined Baxter and curled up next to him.

Seth and I went back out into the living room.

"The dogs seem to have picked that room," I said. "I guess you two will have to take the other one."

Dad lugged Mom's suitcase into the second bedroom. "Wow, fancy." His voice floated out into the living room.

"This place is great," Dad said as he came out of the bedroom.

Vi sniffed. "It's not as castle-y as the hotel. I'll bet there aren't any ghosts, either."

"Most normal people would consider that a good thing, Vi," Dad said.

"Well, normal people think they have to visit the dentist twice a year," Vi said. "Doesn't make them right."

Vi had as much as declared war with that remark. She must have been really irked that Dad was getting so much attention. Dad was a mostly retired dentist and Vi had floated this theory that dentists were "in cahoots" with an unnamed dental overlord to whip up a frenzy of fear of gum disease. She trotted out the theory whenever she was feeling particularly prickly.

"We'll let you get settled," I said. I pulled Vi back outside and Mac followed, pushing her from behind as he swung the door shut before Dad could retaliate.

"Do you have to do that?" I asked.

Vi shrugged and grinned. "Keeps him on his toes."

Kirk was outside again with his snowblower—we could see the plume of snow in the parking lot.

"I'm going to go talk to Kirk about taking a snowmobile down the road," Mac said. "Your Dad gave me the keys."

"We'll come, too," Vi said. "I need to talk to him about my yarn bombing. I really want those knitting needles."

She hooked her arms through ours and dragged us toward the noisy parking lot.

We saw Kirk inside one of those drivable snow throwers slowly working his way along the sidewalk toward the parked cars. Vi waved her arms to attract Kirk's attention. After a few minutes, Kirk finally noticed us and shut the engine off.

I took a moment to enjoy the silence and then followed Mac and Vi as they crunched through the snow to Kirk.

Mac raised a hand in greeting. "I have the keys to the snowmobiles." Mac held them out to demonstrate. "I was hoping you and I could ride out to the road to see if we can move the tree—"

Kirk started shaking his head even before Mac finished explaining his plan.

"This is the biggest snowblower we have. It's almost a

mile down the road to the turnoff. It could take days to try to dig our way toward the road through this. I'm not even sure I can deal with the sidewalk. We have a truck service that comes to do the heavy plowing—now I know why he hasn't shown up yet."

"With the phones out and the tree down, we're stuck here unless we can find some help," Mac said. "We can at least go evaluate the situation."

"Yeah, okay," Kirk said. "Let me just finish up here."

Vi stepped forward, heedless of Kirk's put-upon attitude.

"I've got a doozy of a yarn bombing planned," she said. "But I really need a ladder . . . and someone to climb on it."

Kirk nodded. "When I'm done helping the detective clear the tree, I'd love to do some more yarn bombing." The sarcastic tone was either too subtle for Vi or she chose to ignore it.

"You're the best!" Vi slugged him in the arm.

Kirk cranked up the snowblower again and steered it toward the parking lot.

We turned and waded back through the snow toward the hotel.

Inside, we stomped our boots and hung our coats on the hooks.

"I'll catch up with you later," Mac said and dropped a kiss on my forehead. "I need to get my jeans back before we take the snowmobiles out." He took the hallway that led toward the stairway to the basement.

I followed Vi up the wide staircase toward our room. She wanted to get her knitting organized for the next workshop and I felt like I needed my own notebook to keep track of all of the suspects in this murder. I hoped she would pack her bag and head down to the lounge.

"So, who should we interview while Mac is off riding around on snowmobiles?" Vi said.

I stopped and turned to look at her.

"We aren't going to interview anyone. Mac will get the police involved and then it will be up to them to figure this out."

Vi put her hands on her hips just like my mother always did when she was ready to dig in her heels.

"That's exactly why we need to interrogate people *now*," Vi said. "As soon as the police arrive, we won't have any authority to ask questions."

My mouth dropped open and I quickly closed it. "Vi, we don't have any authority now."

She grabbed my arm and began hustling me toward our room, shushing me the whole time. As we got to the turn in the hallway, she glanced around and said, "You and I know that, but the rest of them don't. They'll tell us their story because they think you and Mac are investigating. We don't have much time."

I followed her toward our room, and we both stopped when we saw the door was open. I held my finger to my lips and Vi nodded once. Someone was humming and banging around in there. We approached the room slowly and peeked around the corner of the door.

Holly Raeburn hummed to herself and pulled the sheets smooth on Vi's bed.

"Oh, it's you," Vi said.

Holly whirled around, her hand to her neck, eyes wide.

"You startled me," she said, and smoothed her skirt.

"Hi, Holly," Vi said. "We didn't mean to scare you. We just came up during the break between lunch and the next workshop."

"I'm sorry, I should have finished with the rooms by now." She began gathering her cleaning supplies. "I can get out of your way."

"No, it's fine, you should stay," Vi said. She nudged me

hard in the ribs. "I'm sure setting up the cottage has put you behind schedule. We don't mind."

I looked at Vi while rubbing my side.

She tilted her head toward Holly, who had turned back to the bed and was smoothing the bedspread.

Vi pushed me in Holly's direction. "Holly, do you mind if I ask a few questions about last night?" I said while glowering at Vi.

Holly stopped fluffing the pillows but didn't turn around.

"Sure, I heard you were asking people what they were doing when Ms. Carlisle . . . died." She resumed her pillow fluffing with increased vigor.

"Come sit by the window, Holly," Vi said. She gestured to the chairs.

Holly set the pillows down and crossed the room to where Vi had already taken the chair with its back to the window. I joined them and we sat in silence for a moment. Holly was quiet. But her eyes held an intensity that was hard to ignore.

Vi took a breath to speak and I held up my hand.

"Detective McKenzie and I are police officers. He works in homicide for Ottawa County and we're investigating until we can reach the Kalamazoo Police. We've been asking everyone where they were last night between six thirty and nine," I said.

"I'm their assistant," Vi said. She hooked her thumb in my direction. "Kind of like a deputy."

I sighed and closed my eyes for a moment. It wouldn't help to argue in front of Holly so I let it slide.

Holly glanced at both of us and cleared her throat. "I finished up with my usual cleaning at around five thirty and went to the kitchen to grab some dinner." She looked at the ceiling while talking as if trying to envision her movements from the night before. "Jessica—Ms. Garrett—had said I didn't need to do the turndown service, so I was planning to go to my room for a little while after I ate and then check with Wallace to see if there was anything else I needed to do."

Vi and I nodded to encourage her.

"On my way to my room, I ran into Ms. Carlisle. She wanted me to do the turndown service even though Ms. Garrett had said not to and the fact that I am the only housekeeping staff in the building. She had already yelled at me earlier in the day about her room not being tidied, so I didn't argue with her and said I would start that at seven o'clock."

I felt my cheeks grow hot when I remembered overhearing Clarissa berating Holly earlier in the day when Mac and I were going down to dinner.

"I went downstairs to my room and saw Kirk." She blushed and twirled her dark hair around her finger. "He was just coming in from outside and we talked for a couple of minutes in the hall. Ms. Garrett came down and asked Kirk if the generators were working, because she was worried about losing power with the storm that was predicted. It happens pretty routinely out here."

She focused on her lap.

"I read a book and rested for a while in my room and then went upstairs to start the turndown."

Vi cast longing looks at her velvet pouch that contained her pendulum. I saw her flexing her fingers in anticipation of questioning it. I shook my head at her and narrowed my eyes.

"I was just finishing in the hallway outside the turret room when I saw one of the knitter ladies—the one with the tattoos—coming out of the stairwell. She seemed surprised to see me and said she had gotten turned around. I showed her the way to her room and then went to finish turndown."

"You saw Tina coming out of Clarissa's room?" Vi said.

She leaned forward and rummaged in her knitting bag. She pulled her notebook from its depths and began scribbling.

Holly watched Vi with interest. "I saw her coming out of the turret stairway, not out of the room. I can't say whether she was in the room."

Vi's lips made a thin line. She snapped the notebook shut.

"How did you get along with Ms. Carlisle?" Vi asked.

Holly looked down. "Honestly, I didn't like her." She raised her head and met Vi's gaze. "She was hypercritical of the staff and I often had to calm one of them down after they'd had a run-in with her." Holly looked at me. "I don't think she will be very much missed by any of the employees."

"Do you have any theories about what might have happened?" I asked.

Holly shook her head slowly. "No one liked her, but I can't see any of the staff actually killing her." She paused for a moment. "I heard she had some history with a couple of the knitters." She lifted a shoulder. "Maybe it was one of them."

"How long have you worked here?" Vi asked.

"Two years. Mrs. Garrett has been wonderful to me." Her eyes teared up and she blinked them away. "I have a five-year-old daughter who has diabetes. If I didn't have insurance through my job, I don't know what I would do. Olivia needs a lot of expensive medication and monitoring supplies. Mrs. Garrett made sure it was all covered and she helps me keep my hours up so I continue to qualify under their plan. I'm taking classes at the community college and working here and Mrs. Garrett is always so supportive and flexible."

"It must be hard for you—caring for your daughter, working, going to school . . ." I thought of my own relatively responsibility-free life. "Where is your daughter right now?" I asked.

"My mom takes her for me when I'm working or in

classes. I called her yesterday and she agreed to keep her for me until the storm passed. The other two housekeepers had to get home to their own kids, so I volunteered to stay. Whenever I can, I try to help out."

"Where were you when the lights went out?" Vi asked.

"I . . . had finished my work and went back downstairs. I was in my room."

"Weren't you scared to be in the basement of a haunted house with no electricity?" Vi continued.

Holly glanced at me and I shrugged. If Vi focused on real evidence and not ghosts and animal messages, she might become a good investigator.

"No. I don't think the castle is haunted and I had a large flashlight with me. I thought the power would come back on pretty quickly—" Holly broke off and stared at the door. "There she is!"

Vi and I turned to look at the door as well. Duchess stalked into the room, surveyed the area, and approached Holly. Purring sounds filled the air as she rubbed her head on Holly's legs. The cat jumped up and made herself comfortable on Holly's lap.

"That's a beautiful cat," Vi said. "I haven't been able to get close enough to see her—she always disappears before I can get near her." Vi cocked her head at Duchess. She sat very still and stared hard at the cat in what I knew was her "receptive" mode. Duchess continued to purr with her eyes closed, seemingly unaware of Vi's focused attention.

Vi quietly stood and approached Duchess. Just as Vi reached forward to touch the cat, she jumped off Holly's lap and zoomed out the door.

Vi tsked. "She's a clever one."

"I thought you said you didn't get along with cats?" I said.

Holly shook her head. "I don't. That's the first time she's let me pet her since she arrived."

"Very strange," Vi said. She stroked her chin and watched Holly.

Holly began to fidget under Vi's glare.

"Thank you for talking to us," I said. I sent Vi a "back off" look. "Please let us know if you think of anything that might help."

Holly nodded, stood up, and gathered her things. She cleared out quickly and didn't look back.

19

Vi had convinced me to come to the workshop with her while I waited for Mac to return from his snowmobiling adventure. We passed Wally in reception. He was huddled over his weather radio and didn't notice us as we passed.

"If I didn't know he was innocent, he'd be my first suspect," Vi said.

"Why? He seems completely harmless," I said and had to quicken my pace to keep up with her.

"That's exactly why," Vi said. "People are never the way they seem."

Miss Marple was Vi's new hero—she'd been talking about her all winter as if Agatha Christie were an up-and-coming new author. Quoting her cynical view of human nature had become a new hobby.

"I think that's going a little far," I said. "Not everyone is up to something."

Vi shook her head and looked at me sadly.

Fortunately, we had arrived at the workshop room. I never thought I would welcome a roomful of knitters, but anything to get Vi off this topic was fine with me.

The knitters sat in a circle near the fire, each one clicking her needles rapidly while a buzz of conversation filled the room. Amy's bright pink head was bent near Mavis's gray one and they counted stitches on a delicate pink baby sweater. Heather, the nurse, sat near Mom and quizzed her on herbal remedies for headaches and allergies. Mom's best friend is an herbalist and she's picked up a few tips through the years. Tina and Isabel knitted brightly colored socks and discussed local yarn suppliers. I glanced back at the door, but Vi grabbed my arm and pulled me forward.

"Clyde! Come sit with me and I'll get you started." Lucille patted the couch next to her. I looked over my shoulder again and saw no easy escape. Lucille had a prime seat next to the small fireplace so I climbed over the bags of yarn and needles and sat next to her.

They explained that this was their sharing workshop, so everyone had brought something different to show the other knitters. Selma had just finished presenting a neon-striped scarf that had to be a gift. She wore a brighter shade of beige today with a soft ivory scarf. I murmured polite compliments as they all showed off their works in progress. Then the attention shifted to me.

"Here, Clyde, you can use this yarn," Mom said. She handed me a soft purple skein that slowly shifted from pale lavender to deep plum. "If you finish a scarf, it will look great on you."

"Thanks, Mom," I said.

Mavis handed me a cord with needles on either end, but Vi intercepted it and traded for two thick straight needles.

"Don't get her addicted to circulars until she learns how to use straights," Vi said to Mavis.

Mavis narrowed her eyes at Vi and sniffed. She turned away from Vi and began vigorously knitting. I was glad I wasn't sitting next to her—she looked like she wanted to kill her knitting, or Vi.

"She should try both," Lucille said. "Which do you want to start with?" Lucille turned to me holding out the needles. I looked at them and shrugged. She might as well have been asking whether I wanted to hold the snake or the tarantula. I decided on family loyalty and chose the straight pair.

Vi sat back and humphed in a satisfied way. Mavis refused to look at me. I consoled myself with the knowledge that we were never going to be friends anyway, what with our competition for Mac's affection and all.

For the next hour I tried to knit using the purple yarn and big needles. Several of the knitters got involved and contributed advice and encouragement. After Lucille cast on for me, she patiently showed me how to put the tip of the needle in the first loop, wrap the yarn, and pull it through. When it was clear that I was a complete klutz when it came to the knit stitch, Isabel got involved and tried to show me the "continental" method.

"Hmmm," she started, "maybe you're a picker, not a thrower."

I looked up at her, never feeling more clueless in my life.

"I knew it," Vi said. "Leave it to Clyde to be a picker when every woman in her family tree has been a thrower."

There were rueful murmurs of agreement around the knitting circle and I wasn't sure if I was being insulted or what I was being accused of. But I did feel that I finally got the hang of it once I adopted Isabel's method.

Heather leaned forward to watch me struggle with the needles and yarn. "I think you're getting the hang of it," she said. "It takes a while."

Amy looked at Heather's gray cabled project. I couldn't tell whether it was a scarf or a blanket. "I remember when you used to be afraid of cable needles."

Heather laughed. "Now look at me!" she exclaimed. She held up her knitting for admiration.

"Now, whatever you do, Clyde," Amy said earnestly, "don't make anything for your detective."

There was a round of nods and murmurs of agreement.

"They're right," Vi said. "I didn't warn you because I never thought I'd see you knit, but you can't make anything for a boyfriend or you'll doom the relationship. You'll break up before the project is finished."

I dropped a stitch and swore under my breath as I tried to put it back on the needle.

Lucille gently took the needles from me and fixed the mistake before handing them back.

"I don't think there's a risk of that," I said. "I'll be lucky if I can make a scarf for myself before next winter."

By the time the clock on the mantel struck four, I had managed six rows of knitting. I'd begun with twenty stitches and now had twenty-two on the needle. And there was a hole beginning right in the middle. I leaned back into my chair and stretched my neck. I did not find knitting relaxing. Between counting the stitches, and keeping track of whether I was knitting or purling, and fielding questions on everything from my love life to my career path, it was downright stressful. Mom and Vi had obviously filled the group in on every detail they knew about my private life.

I put the knitting down and got up to stretch my legs. I wondered what was taking Mac so long, and suspected he was afraid to come rescue me from the knitters. He can be such a coward sometimes.

I was standing by the window, watching the wind make little tornadoes out of the snow, when I heard the snowmobiles returning.

They pulled into the back of the building and I could just see them by angling sideways and peering to the far right.

Mac and Kirk parked the vehicles and climbed off. I couldn't tell whether they had been successful in reaching the police or not. They certainly didn't arrive with a police escort.

They stood with their heads close together, hunched into their coats. I saw Mac put out his hand and Kirk shook it, then Mac headed for the hotel while Kirk pushed the snowblower around the side of the building.

I quickly packed up my knitting and stuffed it into Vi's bag. I whispered to her that I had to step out for a few minutes. She nodded and kept knitting while Isabel walked among the women, offering assistance and advice.

I left the room, took a deep breath, and let it out.

I rounded the corner toward the back of the hotel and almost collided with Mac. He was still wearing the snowman sweater and his jeans were damp from the knees down. I guessed I'd be seeing the pink Bermudas again soon.

"Hi, I was looking for you," he said.

"You found me." I put my arms around his neck and kissed him. His lips were still cold from being outside and he smelled like snow and gasoline.

He had just slipped his arm around my waist to pull me closer when we heard a discreet cough.

Mac's shoulders relaxed and he rested his forehead against mine for a moment.

"Yes?" he said, and turned to see who had interrupted.

Emmett stood there, shifting from foot to foot. He glanced over his shoulder and took a couple of steps in our direction. His face was pink, but he still wore that friendly smile.

"I'm sorry to . . . interrupt," he said quietly. "I've been thinking about Clarissa's death. I didn't think this would matter, but then the more I thought about it, the more I realized that anything can be important, right?"

He had Mac's full attention now. Mac released me and I took a step back to steady myself. We both turned to Emmett and nodded encouragement.

"This probably doesn't have anything to do with your investigation, but there was a meeting on Wednesday afternoon. It was just between Clarissa, Jessica, and Mrs. Garrett."

"Do you know what the meeting was about?" I asked.

"No, but I know that René was really ticked off about it."

"Why?" Mac said.

"He sees himself as a shareholder even though he and Jessica aren't married yet. I don't blame him—he's put his whole life into this restaurant. If sweat equity counted for anything, he'd be the majority owner."

Emmett shoved his hands in his pockets and lowered his voice even more.

"I think he and Jessica had a fight about it. And I think the meeting itself was a bit of a knock-down, drag-out kind of thing."

"What do you mean?" Mac said.

"I saw Jessica and Mrs. Garrett storm out of the meeting and then a few minutes later Clarissa strolled out like she didn't have a problem in the world."

Emmett shrugged. "I got a little nervous because the last time they had a meeting like that a bunch of people lost their jobs. I don't know who they could lose at this point, we're at bare bones as it is, but nothing has come of it so far."

"We'll look into it, Emmett, thank you," Mac said.

Emmett turned to look over his shoulder, and lowered his voice.

"There's something else," he said. "I saw Jessica coming out of the door that leads to the back stairway of the turret room."

Mac had become very still. We exchanged a quick glance of surprise.

"What time was this?" I asked.

"Maybe ten minutes or so before the lights went out," Emmett said. He held his hands out. "I can't say for sure that she was in the room, just that she came out of the stairway door."

We heard a door close down the hall and footsteps heading our way. Emmett waved and melted into the back hallway.

"That was weird," I whispered. "Why didn't he tell us that yesterday?"

"Maybe he really didn't think the meeting mattered, or maybe he didn't want René to hear him."

Kirk rounded the corner carrying the ladder again. He nodded as he passed and went into the lounge.

"Did you get in touch with the police?" I asked.

"No, the road is blocked and the snowmobiles are low on gas, so we didn't want to go looking for a phone. It's almost a mile to the turnoff." Mac leaned against the wall.

"It's too bad Dad and Seth didn't tell the police they were looking for us," I said. "They didn't realize there would be a murder to deal with."

"It's likely anywhere nearby is dealing with the same outages as we are," Mac said. He pushed away from the wall and paced. "The police know the hotel is here. If the phones don't come back on, they'll eventually try to get up here. We'll have to keep working the case in the meantime."

"Vi will be so pleased," I said. "She's identifying herself as one of our deputies now."

Mac rocked back on his heels and looked at the ceiling.

"While you were away she and I spoke with Holly."

"Let me guess, she wasn't much of a Clarissa fan, either."

I nodded. "Holly doesn't even think the cat liked her. She did say she saw Tina come out of the stairwell sometime after seven thirty."

Mac pressed his lips together. "I thought Tina was in the dining room the whole time."

I held my hands out. "I guess not. She also didn't volunteer the information when we were talking to them in the workshop room."

"We'll need to confront her," Mac said. "It also means her friends covered for her. They must have known she left the room."

"I don't like this, Mac," I said. I wrapped my arms around myself to ward off a sudden chill that I suspected had nothing to do with the temperature. "Everyone is hiding something."

The corner of Mac's mouth twitched up in a rueful smile. "It does seem that way. Including the building itself. Which reminds me, I wanted to talk to the Garretts again after finding the secret stairway. With Emmett's news, we have even more reason to question them," Mac said.

"Let's wait to confront them about the hidden stairway until they're together—I want to see how they react," I said. "I think the offices are back here by the kitchen." I pointed down the hallway where Emmett had disappeared.

Mac and I followed the hall until we were almost to the kitchen door. We heard drawers slamming and papers rustling in one of the rooms.

We peered around the doorjamb and saw Jessica

rummaging through a desk. She looked up, startled, when we walked in.

"Hello, can I help?" she said as she quietly slid one of the drawers closed.

"We were hoping to talk to you and your mom again," I said.

"Oh, I see." Jessica straightened the pens on the desktop. "She's really not doing very well today. Clarissa's death has hit her much harder than I would have expected."

"Why do you say that?" Mac asked.

"It's just . . . they never got along that well and they had been arguing over how best to run the hotel." Jessica turned away from us and looked out the window. "Honestly, I thought on some level she might be relieved, but that doesn't seem to be the case. If anything, she's spending a lot of time talking about how wonderful Clarissa was." She turned back toward us. "I finally had to walk away."

Jessica sat in the desk chair and gestured for us to take seats.

"Can you tell us any more about your cousin? Did you grow up together?" I asked.

Jessica snorted. "We never got along, even when we were kids. She was one of those spoiled little kids that was used to having every whim indulged, and she didn't mind stepping on people to get what she wanted."

"How had you been doing since she moved back here and started working at the hotel?"

"Mostly I ran interference between her and the staff. I felt like I was back in high school again, where I had to convince people that, even though we were related, I was nothing like her. The staff started acting scared of all three of us. I suppose because they assumed we were complicit in Clarissa's management style. Basically, I ran around cleaning up her messes."

"What changes was she trying to make here?" Mac asked.

"She had this idea that the hotel could become a destination spa. She wanted to divert money from the restaurant—René had been working on expanding our offerings and trying to get the restaurant Michelin rated—and put it toward the spa," she said. "René was initially outraged and then . . . I don't know . . . he just backed off." She stopped and stared into space for a moment.

"Anyway, I'm sure you don't want to hear about our boring business plans." She stood and gestured toward the door. "Let's go up and see how she's doing."

I opened my mouth to ask more about the business plans, but Mac gave a quick shake of his head. He rested his hand on my lower back and I knew he had his reasons for allowing Jessica to deflect further questions.

Jessica didn't notice as she was already shooing us out of the office and quizzing Mac on what he had discovered when he drove out to the road.

She didn't seem surprised that the road was blocked and accepted it without comment.

We followed her through the back hallways and up the stairs. Jessica knocked on the door and signaled to us to wait a moment while she checked on her mom. I heard whispering inside and then Jessica returned to the door and ushered us inside.

Linda did look like she'd seen better days. The efficient, art-collecting proprietor had been replaced by an old woman with red-rimmed eyes and frizzy hair.

"Please excuse my appearance—I just . . ." Her eyes welled up and I stepped forward to touch her arm.

"It's fine, Mrs. Garrett. Detective McKenzie and I just have a couple more questions for you and Jessica. Until the

Kalamazoo Police can get here, we're trying to find out who could have . . . harmed . . . your niece."

She nodded and sat on the couch. Jessica sat next to her and gestured for us to sit as well.

Mac cleared his throat. I knew he hated talking to people when they were crying. Unfortunately for him, it was part of his job description. Working in homicide meant he had to give bad news frequently and then make things worse by questioning the grieving family.

"Clyde and I examined Clarissa's room today. We hoped to find some clues in the light of day. What we found was a secret staircase that led to the kitchen." Mac gazed from one to the other. I knew he was looking for any signs of surprise or concern. "I assume you knew of the existence of the staircase?"

Both women nodded.

"Is it in regular use?" I asked.

Linda dabbed at her eyes with a tissue. "No, it had been boarded up for a long time. When Clarissa moved into the turret room, she had Gus open it up again and sweep it out. I'm not sure that she even used it, but she had always been fascinated by it. I thought she just liked the idea of a secret passage." She looked at Jessica. "When the girls were little, they were so disappointed that I wouldn't let them play in there, but it hadn't been opened in years and it's so steep."

Jessica nodded. "Clarissa and I went through the passageway just after she had it cleaned out. She was so intrigued by the story that Alastair had built the staircase for a wife who was essentially bedbound."

"How many people know that it's there?" Mac asked.

They looked at each other and then Jessica said, "Probably most of the staff. It wasn't a secret. In fact, it never occurred to me to mention it to you since everyone who works here knows it exists."

Mac nodded. "Well, it does change our questioning a bit. If there were two entrances to the room, it opens up more opportunities for the killer to get to her unseen."

Linda's mouth dropped open. "Of course. I didn't think of that. I'm sorry we didn't tell you. I haven't been thinking straight since I found her . . . body." She dabbed at her eyes again and sniffled.

I looked at Mac and he gave a slight nod.

"Jessica, Linda, we've heard during our interviews that you two had a meeting with Clarissa on Wednesday afternoon that became heated. Can you tell us what that meeting was about?"

Jessica glanced quickly at her mother. Linda narrowed her eyes and looked much less distraught at Clarissa's passing.

Jessica took her mother's hand and I sensed that she was sending her a signal to keep control of herself.

"We had our monthly meeting on Wednesday," Jessica said. "It's always the first Wednesday of the month. It was just the usual thing—staffing, repairs, and plans for the month. Clarissa wanted to talk about the spa. It's all she could think about. She was so convinced that putting a spa here would somehow catapult Carlisle Castle into a destination-hotel category."

Linda sniffled. "The truth is, the hotel has been struggling for a few years now. The winters are always lean. We haven't been able to cover the slow times as well as we did in the past. We aren't near a big city, there's not a lot of shopping in Kalamazoo the way there is in Chicago, and with the economy the way it is, people just aren't taking vacations like they used to."

"Did you two and Clarissa ever argue about how to run the hotel?" I asked.

Jessica snorted. "When did we *not* argue about it?"

"Well, it wasn't *that* bad . . . ," Linda said. She cut her eyes to Jessica and then smiled weakly at us. Linda's knuckles had turned white where she clasped Jessica's hand.

And Jessica's mutinous face had me thinking it *was* that bad and maybe worse.

"Thank you for talking to us again," Mac said. "If you think of anything else, even if it seems small or obvious to you, please let us know. We don't have the same sense of the history of the castle or the hotel that you do, so it will help us to get a better picture of what might have happened if you can give us as much background as possible."

Both women nodded agreement.

Mac and I stood to leave and Jessica followed us out into the hallway.

Jessica leaned into the room. "I'll be back in a little while with some tea, Mom." Jessica quietly closed the door and turned to us.

She put her hands out, palms up. "I'm sorry we didn't mention the meeting or the stairway. I guess we took for granted that those things would be unimportant. We want nothing more than to find out how this could have happened."

"Jessica," I said, "when was the last time you saw Clarissa?"

Jessica looked at the ceiling as if trying to find answers there. "I saw her just before dinner—after we left the lounge we talked in the hallway for a few minutes."

I remembered them *talking* in urgent, angry whispers in the hall.

"Then during dinner, we passed in the hallway. She was leaving, I was going in."

Mac leaned forward. "That was the last you saw of her?"

Jessica looked at us with a wide, innocent stare. She nodded.

Mac looked at the floor and gave a disappointed sigh. "You were seen coming out of the stairway door—much later."

Jessica took a step back. She shook her head. "I didn't see her. I was still angry with her about our earlier conversation and I was going to go talk to her about it." Jessica stopped and took a breath. "I got partway up the staircase and thought better of it. I decided to talk to her in the morning after we had both cooled off."

I crossed my arms.

Jessica looked from me to Mac. "I didn't kill her—I get squeamish if we have to set traps for mice." She shook her head. "I couldn't kill someone and I can't believe that anyone here in the castle would have killed her." Jessica lowered her voice. "As I've said, plenty of the staff might have wished her dead in a passing sort of way, but I work with these people every day and none of them seems like the type who would actually kill another human being." She hugged herself and shivered. "The truth is, it's freaking me out to think I've been working with a murderer all this time."

20

That evening, Seth and Dad returned from the cottage for dinner. Mom and Vi had spent most of the afternoon in the workshop and everyone was tired. The news that the police would not arrive was met with dismay, but spirits seemed a bit better this evening with electric lights and heat to accompany dinner.

Our family took the largest table in the room and the dinner conversation centered on the murder and who might have done it. I wish I could say this was unusual for us, but it wasn't. Only Mac and Lucille seemed surprised at how easily we discussed motives and methods of murder over our beef bourguignon.

"I don't like the idea that I might be knitting next to a murderer." Lucille shuddered. "I don't think any of them could have done it. They're all so nice."

"That's how they trick you, Lucille," Vi said. "They lure

you in with charm while they're out attacking innocent people."

"It doesn't sound like Clarissa was very innocent," Mom said. "You heard what Isabel and Mavis said about her."

"Mavis," Vi said, her voice a low growl. She glanced around the table and lowered her voice. "She probably did it. I hate to accuse another knitter, but I don't trust her."

I covered a smile with my water glass, knowing that Vi's accusation came from a competitive place. The afternoon with the knitters had not been conflict free.

"Why would Mrs. Poulson want to kill Ms. Carlisle?" Seth asked while slathering butter on a slice of bread.

Mom glanced at the other tables and leaned toward Seth. "Apparently, Clarissa bullied Mavis's daughter in high school. The girl got very depressed and eventually committed suicide. Mavis and Isabel have always blamed Clarissa for Teresa's death."

"Oh. That's rough." Seth shook his head. "Girls can be really brutal."

"Shhh!" Mac said to the table. "We cannot discuss this. It's an active investigation." He lowered his voice. "The suspects are all in the vicinity, this isn't a game of Clue."

The table fell silent for a few moments, then Seth asked for the bread basket again and people gratefully began discussing the meal.

Dad leaned toward Mac and said in a low voice, "If incompetence is an indicator of guilt, then you should consider Kirk as your number-one suspect. I don't think he's ever worked as any type of maintenance person before, unless it was just on the landscaping side of things. He certainly knows how to work a snowblower. He has no idea how to fix anything."

"We haven't taken anyone off the list," Mac said quietly.

"If they weren't in the dining room for the whole time that night, then I consider them a suspect."

"I suppose anyone is capable if given the right circumstances," Dad said.

"I still think there's something sketchy about the chef," Seth said.

"What?" Mac said.

"I told Clyde earlier today," Seth said. "The chef claims he's French, but I think he must be Canadian."

"What does it matter?" Vi said.

"That's what Clyde said. But why would he lie about it?" Seth said.

"Jessica did seem impressed that he was from France," Mom said. "It's part of all their literature about the restaurant—that they have a 'real' French chef who trained at Cordon Bleu."

"It can't be hard to check," Mac said.

"It is when the cell service is down and there's no Wi-Fi," Seth said. "I tried to connect this afternoon—it's like the dark ages out here."

"At this point, I'll look into anything—once the phones are back on I'll call Pete Harris and see if he can run a check on René Sartin," Mac said.

Vi leaned forward. "The chef did it," she whispered. "I don't trust the French. I don't care if he's Paris French or Canadian French, he's sketchy."

I wondered if Vi had given up on Kirk as a suspect because Dad thought he was guilty.

Seth's eyebrows came together. "What's wrong with the French?"

"They're snooty and they eat weird food," Vi said as she took another bite of her beef bourguignon.

Mom glanced nervously around the table and decided to

step in. "I'm sure you don't mean that, Vi." She clamped her hand onto Vi's wrist. She looked at the rest of us, particularly Mac and Lucille. "She's joking."

Vi harrumphed and kept eating, but didn't pursue her character assassination of the entire French culture.

There was an uncomfortable silence as we applied ourselves to our dinners and waited for someone to change the subject.

I decided to throw myself under the bus. "I think that new style of knitting that Isabel taught me is easier."

Mom gasped. Vi narrowed her eyes.

"You didn't tell me you learned to knit today," Mac said. He turned in his seat and his eyes sparkled with amusement. Sort of the way I smiled at him wearing the snowman sweater. I would never hear the end of this.

"Didn't you hear we're living in the dark ages?" I gestured toward Seth. "I had no choice but to knit." I sipped my water.

"But I thought you hated knitting," Mac said.

"You do?" Lucille asked.

" 'Hate' is a strong word." I glared at Mac. "I figured I'd give it a try again. Isabel showed me the 'continental' method."

"That sounds fancy," Dad said.

I ignored the stony faces of my mother and aunt. "It *is* fancy," I said. "And *way* easier." I glanced at Vi. "It's probably the way they knit in France."

Violet dropped her fork. "I can't listen to this anymore."

Dad snickered. Mom looked at me sadly and shook her head.

"So, will you be joining us for more of the workshops?" Lucille asked. "If you find a way that works for you, it can make all the difference." She seemed oblivious to the tension rolling off of Vi and Mom.

I shook my head. "I don't think so. I probably should practice some more on my own."

"We'll work on it tonight, Clyde," Vi said. "I'll show you how much easier it is to purl using my techniquc. That continental bunch avoids purling like the plague."

Mac grinned at me as he realized I had successfully distracted the gang from murder by throwing them a more interesting bone.

"Seth, you can come to the classes if you want," Mom said. "We have good snacks all the time. They send in brownies and cakes and cookies."

Seth looked up from his plate at the sound of his name and "snacks" in the same sentence, but he had clearly not been listening to all the knitting talk.

"Huh?"

"I need Seth to help me with some things," Dad said and slung his arm over Seth's shoulder and whispered something in his ear.

"Yeah, sorry. I'll have to get the snacks some other time," Seth said.

Vi pressed her lips together and glared at Dad.

Everyone scattered after dinner to cither his or her own rooms or the workshop room. Dad and Seth ventured back out into another light snowfall to feed and walk the dogs.

Mac and I went in search of Tina.

After we checked the workshop room and the lounge, we found her in the reception area talking to Wally. He stood a couple of feet away from the counter while Tina leaned toward him, talking urgently. They both startled when we approached.

Tina leaned back, cast a threatening look in Wally's direction, and tried to brush past us.

Mac put his hand out. "We need to speak with you if you don't mind."

Tina narrowed her eyes at Mac. "Actually I do mind," she said.

Mac's eyebrows twitched up. No one had refused to talk to us so far.

"We're just trying to establish a timeline of the night Clarissa died," I said.

"I know what you're trying to do," she said. "I also know I don't have to talk to you. I'm not under arrest and I don't have anything to say." She crossed her arms.

Mac glanced at Wally and lowered his voice. "We are talking to everyone who was not in the dining room the whole time that evening—a witness has come forward who saw you in the hallway outside the turret room that night."

Wally pretended to be working on his computer, but his hands rested quietly on the keyboard and I could tell he was listening to every word.

"You'll have to solve your mystery without me," Tina said. "I'm not talking about it." She pushed past us and stalked down the hall toward the stairs.

I moved to follow her but Mac put a hand on my arm.

"We can't force her to talk to us," he said. "She's right. She's not under arrest. But she's just moved way up on my list."

I returned to my room after an hour or so of talking with Mac about the suspects and motives we had already uncovered. Mom and Vi rushed toward me as I shut the door behind me.

"Finally!" Vi said. "Where have you been?"

"Mac and I were downstairs talking." I noticed the room was lit by candles and all the electric lights had been turned off. I got a queasy feeling.

"We need to get busy here," Mom said. She swung her arm in the direction of the sitting area.

I looked at the coffee table and saw what they were so excited about. Mom's tarot cards were poised to share the secrets of the universe and Vi's pendulum glinted in the candlelight.

"Mom, how come you didn't go back to the cottage with Dad?" I worried there would be a night of psychic interrogation.

"He and Seth can deal with the dogs," Mom said. "This is more important. I know you and Mac are working on things in your own way, but I think we can help." She gestured at her cards.

In the past I would have pushed back against the tarot and pendulum, but now that I was working on my own talents, I understood their need to contribute in any way they could. "What do the cards have to say?" I asked.

"I haven't looked yet," Mom said. "We were waiting for you. We think that the cards, the pendulum, and maybe an eyewitness will be useful."

"Eyewitness?" I said.

"I've been trying to find that cat all day, but she's disappeared," Vi said. "She might know something."

"Oh. The cat. Of course."

I yawned. Even though I was tired, I wasn't looking forward to another night alternately listening to the wind and Vi's snoring. Day two in Mexico would have found Mac and me at some romantic restaurant followed by a stroll along the moonlit beach. Tarot cards and pendulums would *not* have featured in our plans.

"Let's get this over with," I said, and sat near the coffee table.

Vi clapped her hands and sat next to me.

"What are we asking tonight?" I asked.

"It seems like Mavis and Isabel had a good reason to want Clarissa dead, if you think that revenge is a reasonable motive," Vi began. "Tina was seen in the hallway, but I have no idea why she would want to hurt Clarissa. None of the staff liked her very much, but that doesn't mean any of them would kill her. Lots of terrible bosses live through their employee's anger."

I nodded. Vi had summed up in four sentences what Mac and I had discussed for an hour.

"I agree, Vi," I said.

She smiled. "I've been thinking . . ."

She paused and looked at Mom, who tilted her head and gave a subtle nod.

"I want to open my own detective agency," Vi said in a rush.

I stood up quickly to put some distance between Vi's crazy idea and myself. "You don't know anything about detective work."

"I've been reading up on it," Vi said. "It doesn't seem that hard and I have some natural talent—I took a test online."

"I can't talk about this right now," I said. "I really need to get some sleep and you two obviously have plans to search out a psychic answer to this mystery." I gestured at the cards and pendulum.

"Okay, you're right," Vi said. "Let's focus on the problem at hand. It will give me some practice for when I have my own cases."

Mom was already flipping cards onto the table. I noticed

she was using the queen of swords again. That was the card she used to indicate me in her queries. I had had this argument with her enough times to let it slide. She would say that she needed to determine how I would affect the situation. Mom and I don't usually agree on things psychic, but after spending time with Neila Whittle, I was softening toward Mom's view. I had been leaning toward the "if you can't fight it you might as well use it" camp.

"Okay, the cards indicate that you will have a lover's quarrel—oh, my. I didn't ask the cards about you and Mac. . . ."

"Maybe they'll fight about who the killer is," Vi said. "Or Clyde will get tired of seeing him in that snowman sweater."

I grinned at Vi. "That's already happened. Don't worry about Mac and me. We're fine. What else do the cards have to say?"

Mom shook her head. "It looks like this will be a tough case. There are many secrets surrounding the situation and some of them are still hidden."

In the past I would have said something like "super helpful as usual" but my new leaf dictated a more tolerant view. "Thanks, Mom. We can ask again when we know more."

"Let me have a try," Vi said. She grabbed the pendulum and set up her piece of paper with the big plus sign indicating the yes and no directions. The pendulum is only able to answer if given two choices.

"What are you going to ask it?"

"I'll ask whether the killer will be caught before the weekend is over."

Vi stabilized the pendulum and let it go. It hung from its chain, unmoving. Slowly it began to move in the yes direction.

"Well, that's good news," Mom said.

"Was the killer a knitter?" Vi asked the pendulum.

The pendulum swung rapidly in the yes direction. Vi looked up, her eyes intense.

Unfortunately, the pendulum seemed to sense Vi's eagerness and refused to identify any of the knitters as the killer. By the time she had run through the list it was almost midnight and I could barely keep my eyes open. Mom and I both begged her to give it a rest.

I walked Mom back to the cottage and hurried through the snow back to the hotel.

By the time I got back to the room, the cold had seeped into my core. I wore a pair of Vi's wool socks, three T-shirts, and my jeans to bed and still shivered. I was sort of wishing I had Mac's snowman sweater as I struggled to get warm enough to fall asleep.

21

I am running through the snowy woods. The wind sucks the air from my lungs and snowflakes pelt my face, so I can't see where I'm going. My heart races and I feel the panic rise in my chest. I'm looking for someone and getting more and more worried. I realize that I am lost. I can't see the castle anymore and none of the trees look familiar. The snow is piling up so fast I can barely keep moving. My thin sweater doesn't protect me from the cold and I am shivering.

Then I hear a weak cry. "Clyde . . ."

I run in the direction of the voice, then I hear it behind me—is it an echo? The sound is getting weaker. "Clyde . . ."

A gust of wind knocks me to my knees and I can't breathe. Just as I fall into the snow on the forest floor I hear it again. "Clyde . . ."

I jerked awake in an unfamiliar bed and realized Vi was shaking my shoulder and saying my name.

"Clyde, wake up!"

I sat up quickly and still felt panicky from the dream.

"Vi, what is it?" I felt like I should have paid more attention to the dream. Something was wrong.

"I think I heard a noise in the hall," she said. She pulled her fluffy robe tightly across her chest. Her hair was in a braid, but pieces had come loose while she was asleep. Her brows drew together and she looked every one of her seventy-three years.

"It's a hotel, Vi. It's probably someone going to their room." I rolled away from her and pulled the covers over my head, trying to get warm and slow my heartbeat.

"It's three o'clock in the morning," Vi said. "This isn't a party cruise. Everyone is asleep."

Grumbling, I swung my legs over the edge and clicked on the lamp by my bed. I stood and walked to the door, cracked it open, and listened. There was a cold draft in the hall. I stepped into the darkened hallway with Vi. I was about to head downstairs to see where the draft originated when a door banged shut. The cold air stopped abruptly and I realized that the slamming door was in the turret room.

Vi grabbed my wrist and pulled me toward the turret stairs. "It came from up there."

We started to climb the stairs and then a low moaning sound began and increased to a shrill shriek.

"It's the ghost!" Vi said. Her bony fingers dug into my upper arm and she slipped behind me on the stairs but I felt her pushing me upward.

"It's not a ghost," I said. I gripped the banister tightly and willed myself to continue up the stairs.

"Then what's that noise?"

"It must be the wind," I told her and tried to sound brave and not at all freaked out.

We made it to the closed door at the top. The noise was coming from inside the turret room.

I looked at Vi, took a deep breath, and turned the knob.

The door didn't swing easily open, but as soon as I pushed it a few inches, the noise stopped. Just as we were about to step into the room, the white cat rushed out just like the night before when we had found Clarissa.

"She's really spooked about something," Vi said as we watched her race down the steps.

Inside, the room was frigid. I caught movement out of the corner of my eye and spun to confront it. White filmy curtains billowed in the wind. Both windows were fully open and snow blew in onto the carpet.

Vi and I rushed forward to slam the sashes shut.

"What's going on?" Isabel said from the doorway.

We turned quickly to see Isabel and Jessica standing just inside the room.

"We heard noises up here and came to investigate," Vi said.

"Someone opened the windows, and the wind shut the door and trapped the cat," I said.

Isabel and Jessica exchanged a look and they both relaxed.

"Mavis is downstairs in a state of high anxiety," Isabel said.

"She claims she saw a ghost," Jessica said.

"Mavis saw the ghost?" Vi sounded disappointed that we had only found a cat.

"She pounded on my door a few minutes ago," Isabel said. "I had her wait in my room with Selma while I went to find Jessica."

"It was so cold in the hallway," Jessica said. "I checked all the doors to be sure they were locked and closed and then, while we were reassuring Mavis that everything was fine, the cat streaked past the doorway and downstairs into the lounge."

"Why was she wandering the halls in the middle of the night?" Vi demanded.

Isabel's lips thinned. "She claims she heard a noise in the hall."

"What did Mavis see?" I asked.

"It's not clear," said Isabel. "She thought she saw someone walking down the stairs wearing a white old-fashioned nightgown, but when Mavis called to the person she just kept walking and then seemed to disappear."

"Let's go down and talk to her," I said.

Every door was open and the knitters were milling about talking to Mac when we arrived back in the hallway. He was in plaid drawstring pants and an old Michigan State T-shirt. His hair was rumpled and he didn't look happy at being dragged from his bed for a ghost sighting. Lucille stood next to him in a deep green quilted satin dressing gown. Her spiky hair was a bit lopsided and she looked more fascinated than annoyed.

"Phillip, I think you should go down there and check things out," Lucille said. "I'm sure we'd all sleep better knowing there isn't a ghost roaming the halls."

Mac ran his fingers through his hair, making it look almost as spiky as his mother's.

"We'll go with you," Vi said as we approached.

Mac turned and I saw relief and annoyance flash across his face.

"There's no ghost," Mac said. "I don't know how to prove the castle is safe from something that doesn't exist."

Vi gave him a pitying look.

"We can go downstairs and check for cold spots," Vi said in a tone that should be reserved for kindergartners. "If there was a ghost, there will be cold spots."

"I think the whole castle is a cold spot, Vi," I said. "The window let in enough cold air for twenty ghosts."

Vi sighed. "You're probably right. It's not like we'll be able to tell the difference between regular cold and ghost cold now. Whoever opened the window was pretty clever."

"Do you think the ghost opened the window?" Lucille asked.

Vi considered this and then shook her head. Mac and I exchanged a "how did we get here" look.

"I doubt the ghost would have messed with the windows," Vi said. "It usually just walks the halls or looks *out* the window. Isn't that right, Jessica?"

Jessica drew in a sharp breath at being pulled into the ghost discussion.

"I don't know, Ms. Greer," Jessica said. "I'm not a ghost expert."

"Obviously," Vi said. "But you know the stories about *your* ghost. Has it ever opened the windows before?"

Jessica shook her head, and took a step closer to Isabel.

"It's too bad we can't get some ghost hunters out here with the storm and all." Vi stroked her chin in an exaggerated gesture of thinking.

"I think it would be more useful to get the police out here," I said.

"They won't be any better at dealing with this than you and Phillip," Lucille said.

Mac held up his hands and I saw his cheek muscles twitch.

"Look, Clyde and I will go downstairs and check out the whole ground floor," he said. "Jessica and Isabel, maybe you can calm Mavis and Selma and get them back to their room." Mac turned to Tina, Heather, and Amy. "If you wouldn't mind returning to your rooms, we'll take care of it from here."

Heather and Amy nodded. Tina narrowed her eyes at Mac and opened her mouth to speak, but Heather jabbed her in the ribs and pulled her down the hall. I watched them go, wondering why Tina had an issue with Mac. She bristled every time he tried to take control of the crowd.

Isabel and Jessica nodded and ducked into Isabel's room. Mac and I walked toward the stairs. I heard shuffling behind us. I stopped and Vi bumped into me.

"What?" she said. "Neither of you have any experience with ghosts. You'll need me along to help deal with it."

"What experience do you have?" I crossed my arms.

"I've done a lot of reading on the subject," Vi said. "And I've talked to lots of ghost hunters."

"Fine, Ms. Greer, you can come with us," Mac said.

I twisted around to look at Mac and probably looked just as mutinous as Tina had. Vi grinned and we set off again for the stairway.

Even with the electricity back on, the sconces in the hallway had been dimmed for the evening and the three of us cast hazy shadows on the stairs as we descended. It was definitely spookier than during the daytime and I was glad I wasn't alone. I took Mac's hand and Vi slipped her arm through mine on the other side.

A thorough search of all the main-floor rooms yielded no ghosts. Everything was as it should be. The library was ready for the next day's workshop, with yarn and needles laid out on the tables. I noticed striped scarves on all the statues in the reception area. That was new. Maybe the ghost had been doing some yarn bombing.

In the lounge, several of the decorative vases had been covered with neon jackets and knitted flowers nestled among the real ones.

"Maybe Mavis saw a yarn bomber," I said. "That would explain why the person didn't respond and then ran away." I turned to Vi. "The whole point is to not get caught, right?"

Vi examined the knitted flower. "I think I know who did this one."

She turned to us. "Linda must be feeling better."

"What do you mean?" I said.

"She makes these flowers," Vi said.

"I didn't know she was part of the conference," I said.

Vi wandered the lounge inspecting the new yarn installations. "She comes when she can, in between whatever she has to do with the hotel. But she's the one who started the workshops ten or so years ago. She's a big knitter."

Mac and I managed to drag Vi away from the knitting and back out into the hall.

The only place we hadn't checked was the kitchen. We turned down the darkened hall that led to the staff entrance to the kitchen. There was a line of light under the door.

I pushed it open and we were all surprised to see Linda there at the stove stirring a small pan. A thin cord ran from her pale gray robe pocket to her ears and she seemed oblivious to our entrance.

She whirled around when we moved toward her and then quickly relaxed.

"Oh, you startled me!" she said and tugged the earbuds out of her ears.

"Sorry Mrs. Garrett," Mac said. "We're searching the area because Mavis Poulson thinks she saw a ghost.

Linda chuckled. "Mavis always did have a wild imagination. Where did she see the ghost, exactly?"

"She thought it came down the stairs about twenty minutes ago," Vi said.

Linda shrugged. "She probably saw me."

"It's possible," I said. "Did you come down the main stairs?"

She nodded. "I couldn't sleep." She stopped and blinked back tears. "I haven't slept much since Clarissa died. I just can't get the picture of her lying there, dead, out of my mind." She gestured at the pot. "I thought some warm milk might help."

"She says she called out to the ghost and it didn't stop," Mac said.

Linda pulled her iPod out and showed it to us. "I like to listen to Mozart when I can't sleep." She dropped it back in the pocket. "I wouldn't have heard her with my earphones in. Plus, at three in the morning, I wouldn't have been expecting to meet anyone in the hall."

Mac and I exchanged a tired look.

"That's probably exactly what happened," Mac said.

We turned to go. As we reached the door, I stopped. "You weren't in Clarissa's room tonight, were you?"

"No. I don't know if I'll ever be able to go in there again," Linda said. "Why?"

"Someone was there and they left both windows open."

"That's strange," she said. "Why would anyone do that?"

"Don't worry, we'll figure it out," Vi said. She flapped her hand as if it was already handled.

Mac sighed and held the door open for us.

He walked us back to our room in silence. We all seemed to be mulling over what we had discovered, which wasn't much.

He gave me a quick kiss and said he'd see me for breakfast. It didn't take long to fall asleep again and this time I didn't dream at all.

22

After the ghost sighting, Saturday morning came too early. I rolled out of bed, and quietly opened the door. Mac and I had agreed to meet early again, before the knitters descended on the lounge. Wally approached Mac and me out of breath, but with a huge smile, as we walked downstairs.

"The phone lines are working!" he said.

"Fantastic," Mac said. "Let's call the police."

We followed Wally out to the front desk. "I was going to call myself, but I thought you might want to talk to them."

The old phone was ringing when we got to the counter. Wally pressed his lips together. "I plugged this old one in when the power went out. It's been ringing off the hook—that's how I knew it was working. Several of the guests received phone calls from family who were worried about them when the cell towers went down."

Wally answered the phone, took a message, and hung up.

He then took the phone off the hook and handed the receiver to Mac.

"Let me know when you're ready and I'll dial—we have to be quick before another call comes through."

Mac nodded at him and Wally dialed.

From what I could glean by listening to his side of the conversation, it sounded like Mac was being put straight through to homicide. I began plotting how long we would likely have to stay after the police arrived.

Mac turned to Wally. "Let's keep this between us for now," he said. "I'm not sure how quickly they can get here with that tree blocking the road—there's no need to raise everyone's hopes."

Wally nodded agreement. "I'll just tell the rest of the guests when they come down that the phone is working in case they need to check in with family—it might limit the phone calls coming in," Wally said.

We sat in the lounge while we waited for the dining room to open. The hours were later on the weekends and I was getting antsy without my caffeine.

"I'll be glad when the police arrive and they can remove the body," I said. "It's creeping me out, knowing she's outside in the shed."

Mac nodded. "They'll take over the investigation and maybe we can get out of here."

"Should we write up what we know so far so we can turn it over to them?"

Mac pulled his notebook out of his back pocket and flipped it open. "It wouldn't hurt."

I scooted closer to him so we could read his notes together.

"Clarissa left the cocktail party at six thirty and we saw her arguing with Jessica in the hall." Mac made a note.

"Isabel, Mavis, and Tina were all out of the dining room at some point before Clarissa's body was found," I said.

"And as far as staff members go, we can only rule out Wally." Mac put a line through Wally's name.

"By refusing to talk to us, Tina has guaranteed my suspicions. I don't like it that she tried to cover up the fact she left the room." I leaned back against the cushions. "It's weird. How did she think she would get away with it? We were all there—someone was bound to remember that she had stepped out."

"People don't always make good choices." Mac shook his head. "Maybe she's scared. She hasn't acted thrilled that we're investigating."

"I suppose." I took Mac's notebook and flipped a couple of pages. "Who had a motive?"

Mac ticked names off on his fingers. "Jessica and Linda had been fighting with Clarissa about the hotel. Mavis and Isabel hold a past tragedy against her. Holly was likely bullied and may have been afraid of losing her job."

"What about Kirk?" I said. "He's at the top of Dad's list."

"Incompetence isn't a crime. We can't forget René," Mac added. "If Clarissa interfered with his plans for the restaurant."

"At least we can give the police somewhere to start," I said and handed his notebook back.

"They'll probably want to do their own interviews," Mac said. "I hope we can turn this over to them and head out before the weekend is over."

"We probably can't make it to Mexico at this point—where do you want to go?"

"Anywhere but here," Mac mumbled as his mother waved from the doorway and headed in our direction.

"Hello, you two! Did you hear that the phones are back on?"

We nodded. "We just called the police to come and deal with Clarissa's death," Mac said.

"Oh. You won't be working on it anymore?" Lucille said. "I'm surprised you can just walk away after all the time you've put into it so far."

Secretly I had to agree with Lucille. Mac was like Baxter with a bone when it came to solving a murder.

"I don't think I'll have a choice, Mom. It's not my case. I only stepped in because we were all stuck here. I'll turn over all the information I have and let them get on with it."

Lucille held his gaze for a moment. "We'll see," she said. She walked around the room to admire the newest yarn creations. The lounge had taken on a surreal character with all the brightly colored yarny things stashed everywhere.

"Do you think we could stay and finish what we started?" I whispered.

Mac turned to me. "Is that what you want?" he said, and a slow smile began.

"I hate to leave a case right in the middle. If they'll let us continue, I think I'd like to see it through."

Mac let out a breath and I saw his shoulders relax. "Me, too. I just feel bad that our vacation is ruined."

"We'll still take that trip—just later than we planned."

Mac took my hand and squeezed. "Are you sure you want to leave police work? You obviously love it as much as I do."

I pulled my hand away. "I love solving the puzzle—I don't love the hierarchy and the paperwork and the hours."

Mac waited. I was very aware of Lucille wandering through the room, examining the knitting. I lowered my voice.

"I don't think I'll be able to go back to it after everything that has happened."

"What will you do?"

I shrugged. I had hoped to avoid this conversation for a little while longer.

"Are you two coming in to breakfast?" Lucille said from the doorway.

I hopped up. "Yes, I'm starved."

I took Mac's hand and pulled him toward the door.

Mac and I walked to the dining room and I went straight for the tea. The buffet was more elaborate than before—apparently with electricity came homemade waffles.

We heard voices in the hall as we sat down with our plates loaded with waffles and whipped cream.

I recognized Vi's voice first. She was telling the ghost story *again*. It got more and more lurid with each iteration. She entered the dining room with Seth. His eyes were wide and his mouth hung open while Vi told her tale. He caught sight of Mac, Lucille, and me and raised his hand in greeting. The rest of the knitters followed and Mom and Dad took up the rear, holding hands.

Seth veered toward the buffet. Even a really good ghost story would not deter him from obtaining food. The noisy group swarmed the buffet and settled at tables in groups of four or five. Vi and Mom clattered their plates as they joined us.

"You were up early," Vi said.

I nodded and suppressed a yawn.

"What's the plan for today? Have you interviewed all the suspects?" Vi dumped half the cream pitcher into her coffee.

"This whole thing makes me very nervous," said Mom. She leaned forward and glanced side to side. "There's a murderer among us!"

Seth took a moment from his food to glance at Mom, but quickly went back to the task at hand.

Dad patted Mom's hand. "It's not like it's a crazed lunatic. It sounds like this Clarissa had at least a couple of enemies."

Dad must have heard the whole story from Mom and Vi.

"Baxter's been acting really weird since we got here," Seth said. "Usually Tuffy is the one who sits and shivers and acts scared."

"Baxter's been acting scared?" I said.

Seth took a gulp of milk and swallowed. "He's just not himself. I guess I'd say he's a little skittish. He doesn't like my room in the cottage."

"He ran right in there yesterday," I said.

"I know, right?" Seth said. "Dogs are strange." He shook his head and dumped more syrup on his waffles.

"I hope he's not sick," I said. I examined my plate. Suddenly I wasn't hungry. I had gotten attached to the big lug. I didn't know what I would do if anything happened to him.

Vi had been talking to Mac about her idea of opening a detective agency. He seemed to have lost his appetite as well. He pushed his plate away and sat back, looking a bit green.

"Isabel has a full day planned for us knitters," Vi said to the rest of us. "I'm considering skipping her workshop on intarsia. I hate intarsia. It's someone's sick joke and actually takes all the fun of knitting and turns it into torture. That way I could help you and Mac."

"What's intarsia?" Seth asked.

I had been too late in my attempt to signal him to just let it go.

"It's when you knit in multiple colors to make a design," Mom said. "Like a letter, or a pattern."

"Oh, like those sweaters Mrs. Weasley made in the Harry Potter books?"

"Yeah, but she used magical knitting needles and didn't have to sit and read a chart and twist all the stitches and fix all the holes and weave in all the ends," Vi said.

Mom smiled at Seth and leaned toward him. "It's really not that bad."

Vi huffed and turned her attention to Lucille. I noticed Mac kept his eyes on his plate and didn't engage in the knitting conversation. I put my hand over his on the table.

"Do you like intarsia?" Vi asked Lucille.

"I'm more of a cables-and-lace kind of gal," Lucille said.

Vi slapped her on the back. "I knew I liked you. Maybe we can get Isabel to skip the intarsia."

"Given that her most recent pattern book is *all* intarsia, I doubt it," Mom said and narrowed her eyes at Vi.

"So what's with all the socks on the furniture?" Seth said after returning from his second trip to the buffet.

"That's the yarn bombing. It's a hoot!" Vi said.

"That reminds me, Violet," Lucille said. "I brought a few items with me. Will Wally help me put them up?"

Vi shook her head. "No, you want Kirk. He's got a ladder. Unless you want to bomb a low-lying area, which is fine but not as showy . . ."

"I'll help, Mrs. McKenzie," Seth said.

"Thank you, Seth." Lucille smiled at him. They had become close over the past couple of months. Seth had moved in with me just before Thanksgiving, and Mac's mother discovered that Seth would eat just about anything. The two of them bonded over her desire to bake and Seth's desire to eat.

Mac put his hand on my back and whispered, "Ready to go?"

I nodded.

Mac pushed his chair back while gulping the last of his

coffee. "Clyde and I have some work to do this morning. We'll see you all at lunch."

"I hope you'll think about what I said, Phillip," Lucille said as we stood.

Mac's face turned a bit pink and he clamped his lips together. He gave her a curt nod, grabbed my hand, and pulled me toward the door.

"What was that about?" I said while jogging to keep up.

"You aren't the only one with an interfering family," Mac said.

23

Wally rushed up to us as we exited the dining room. "Detective McKenzie! Detective Harris is on the phone—he needs to speak with you."

Mac and I followed him to the front desk.

Wally silently handed the phone to Mac.

"Pete? What's up?" Mac said.

Wally and I watched Mac as he listened.

"I'm not surprised. No, that's fine. We'll see what we can do from our end."

Mac caught my eye and gave a small shake of his head.

"Okay. Yup. We'll see."

Mac hung up and Wally and I almost pounced on him.

"They can't get through. The tree that came down took some power lines with it." Mac grimaced. "I'm glad Kirk and I didn't touch it or wander around too much in the vicinity."

"So, are they going to clear the tree?" Wally asked.

Mac nodded once. "They have to get the power company

out to secure the lines and then they'll have to cut the tree into pieces to move it. It might take a while. They're dealing with power outages all across Southwestern Michigan."

Wally left us in the reception area and went to herd the knitters into the lounge for the big reveal of more yarn bombing.

We sat on one of the comfy couches that graced the entryway. I looked out at the white landscape, the trees outlined in snow, and the drifts that had piled up outside. After a few minutes we heard them noisily make their way to the library.

I wondered how long we would be stuck here with our families and the progressively more anxious knitters. "What was your mother talking about?" I said.

"Nothing. We had a little argument last night."

"What about?"

Mac sighed. "About you."

I opened my mouth to speak and we heard a shriek from down the hall followed by screams and exclamations from multiple voices.

I got to the hallway before Mac and we both raced to the workshop room.

The knitters were crowded around a pile of yarn, talking and pointing and wringing their hands. Yarn and needles lay on the floor near the chairs as if they had all jumped up and flung their projects down. It must be something serious.

Isabel gestured at everyone to stand back.

"What's going on?" I said over the noise.

Isabel pointed a shaky finger at a pile of yarn.

I stepped closer and saw what was causing the ruckus. A Maglite sat halfway buried by the yarn. A brownish-red substance covered the side and part of the bulb. Of course, without a crime lab, we couldn't be sure, but I was convinced that this was the murder weapon.

Mac held his arm out to keep everyone back and knelt

down to examine the flashlight. He pulled out his cell phone and took a picture and then asked the knitters if anyone had a large paper bag. Isabel opened a box in the corner of the room and pulled out a folded shopping bag.

"Can I use one of these?" Mac asked, pointing to a box of zippered plastic freezer bags that sat on the coffee table. According to Vi, knitters stored projects in plastic bags to protect the yarn from dust and moths.

Isabel nodded and handed him the now open shopping bag.

Mac used the plastic bag as a glove and gingerly picked up the flashlight and yarn. He placed it in the paper sack, turned the plastic bag inside out and stuffed it in along the side of the paper one.

"We'll need to keep the yarn for evidence," Mac said.

"Evidence?" Isabel squeaked.

"It looks like you just found the murder weapon."

A murmur went through the crowd, punctuated by Vi's "I knew it!"

Selma covered her mouth, her eyes large. Mavis clutched Selma's hand. Amy and Heather backed away from the bag of yarn while Vi and Mom stepped closer to it.

"At least the murderer hid it with the acrylic," Tina said. "If they had put it in with the silk-mohair there might be another murder."

Nervous chuckles spread among the group.

"How could this happen?" Selma asked. "I thought the room was locked up at night." Her face was pale and I worried she might faint.

"Unless it was one of us," Mavis said. She glowered at Vi and then turned angry eyes on Isabel.

"It doesn't matter who it is!" Selma said. "We're all stuck here with a murderer. We could all be dead by the end of the weekend just like that Agatha Christie story."

Mom went to Selma and patted her on the back. She talked quietly to her and I saw Selma's shoulders relax.

"*Was* the room locked?" I asked Isabel.

Isabel tore her gaze from Selma and looked at me. "I haven't locked it the whole time we've been here." Isabel held her hands out. "I didn't see the point. We're the only guests, and it's not like there's a black market for knitting supplies."

The knitters murmured agreement and Mavis humphed.

"Clyde and I will take the light and yarn and store it in case we need to send it to a lab," Mac said.

"*If* we ever get out of here," Selma said.

"The snow will melt eventually," Mom said in her "look at the bright side" voice. "In the meantime, we should enjoy the time we have to knit." She went back to her seat and pointedly picked up her needles.

Mom was a professional worrier, but she also was great in a crisis. It was one of her many contradictions.

The rest of them also returned to their seats and rescued their projects from the floor.

Mac spoke quietly to Isabel, who nodded and darted glances at her group.

"Okay, ladies," she began. "Let's try to get back to work." Her hands shook as she picked up her needles and yarn.

We left the workshop room with the offending flashlight and yarn. Mac gestured up the stairs.

"I want to put this somewhere safe," he said.

We walked down the hallway to the room he shared with Lucille. He pulled the old-fashioned key from his pocket and slid it into the lock. I couldn't remember the last time I used a key at a hotel. The sound of a real lock is more satisfying than the beeps of the key-card locks so many hotels use.

Mac swung the door wide and gestured inside. I stepped in and surveyed the room. It was decorated in light yellow and green with dark wood twin beds flanking a large bureau. They also had a small sitting area near the window. Their room boasted a view out the side of the building and down the hill into the woods. I wandered to the windows while Mac rummaged in the closet with the wall safe.

I glanced at the small table between the chairs and caught my breath. A manila file folder sat on top of a knitting magazine. Stamped on the front was the seal of the Ann Arbor police department and my name was typed on the tab. The envelope with my name scrawled on it sat on top.

I took a deep breath and glanced at the closet. Mac was mumbling to himself about old safes. I flipped open the file and saw exactly what I was expecting—a report on the shooting that had occurred almost a year ago.

It had been the catalyst that sent me back to Crystal Haven. My partner and I had chased a suspect through backyards and eventually ended up in a cemetery. When the man had turned to face us, I was certain he held a gun. I didn't actually *see* the gun. I *felt* the malicious intent with some other sense. I shot him, but aimed for his leg and he went down. That one decision had effectively ended my career, at least as far as I was concerned. If I was sure he was aiming a gun, I should have aimed for the largest target—his torso. In that situation the surest way to protect myself and my partner would not be to simply wound the gunman. However, he wasn't holding a gun. I was thankful that I hadn't killed him, but he would always walk with a limp and had to undergo surgery to repair his knee. He was only seventeen, not much older than Seth. The guilt from harming another person ate away at me and the knowledge that I couldn't shoot to kill ate away at my reputation with the other officers.

I picked up the file and flipped through the pages. Interviews and witness accounts were followed by my report of the shooting. I flicked the folder shut and realized Mac was now quiet.

I turned and saw him looking at me with a mixture of concern and obstinacy. We had been over this ground before. But just before Christmas I thought I had finally convinced him that I didn't want to pursue any more investigations into the shooting. Apparently Mac had other ideas.

"Clyde, let me explain," he said. He took a step toward me.

I held up my hand. "There's nothing to explain, Mac." I dropped the file back on the table. "You're checking up on me even after I asked you to let it go."

"No, I wasn't checking up on you." He took another step forward and stopped when he met my gaze.

"Then what are you doing with the police report on the shooting?"

Mac sighed and looked away from me.

"I planned to talk to you about it while we were on vacation," he said.

"Talk to me about what?"

"I think you're being much too hard on yourself," he said. "Your lieutenant says you won't even consider his opinion that you acted well within the bounds of what would be expected—"

I stepped forward and held up my hand.

"I don't want to talk about it. I completely misread the situation and shot an unarmed man. Nothing will change that fact." I stopped and took a moment to control both my anger and my sadness.

"Clyde. You have to listen to me," Mac said. He held his hands out in a pleading gesture. "You did what you were trained to do."

"I need a few minutes, Mac." I strode to the door and pulled it open. "I'll see you at lunch."

24

I went straight to my room, figuring I could grab a few minutes to calm down and get some perspective. Mac and I had covered this ground before. He felt I was overreacting and that all police officers face this kind of guilt along the line. He also didn't want me to throw away my career at such an early point.

We frequently found ourselves at an impasse, and my reluctance to name another career seemed to prove Mac's point that I needed to return to my job in order to be happy. I knew that I was dragging my heels and was grateful that my financial situation allowed me the time and space to figure things out. I needed to decide what to do with my life now that I had stopped running from who I was. But I wasn't ready to share all of that with Mac yet and so he didn't understand my reluctance to return to my old job.

I shook my head to clear it as I turned to shut the door behind me.

"Oh! I didn't expect you," Vi said from the couch by the window.

I'm embarrassed to say I actually jumped at the sound of her voice. I had been so intent on my own thoughts I didn't see her sitting there in her multicolored array of shawls.

"Vi," I said, "I thought you were at the workshop."

She shook her head. "I needed a break from the knitting." She said this while clicking her needles along a sage green scarf.

I cocked an eyebrow. "I see."

She glanced at her hands and snorted. "Not that kind of a break. The gang couldn't stop chattering about the blood-covered flashlight. Selma has them all thinking they'll be murdered in their beds. I needed to think."

"Me, too." I sat on my bed and stared at the whiteness outside.

"I'm glad you're here," she said. "I've been hoping we could go over the case together."

"I really—"

"I know what you're going to say," she said and held one hand up to stop me. "You want me to just sit back and let you and Mac have all the fun."

"I hardly think of trying to solve a murder as fun. Especially when the murderer is likely having dinner with us every night," I said stiffly and again wondered how Vi always managed to make me feel like the older, more mature person in the room.

"Okay, you keep telling yourself that," she said and went back to her knitting.

"What are you talking about?" She was irking me despite my intention to remain calm.

"I mean you're made for this kind of thing." She set her project down and turned to face me. "You loved working cases when you were a police officer and you've loved solving the murders in Crystal Haven this past year."

Great. Another person trying to push me toward a calling that wasn't mine.

"I don't want to go back to police work, Vi."

"Who said anything about the police?"

My head snapped up and I narrowed my eyes at her. "You just did. I can see right through you. You want me to join the Crystal Haven police force, and move back home for good."

Vi came to sit with me on the bed. She put her arm around my shoulders.

"I do want you to move home for good, but I think you'd lose your mind if you joined the Crystal Haven police. You'd have to work with li'l Tom Andrews and take orders from Mac whenever anything interesting happened."

Tom was a junior officer on the force, but Vi still saw him as the twelve-year-old neighborhood hooligan—her words. And Mac's job as a homicide detective meant he took the case whenever there was a murder in Ottawa County.

I laughed and turned toward her. "Then what are you talking about?"

"I'm talking about you and me. We should open our own business."

My mother and Vi had been nagging me to join the family business for years. They each had a psychic niche—Vi as a pet psychic and Mom as a tarot reader—but felt they could build an empire if I joined them and used my premonitions and touch sensitivity to tell clients their future, help them find lost objects, or warn them of doom.

I shook my head and stood up to get away from her.

"We've covered this, Vi," I said. "I'm not interested in a psychic career."

She sniffed and looked away from me. "I gave that up a long time ago."

"What? You did?"

"Of course," she said. "You made it very clear how you felt and these past few months I noticed that you only really seem satisfied when you have a puzzle to solve. Psychics don't tend to solve puzzles."

"So, what are you suggesting?"

"Well, I don't want you to become a fortune teller, but if you use your gifts and your police training you could help a lot of people." She paused and held my gaze. "I think we should open a detective agency—together."

I laughed, so glad to realize she was just trying to cheer me up.

"That's a good one," I said, still giggling. "I needed a good laugh—thanks, Vi."

Her face turned stony.

"I'm not joking."

My stomach dropped. "What?"

Vi took a step toward me. "Think of it, Clyde. It would be great. You could help people find things they've lost, and solve mysterious disappearances. And I could deal with any strange psychic events. Plus, I'm going to learn more about ghost hunting."

I shook my head and backed away from her.

"With my ability to interview animals, and your multiple abilities to see the future and find things, we'd be great together. Your mom said she'd pitch in with tarot if we need it."

"Mom is in on this as well?"

"Yeah, we all think it's a great idea."

"Who thinks it's a great idea?"

"Me, Rose, Lucille, and your father."

"You've all discussed this? Dad would never think it's a good idea. And what about Seth? Does he know?"

Vi shook her head. "We couldn't risk telling Seth—he can't keep a secret."

I took a deep breath. If Vi only knew about the secrets Seth could keep.

"And why are you discussing this with Lucille?"

Vi looked down and hung her head. "That was an accident. Your Mom slipped up and mentioned it. Lucille thinks Mac is worried you might move away when your year is up."

"Wait, what?" Mac thought I was going to leave? Now I was less concerned about the detective agency and more concerned about my mother and Lucille discussing my life.

"We all want you to be happy and to stay in Crystal Haven." She stood up to pace and gesture wildly to make her point. "I think this would solve everything."

"And all of you have *decided* this is a great idea?" As usual, Vi ignored my threatening tone.

She nodded and grinned. "They see what you're good at and know we'd make a great team. C'mon, it'll be great!"

"No offense, Vi, but you don't know anything about solving murders." I turned away from her.

"I think I've done a good job so far when it comes to asking the right people the right questions. I could figure it out. You aren't the only one with a deductive mind."

I snorted and sounded like Vi. Then I sighed. Everyone had ideas on how I should live my life.

Vi and I could argue about this until the next winter, but I didn't have the mental energy to keep fighting her. And yet, I needed some space, so I told her what I knew she wanted to hear. "Let me think about it."

She shook her head. "No. I know what that means," she said. "You'll just keep putting me off, hoping I'll give up."

Damn, I hated it when she did that.

I opened my mouth to respond, but she wasn't finished.

"I have a deal for you," she said.

This was classic Vi. With nothing resembling a winning hand, she would continue to up the ante.

"Okay, let's hear it." I crossed my arms.

"Let's have a contest," she said. "If I solve this murder before you do, you'll give the business a try for one year." She held up one knobby finger. "If you solve it before me, and without any help from me, I'll let this drop."

"You'll move on with no more sneaky plans to get me to change my mind?"

"Correct. If you solve it first, you're free to make your own plans."

I chose not to point out that I was *already* free to make my own plans without her blessing. This was going to be interesting. At the very least, it would leave Mac and me to investigate on our own. Vi would have to gather her own information and wouldn't be badgering us. I wondered what Mac would think of it. I didn't know if he would love it or hate it. However, if I lost the bet, Mac wouldn't have to worry that I would leave Crystal Haven anytime soon. I was almost willing to just agree to work with Vi for a year to get Mac to back off on the police idea. And to reassure him that I was sticking around.

"Okay, Vi, you've got a deal."

She grinned.

I stuck out my hand and we shook on it.

25

At lunchtime, I walked into the dining room after the knitters had already arrived. René had set up another buffet and Emmett was busy refilling serving platters. The knitters seemed subdued and were not chatting as animatedly as they had at other mealtimes. Finding a murder weapon among their things must have put a damper on their spirits.

I spotted Dad and Seth across the room and headed in their direction after filling my plate with beet salad, risotto, and grilled salmon.

I sat between them, feeling cowardly. I was still unsure of just how mad I felt about Mac snooping around behind my back. And Vi's comment that he thought I would leave Crystal Haven bothered me. We hadn't really talked much about the future—our future—but I thought he knew I planned to stay. And to give us a chance. I wasn't ready to talk to him just yet and didn't want to give him an opportunity to engage me in conversation. I planned to use my human buffers to keep him at a distance. I glanced at Seth, who had nodded at me in between bites when I sat down.

Dad leaned over and whispered, "I've been keeping an eye on that maintenance guy." It took me a moment to remember why he had it in for poor Kirk.

Dad didn't like posers and he had pegged Kirk as a fake from the moment he fixed the generator.

"I know that everyone's a suspect, but I really think he's just new at this, Dad," I said. "It doesn't mean he's up to anything."

"Maybe, but I don't like coincidence." Dad tore off a piece of French bread and stuffed it in his mouth. He took a swig of water and continued. "Doesn't it seem strange that that poor woman was killed right after the power went out *and* the man in charge of the generator is incompetent?"

I shrugged, letting Dad know I really didn't want to engage much. Plus, my own suspicions were in a different camp entirely and I didn't want to encourage Dad's speculations.

"I saw him outside working on the snowblower," Dad continued. "He had the whole thing torn apart and then he put it back together and got it working again—all in about ten minutes."

I looked at Dad and must have appeared as clueless as I felt.

Dad huffed. "If he can fix a snowblower in a few minutes, how come he couldn't fix the generator in many hours?"

"You think he *wanted* the power out all that time?" I said.

Seth leaned forward.

"Papa, if he wanted the power outage to give him a chance to kill someone, why wouldn't he just fix it after he was done? There's no reason to keep everyone in the dark and cold."

I agreed with Seth. Kirk had seemed sincere in his efforts

to fix the generator. Plus, I was having a hard time imagining the guy who was assisting with the yarn bombing wielding a flashlight as a weapon.

"To deflect suspicion, of course. It's clearly working on you two," Dad said. "If he had conveniently fixed it later, then you would have suspected that he had left the power off on purpose to suit his nefarious schemes."

"Nefarious?" Seth said.

I put my head down and smiled.

"It means—" Dad said.

"I know what it means," Seth said and held up his hand. "Just seems like something Vi would say."

Dad's quick intake of breath indicated that Seth had wounded him with that remark.

"No offense," Seth said and held up both hands.

"I would prefer not to be compared to that person," Dad said stiffly.

"What's the matter, dear?" Mom put her plate on the table across from Dad. "You look like you don't feel well."

Seth snickered and I put my hand on Dad's back. "Dad's still worked up over the generator," I said.

"Not that again, Frank." Mom sat and opened her napkin. "That poor man is doing his best. Not everyone can fix machinery the way you can."

Dad seemed mollified at this and went back to his meal.

The conversation had started me thinking again. There were plenty of suspects and I was wondering how to narrow the list without tipping off Vi, when Mac and Lucille walked in.

He caught my eye and gave me a half smile. I knew that was his first attempt at an apology.

Vi breezed in and skipped the line to rush over to our table. "Have you told them?" she asked me.

I started shaking my head the moment she approached.

I didn't want everyone knowing about our bargain, especially Mac, who I knew was only a few minutes away from joining us. I narrowed my eyes at her and tried as hard as I could to send her a message to keep quiet.

"Told us what?" Mom said.

"Um." Vi hesitated. "Wally said there's another storm due in this afternoon."

Dad groaned and Mavis and Selma, who sat at the table next to us, joined in.

"When will we ever get out of here?" Mavis said.

Vi winked at me and turned her attention to Mavis.

"He says we're looking at another six inches tonight. Kirk barely has the front walk cleared—I don't know when we'll be able to get out," Vi said with more authority, and not sounding nearly as disappointed as the rest of us at this news.

"At least we have power and the phones are working again," Selma said.

"And we have plenty of yarn," Mom added. "In some ways this is like a knitter's dream. Our real lives have to be put on hold and all we can do is knit. I can't tell you how many times I've wished for a few days away from my real life. . . ."

"I'm sure the dead lady would disagree," Seth said in my ear.

"Rose is right," Vi said. "This is an opportunity—we are in a beautiful haunted castle in the middle of a winter wonderland, where we're required to enjoy knitting."

"Maybe Rose can get her tarot to tell us how long we're going to be stuck here," Lucille said as she joined us. She had obviously been listening while she visited the buffet.

Mac followed his mother and glanced around the table. The closest he could get was across the table and two seats down from me. His lips were a thin line and I knew the buffer of the rest of our group irritated him.

As soon as Seth finished his sandwich and pushed his plate away, I shoved my chair back and grabbed Seth's elbow.

"See you all in a while!" I said. "We have to go walk the dogs."

I hustled Seth out of the dining room. He balked as we passed the fresh tray of homemade macaroni and cheese. I felt slightly guilty since René had likely made it with Seth in mind.

"I wasn't finished, Clyde," Seth said, shaking my hand off his arm.

"You made three trips to the buffet," I said. "I'm sure you can survive until dinner."

"What's the rush, anyway?" He rubbed his arm where I had gripped him as if he'd been mortally wounded.

"I have to talk to you." I gestured down the hallway toward the front desk. It tended to be less crowded than the lounge since there was no fireplace and only a view of the piles of snow. The beauty of the snowcapped trees had lost its charm.

I led him to the couch that faced the desk and the hallway so I could be sure we wouldn't be overheard.

"I've done something really stupid," I said.

Seth cocked his head and settled back in the couch, a smile beginning on his lips.

"Don't look so amused," I said. "Vi could drive anyone to madness."

Seth leaned forward and sighed. "What now?"

"I made a deal with her that if she figures out the mystery before I do, I will go into business with her." I put my head in my hands, not wanting to see Seth's reaction.

"You what?" Seth said.

I didn't have to look at him to know his eyes were wide and his mouth hung open.

"You've been fighting them off for years," he said. "And

now you're just going to give in? Is it because you've learned stuff from Ms. Whittle and you want to test it out?"

"No, not a psychic business," I said. "She wants to open a detective agency."

"Oh, now *that* would be cool," Seth said.

"What?" I said.

"You're really good at solving mysteries." Seth ticked his points off on his fingers. "You definitely have some kind of sixth sense, and it might keep Aunt Vi busy."

I shook my head. "No, no, no. You don't get it. Can you imagine the trouble I'll deal with if I have to babysit Vi through 'cases' and keep Mac from killing us both? It will never work."

"So, why did you agree?"

I stood up and walked to the window. "I don't know. I was mad at Mac, and Vi was pressuring me with her theories and I just . . . didn't think it through."

"It's not that big of a deal," Seth said. "Vi isn't likely to win the bet and even if she does, you can wriggle out of it."

I knew Seth was right. What bothered me the most, and what I didn't share with him, was that I was starting to like the idea.

"Will you help me, Seth?" I said.

"Sure."

"Keep an eye on Vi and let me know what she's up to. Once we get an idea who might have killed Clarissa, I'm going to need you to steer her in the wrong direction."

"You want me to spy on my great-aunt, and then mislead the poor woman?"

I tilted my head at him, feeling a bit guilty when he put it that way. Although, "poor woman" hardly applied to Vi. I shrugged and nodded.

"Okay," he said. "We really do need to walk the dogs."

26

The walk didn't last long due to the weather, which had turned nasty again. The earlier sense that maybe we had seen the worst of it faded and I moved on to that sense of stoic tolerance that was necessary to get through a Michigan winter. Tuffy had been carried most of the way home. Even when Seth shoveled an area for him to walk in, he didn't like the snow or the cold feel of ice on his feet. He walked along shaking each foot as if he could brush off the cold and finally started limping on all four feet. Not easy to do. Even Baxter seemed to roll his eyes at the dramatic display.

The wind had picked up again and the temperature had dropped. I couldn't believe we would get even more snow. We brought the dogs back to the cottage and brushed as much of the cold stuff as possible off of them before letting them inside. I grabbed the door as it flew inward with a gust of frosty air. We hurried inside and unclipped the leashes.

Tuffy sat and shivered, glowering at both of us from under

his fringe. He tended to blame me for almost everything, but this time he included Seth in his disgruntlement.

A walk in the winter weather, on the other hand, had rejuvenated Baxter. He raced through the cottage on a continuous loop while Seth chased behind him with a towel. Baxter sideswiped me a couple of times, which was his way of inviting me to chase him.

Tuffy sighed, lay down on the front door carpet, and watched. Baxter calmed down a bit and then took up sentinel duty at the door to Seth's room and barked. When we ignored him, he barked again, a bit more sharply. Baxter usually left the barking to Tuffy, so I approached him to see what was bothering him. He backed away from me, moving farther into the room, threw himself on the floor, and moaned.

"What's wrong with him?" I asked Seth.

"I'm not sure." Seth knelt next to Baxter and rubbed his ears. "He's not really giving me much to go on. He just feels uncomfortable." Seth felt along Baxter's legs to see if he had hurt himself during his mad dash through the cottage.

Seth stood up quickly and backed away.

"What is it?"

Seth shook his head and crossed his arms.

"He thinks there's something under the floor."

"What?" I moved toward Baxter and sat next to him. "What does that mean?"

Baxter dropped his heavy head onto my legs and crawled forward as if he thought he would fit in my lap.

"I don't know. Like I said before, he acted funny in here last night. He kept skirting around that area, but now he's planted himself right on it."

The cottage had wood floors with large throw rugs in each room. I managed to stand up again even with Baxter pressing his chin into my knees and he quickly jumped up as well and stood looking at me with a big doggy smile.

I knelt back down and felt the floor where Baxter had been sitting. I hadn't been trying to sense anything but an image of a dim tunnel popped into my mind. I saw a wooden door at the end and pulled my hands away before I saw any more. I felt slightly nauseated.

Seth knelt next to me.

"Are you okay?"

Baxter pushed his forehead into my shoulder.

"Just dizzy for a second," I said. "I think Baxter might be onto something."

I pushed myself up to stand and patted Baxter's head. "Let's pull this carpet back and see what's bothering him," I said, fearful of what we might find.

Seth and I shifted the bed to the far edge of the room and rolled the carpet toward the bed.

The floor underneath the rug was slightly darker, and less scratched, but otherwise looked the same. I didn't understand—the tunnel had seemed so clear. I still had a lot of work to do before I could rely on any other senses. I started to push the roll of carpet away from the bed and back toward the wall, when Seth stuck his foot out to block it.

"What's that?" He pointed to a spot on the floor that seemed to coincide with where Baxter had been sitting when the rug was flat.

I pushed the bed a little more and we both rolled the thick carpet farther.

We revealed a square cutout with a recessed ring in the middle. It was perfectly flat. Seth pushed on a tab near the ring and it raised just enough to be able to grip it and pull it out.

"Wicked," Seth breathed. "I think this is a trapdoor."

We wrestled the carpet all the way off the door and stood

looking down at a metal ring that was right in the middle of a square cut in the floor.

Baxter barked and wagged his tail. Tuffy came in cautiously and lurked in the doorway, whining.

Before I could stop him, Seth grabbed the ring and pulled. Nothing happened.

I told Seth to stand back and grabbed the ring and pulled. Still nothing. I couldn't see any hinges and wasn't sure which way to pull. When I tried pulling in a different direction, I felt the ring swivel.

Seth must have seen it move. He pushed my hand away, gripped the ring, and twisted. We heard a loud squeak of metal on metal and then a click like a lock tumbling into place.

We pulled together on the ring and watched as the trapdoor opened. Baxter rushed forward and stuck his nose in the crack, breathing deeply. Tuffy's whining got louder.

I peered into the opening and caught a whiff of damp air. Seth and I leaned over the opening and saw a rope ladder hanging into the darkness below. The mid-afternoon light, a faded gray due to the impending storm, had crept in through the small window and cast a weak silver-blue patina on everything in the room. It only penetrated a foot or two into the opening.

Seth went to his duffel bag and pulled out a flashlight and a headlamp.

I looked at him with one eyebrow raised.

"What?" he asked.

"Do you always carry flashlights in your duffel?"

He flashed the Boy Scout hand signal. "Be prepared—that's my motto. Especially if Papa is involved." He switched on the light. "What are we waiting for?"

I grabbed Seth's arm to stop him from climbing down the ladder.

"No. You stay here. We don't know what's down there. And someone has to watch them." I jerked my head in the direction of the dogs. No surprise that Tuffy cowered in the corner, but Baxter was right next to him. A low growl emanated from Baxter's large chest.

Seth rolled his eyes and leaned into the opening to shine the light into the gloom.

"They're just overreacting," Seth said. His voice sounded hollow as he hung his head into the opening. "It looks like there's a tunnel down there."

I knelt next to Seth and Baxter whined.

I started to wonder just how many secrets there were in this castle. Realizing that if Vi had discovered the trapdoor, she would already be down there, I finally convinced myself to climb down the ladder. She'd be harassing us for "dillydallying."

"Okay, I'll go check it out," I said.

"What about the dogs?" he asked.

"What about them?" I put one foot on the ladder and gently eased my weight onto it. It held.

"They might fall in if we're down there."

My left foot was below my right, feeling for the next rung. I stopped.

"That's why you're staying here," I said. "It might be dangerous and you need to watch the dogs."

"Awww, man," Seth said.

"Hold the flashlight on the ladder so I can see what I'm doing—then you can toss it down to me."

He held the flashlight as I asked. When I reached the bottom, I heard scrabbling and squeaking and figured I had disturbed some rodent in his daily rounds. Mice don't bother me much. Rats are another matter. And I knew there would be spiders. There are always spiders.

"Okay, toss the light," I said. My voice echoed off the sides of the tunnel.

He dropped it down to me. "What's down there?"

I shone the light in one direction and found a wall about three feet from where I stood. The other direction, which led toward the castle, did indeed have a dim gray tunnel that disappeared into the gloom at the edge of my flashlight beam.

"There's a tunnel, and I think it leads to the castle," I said.

"Wicked," Seth said. His voice sounded very close and I looked up to see him hanging his head into the opening again.

"I'll be back in a couple minutes—stay there," I said.

Seth sighed dramatically.

I was in a tunnel under the ground between the cottage and the hotel. I remembered Vi asking Jessica about Prohibition and rumrunners. Maybe the rumors were true and there was a secret hiding place. I walked slowly, shining the light along both sides of the tunnel to be sure there weren't any doors or off-shoots. I had been counting steps and when I got to fifty the tunnel ended in a wooden door. There was a heavy metal ring where a doorknob should be. I pulled on the ring and the door didn't budge. I heard a scrape on the floor behind me. It sounded bigger than a rat. I spun around, raised the flashlight to strike if necessary, and saw Seth.

"I told you to stay there," I said. I put one hand on my hip and used the other to shine the light in his face. "You never listen to me."

He put his hands up like he was under arrest. "I listen all the time," he said. "I'll bet my percentage is better than ninety percent—that's an 'A' in listening." He grinned.

"What did you do with the dogs?" I lowered the light.

"I put them in the living room and closed the door so they wouldn't fall in."

"All right," I sighed. "I think this is the end anyway." I gestured at the door. "It won't open."

Seth reached out and pulled on the ring. The door didn't move. I grabbed hold and we both pulled. Then we pulled and leaned all of our combined weight into the job. A scraping sound of stone on metal accompanied the slow movement of the door.

We opened it just far enough to squeeze through and found ourselves in the basement of the hotel. It didn't look like it was a well-used area. Cast-off furniture and household items lined the narrow hall. There was a gap in the junk just ahead of us.

Another wooden door greeted us. Seth and I repeated our earlier exercise and almost fell on top of each other when the door swung easily.

"Wicked," Seth said when he saw what was inside.

The room was about ten by ten feet. It contained a table and one chair, and at least ten boxes of cell phones. They seemed to be organized by type. Several boxes of iPhones sat next to Android versions. There was even a small box of BlackBerries. VERTEX WHOLESALE was stamped in large block letters on the side of each box.

"Whoa!" said Seth. "Are these all stolen?"

"I think so," I whispered.

It had been all over the news just before Christmas. Vertex Wholesale had been busted for purchasing stolen cell phones. According to reports, the storefront was known in the Detroit neighborhood as a place to get cash for phones, no questions asked. Police had raided the store and there were rumors that there was a connection to Kalamazoo. Seth and I had just stumbled onto the connection.

Seth stepped forward with his hand out toward a box. I grabbed him by the hood of his sweatshirt and stopped him.

"Don't touch anything," I said.

I shrugged off Vi's sweater and used it to pick up one of the phones. I chose a BlackBerry since it had buttons and carefully turned on one of the phones. It had been wiped clean of data.

Seth pointed to a printed stack of papers on the table. They listed cell phone brands, number of units, and prices. There was another column listing possible destinations. "Looks like your murder mystery just got a lot more complicated," he said.

I nodded absently, trying to fit this piece of the puzzle into everything else we knew. The dollar amounts were big enough to be a motive for all sorts of crimes.

"I've heard it's a big deal," he continued. "They sell for way more overseas than here. The gangs steal them from Americans and ship them to Japan or Europe, where they can get hundreds of dollars for each one."

I turned to him. "How do you know about all this?"

He lifted one shoulder. "I grew up in New York City. I've seen black-market dealers—usually the stuff is fake, though. Plus, I looked it up online after that police bust in December."

"We better get out of here, Seth," I said, and placed the phone back in the box.

Just as we turned to head out of the room, the door slowly swung inward and clicked shut. Seth and I ran to the door and pounded on it.

"Hey, let us out!" Seth shouted.

I wasn't sure our pounding could even be heard on the other side of the heavy door, much less Seth's pleas for release.

"Now what?" Seth said as he gave up on his hammering of the door.

"For one thing, I think I'll listen to Baxter a bit more," I said. "He really didn't want us to come down here."

Seth's face was white and his brows were scrunched together.

I put an arm over his shoulder. "Someone will find us."

I just hoped it was a friend and not the person who had put these phones here.

27

The room had been quite cold when we walked in and an hour later, it felt like the temperature had dropped even further. We'd shut off Seth's headlamp to conserve batteries and because every time he swung his head the wild dance of light on the walls made me dizzy. About an hour into our stay, my flashlight died. Seth quickly clicked his on and I made my fiftieth trip around the room to check for a way out. I had it in my head that with all the secret passages and stairways, maybe there was another way out of this secret room. Unfortunately, it had been designed to hide things. There were no windows, no heating vents, not even an electrical outlet or a pipe to bang on in the hopes that someone would hear us.

Neila's prediction about my mother attending a child's funeral flashed unbidden into my mind. Panic wouldn't help anyone. I knew that Mac would search until he found us and with our canine guards outside the room, it couldn't be much longer now.

Seth sat on the floor and shivered.

"I'm hungry," he said.

"We haven't been here that long. We just had lunch."

He shrugged and chewed on his thumb.

I held my watch in the beam of Seth's headlamp.

"Someone will notice we're missing and they'll find us. Baxter will be sure to show people the trapdoor."

"Yeah, but when? How long is the workshop today? What if they go straight in to dinner and we miss it?"

"I'm so glad you have your priorities straight," I said.

"I wish Vi was better at understanding the animals. Baxter would tell her right away where we went."

"They'll find us, don't worry," I said as much to Seth as to myself.

The headlamp flickered and went out.

Seth's disembodied voice said, "Great."

I took a step in the direction I thought the iPhones were boxed up.

With my hand covered by my sweater, I reached in and grabbed a phone. It took me four tries to find one that still had some power, but I was able to at least find Seth on the floor and sit next to him using the dim light of the iPhone screen.

"I thought we weren't supposed to touch those," Seth said.

"I'm only using the one so we can keep checking the time and avoid losing our minds."

I clicked the phone off and sighed.

Yet again, I had stumbled into trouble and dragged Seth along with me. If his mother had even an inkling of my guardianship track record, she'd have him home immediately. I had had plenty of time to think while we sat in this room. It seemed the more we discovered, the more complicated the mystery became. Clarissa had alienated her family and most of the staff. Several of the knitters had a grudge against her. And now we had a room full of stolen cell phones. Was that connected to Clarissa, or had we stumbled onto a whole different crime? There were too many possibilities and it seemed almost everyone we interviewed had kept something from us.

But, I knew Seth and Vi were right. I did love to solve puzzles. And my work with Neila Whittle had improved my ability to interpret the messages I received. I'd always been good at finding lost items. Maybe Vi's idea would work. But could I work with Vi?

Seth sighed. Every sound was amplified in the close, dark space.

Seth's breathing, my stomach, and then, as faint as possible but still audible, I heard what might have been footsteps outside the door.

I clicked the phone back on and looked at Seth. He had heard it, too. We stood up and started pounding on the door again.

We continued to pound even after the door began to swing open.

"I knew it!" said Vi.

She rushed forward to hug Seth, while Mac took me roughly into his arms as if he wasn't sure whether he was mad or glad to see me. I held on to him tightly and felt the scratchy wool of his snowman sweater against my cheek. At that moment, nothing could have been better.

"How did you get in here?" Mac's voice was low and gravelly against my hair.

"Did you figure out the murder?" Vi tapped me on the shoulder.

"Did we miss dinner?" Seth said.

I reluctantly pushed away from Mac and we all laughed in relief. I brushed past Mac and Vi to get out of the room and into the no-less-spooky passageway.

Mac stepped farther into the room and shone his light into the boxes of cell phones. He whistled low and long.

"Somebody's been busy," he said.

Mac took about twenty pictures with his phone before he would let us leave.

We all trooped in the direction of the inn. Mac wanted to be sure the tunnel connected to the hotel. We passed through the hallway that held over a century's worth of cast-off junk. Old baby cribs and strollers sat next to chairs with broken legs and assorted sporting equipment. It seemed that the members of the Carlisle family didn't like to throw anything away.

We finally got to the area where the staff rooms had been built. The paint was clean and new looking and there was a small room with a freezer and a large refrigerator. Next to that room, we peeked into the utility room, where the generator hummed next to the furnace.

Satisfied that the tunnel did connect all the way from the cottage to the hotel, we went back the way we had come to get to the cottage trapdoor.

When I reached the top of the ladder I was almost knocked back down into the passageway by an exuberant Baxter. Fortunately, Seth was already at the top and pulled him away from the opening. Baxter was so excited to see me that he ran rings around me while hopping up and down. Tuffy shivered in Seth's arms.

I helped Vi climb out of the hole. Mac was the last one up and he and Seth closed the trapdoor.

Mom and Dad were waiting for us.

"We were so worried about you two," Mom said. She rushed forward to hug Seth and me.

"That was amazing!" Vi said. "I've never seen anything like it. I love this castle."

"I could do with a few less secrets," I said.

"What do you think they used that room for?" Seth asked.

"It has to be where they kept the alcohol during Prohibition," Vi said. She slung an arm over Seth's shoulder and they walked into the living room chatting about gangsters and bootleggers.

"I'd better go call off the outdoor search party," Mac said. He walked to the front door, turned, and pointed at us. "No one goes anywhere."

"He's kind of bossy," Vi said after he was gone.

"He was really worried, Vi," Mom said. "You saw him. I thought he was going to tear the place apart, stone by stone."

We had settled in the small living room of the cottage to await Mac's return.

"I would have helped him," Dad said. He'd been left behind with Mom to coordinate with the other searchers.

"I knew you were fine," Vi said. She waved her hand dismissively, and put her feet up on the coffee table.

"You did not." Dad swiveled in his chair to look at her. "You were just as frantic as the rest of us."

Vi scowled at him and crossed her arms.

Mom paced in front of the window, watching for Mac, I assumed.

"Is there anything to eat in this place?" Seth asked.

"I'll check the cupboards, Seth," Mom said. "There's probably some snacks in there."

Mom and Seth went into the small kitchenette together

and we heard doors opening and closing. Then we heard bags rustling.

Mom returned with a plate of cookies and set it on the coffee table. She sat next to Dad and he slipped an arm over her shoulders.

"Are we just going to sit here, or are we going to make a plan?" Vi said.

"I think we should wait for Mac," Mom said. "Besides, I thought you and Clyde had a contest going . . ."

I glanced at Vi. "So everyone knows?" I said to the room.

"I don't like to root against my own daughter, but you really need a job," Mom said. "This business with Vi might be just the thing."

I looked at Dad, who was carefully avoiding my eyes. "You, too, Dad?"

He was saved from having to answer by a blustery gust of wind that blew Mac back into the room.

He stomped on the rug by the door and shed snowflakes.

"It's getting really bad out there again," he said. "I'm glad they hadn't gotten far, it would be horrible if someone got caught outside in this for very long."

He came and sat next to me and carefully took my hand. I thought it was a nice gesture until he squeezed a little tighter and said, "Tell us why you were stuck in an underground dungeon and hadn't told anyone where you were going."

Fortunately, Seth wandered in crunching on potato chips just as Mac asked his question.

"It's not Clyde's fault," he said through a mouthful of chips. "It's Baxter's."

Baxter lifted his head off his paws at the sound of his name. He'd calmed down once everyone had reappeared from the scary hole and lay curled in front of the fire. Tuffy was glued to Seth's leg and watched every move of his hand from bag to mouth, hoping Seth would miss.

"How was it Baxter's fault?" Mac asked. "He seemed to be the only sensible one—he stayed here in the cottage, where it was safe."

Baxter put his head down and closed his eyes. He, like the rest of us, could probably sense that Mac was winding up for a safety lecture. I would have closed *my* eyes, but Mac's death grip on my hand kept me vigilant.

Seth, self-appointed as my backup in almost every situation, sat on the floor near Dad. "Baxter had been acting weird since yesterday," he said. "He didn't like the room and acted like there was something wrong with the rug. I told Clyde about it and we decided to check it out."

Vi picked up her knitting and scowled at us. Mom passed a plate of cookies around the room to dispel the tension.

"We didn't think we needed a whole gang to just check out the trapdoor," I said. "We got stuck in the room by accident. I didn't know the door would lock from the outside."

Mac's grip was loosening; I hoped that meant he had calmed down.

"I think we should make a pact—nobody goes into unknown secret tunnels without leaving a lookout behind, like we did with Frank," Vi said.

I cast a "told you so" look in Seth's direction. He looked away.

"That's a very good idea, Vi," Mom said. She smiled at the rest of us to encourage agreement.

"Okay, that's a good idea," Mac said. "As much as possible we need to be safe. Something is going on at the castle and now that Seth and Clyde have discovered the cell phones, I'm worried we've stumbled onto a bigger problem than a disgruntled employee."

"What cell phones?" Dad said.

We explained about the boxes of cell phones and how they could be connected to a black-market ring.

Dad whistled. "I read about that happening in Detroit. You think they're linked? When they said there was a connection, I just figured one of the suspect's families lived here or something."

Mac let go of my hand, finally, and I surreptitiously rubbed the sensation back into it. He leaned forward and glowered at everyone. "This information stays here, in this room. If someone at the castle is involved in selling stolen goods, he or she could be dangerous." He waited until we had all nodded consent.

"I'd been working on the assumption that Clarissa had been killed because she seemed to make enemies everywhere she went; maybe it was simpler than that," Mac said. "Maybe she knew about the phones or was involved somehow and that put her in danger. Now that we know about the phones, we could be in danger as well. So we all keep quiet, right?"

We murmured agreement. I took a cookie and crunched it quietly.

"This mystery is getting very twisty," Vi said. "Maybe we should all list our theories and figure out which one is best."

I was already shaking my head. "No, you said we can't work together," I said.

"We shouldn't put a small wager between solving the mystery and not . . ."

"What wager?" Mac said.

"I'll tell you later," I said.

Mac held my gaze for a moment, but backed off. He probably was still feeling guilty for the AAPD file he had stashed in his room. I was not above using his guilt to avoid a full-fledged fight right in front of my family. And I knew the last thing Mac wanted was my family even more involved in our relationship. I was good as long as I stayed near them.

Mac stood up and pulled me to a stand beside him. "Clyde and I are going to go talk through a few things. We'll see you all at dinner."

So much for safety in numbers.

Seth gave me a sympathetic smile and then focused on devouring the cookies.

28

I shrugged into my jacket and followed Mac out into the wind and snow. It was an unpleasant sixty seconds as we ran toward the hotel. I dreaded the conversation to come, but didn't want to dawdle in the storm.

"We'd better go tell the knitters that you've been found," Mac said. "Vi made a big deal about going in search of you two."

Lucille rushed to the door when we entered the library and gave me a brief hug. "We've been so worried. Did one of the dogs run away? Did you get lost in the snow?"

"No, Mom, I'll tell you about it later," Mac said quietly. "Seth and the dogs are fine as well." Mac raised his voice so the rest of the group could hear him. "Everyone is fine, and back inside safe and warm."

The knitters thanked Mac for coming to tell them, and told me they were happy no one was hurt.

We said we'd see them at dinner and turned toward the lounge. Mac and I sat in our spot by the fire.

He put his arm around me and rested his head on top of mine.

We were quiet for a while. Even though we'd argued earlier, I snuggled as close to him as I could get and allowed myself a moment to enjoy feeling safe and happy.

"I think I aged five years in the hour or so we were looking for you," he said. "I've never known anyone to get into so many dangerous predicaments."

" 'Predicaments'? You've been talking to the old ladies too much," I joked. "Next thing, you'll be calling Seth a whippersnapper."

With my head against his chest, I heard the low chuckle and knew he wasn't really mad.

"He is a whippersnapper," Mac said. "I liked it better when he called me Detective and acted afraid of me all the time."

"You did not," I said. "Plus, he's spending too much time with your mother to be afraid of you. You should hear the stories she's been telling him about your younger days."

Mac groaned. "How am I supposed to keep my air of authority with that going on?"

"You'll just have to terrorize your junior officers and leave it at that."

"Speaking of officers, I'd better let Pete Harris know about the phones you found."

I sat up and turned to face him.

"How do you think it relates to Clarissa's murder?" I asked. "It has to be a staff member using that room. Does that put all the guests in the clear for her death?"

"I think we need to seriously consider one of the Garretts as the murderer," Mac said.

"I was thinking the same thing. Linda seems devastated by her death, Jessica not so much, but one of them must be involved with the cell phones," I said.

"I agree," Mac said. "I suppose it's possible that a staff member knew about the secret room and decided to use it to hide the phones, but the Garretts are right up there on my list."

"It's less likely it was a knitter since none of them are from here. They are at least innocent of stealing the phones," I said. "Unless the two things aren't connected at all. . . ."

We fell into an uncomfortable silence. I was happy to be sitting with him, discussing the case, but I was still annoyed that he'd been snooping on me behind my back.

Mac turned toward me. "Clyde, I'm sorry about the file. I didn't think I was betraying any trust by looking at it."

"How *did* you see it then?"

"I wanted to see if there was any truth to your impression that you had done something wrong"—he held up his hand when I started to interrupt—"and there wasn't. You acted just as you should have."

I shook my head. "You don't understand."

"Then tell me." Mac took my hand, but more gently this time.

"I shot that boy because I *sensed* a gun. I *felt* that he was a threat, but didn't have any proof. After all the years of telling my family I want nothing to do with psychic input, during an emergency situation, that's exactly what I relied on and it was wrong. As usual."

I stood and stepped to the fireplace, my back to Mac, and stared into the flames.

"What do you think any seasoned cop relies on in a situation like that?" he said. "They turn to experience and gut feelings and impressions that are informed by years of dealing with suspects and criminals. No matter what sense it was that told you he was dangerous, it was no worse than any other gut feeling that an officer has to tap into when he or she makes a split-second decision. You rely on your training and your senses—however many you have."

I turned and must have looked surprised because he quickly rushed on.

"And, in this case, your *sense* wasn't wrong. Jadyn was dangerous, and had planned to kill someone that night."

"What?" I sank onto the couch facing Mac. The feeling had been so strong that night. I hadn't admitted it to myself, but I had been devastated to find out how wrong it had been. I swallowed and blinked back tears of relief.

"He's recently confessed that he was out on an initiation that night. He was supposed to pick someone, anyone, and shoot them to prove that he had what it takes to be in a gang. The thing is, you interrupted him. He had an older gang member with him to verify his kill. That kid took off in the other direction with the gun. There's no mention of another suspect in any report—I assume no one saw him. Jadyn said he would have returned to finish the job if he hadn't been injured."

"Still . . ." I said. It didn't erase the guilt I felt, but knowing my instincts had been right at least gave me a small sense of peace.

"He confessed because his injury saved his life. He turned himself around while he was in the hospital. He had a chance to think about the direction his life was headed and understood that you just as easily could have killed him. He came forward recently because his younger brother is caught up in the same trap and he wants help getting him out. So, you actually saved him that night, and by extension the brother as well."

My head was reeling with this new information. It was already spinning from the whole cell phone cache discovery, but now I had to rethink all my assumptions over the past nine months since the shooting. I stood up again and stepped closer to the fireplace. Even near the fire, I felt cold and hugged Vi's sweater tighter around me.

"I'm going to need a little time to think about this, Mac."

He nodded. "I just wanted you to have all the information before you decided to leave police work permanently."

I turned toward him. I might as well tell him. "I already decided to leave police work."

"But—"

"No, listen. It's not because of the shooting. It never really was. I don't like police work—I'm not cut out for it."

"I thought it was the shooting that sent you back to Crystal Haven."

"It was, at first. I felt terribly guilty and I was angry that my psychic information had let me down—again."

"But now, you want to . . . be psychic?"

"I don't really have a choice about that. It just is. I can't block it out, I can only learn to interpret or ignore or maybe even understand it. What I can do is choose whether to let it control my life."

"So, what will you do?"

"I want to stay in Crystal Haven. I have a few ideas for a slightly different career—don't worry, it won't involve me reading tarot cards or telling fortunes."

"And you'll be happy here? Even with your family around?"

I nodded.

"Clyde, I was afraid that when your year is up in the house, you would sell it and move back to Ann Arbor."

"No. Why would you think that?"

Mac shrugged and wouldn't look at me.

"I'm sorry, Mac. You're stuck with me."

He stood and pulled me toward him. As he kissed me, I felt all the uncertainty melt away. The heat from the fire finally penetrated. I felt warm, happy, and safe for the first time in a long time.

We heard a crash in the doorway. "Oh, sorry. I didn't mean to . . . I only wanted . . ." Kirk and Wally stood in the doorway. Wally had dropped his end of the ladder and stammered his way through an apology.

"It's fine, come in," Mac said. "More yarn bombing?"

Kirk nodded once and sighed as he began to set up the ladder.

29

Dinner that evening was even more stressful than usual. Every time Vi opened her mouth, I tensed up, certain that she would start discussing the cell phones. She didn't. She did discuss Kirk and his position at the top of her suspect list.

"So the way I see it," Vi said and lowered her voice while glancing at the other tables. "Dory is our best suspect."

"Who?" Mac asked.

Vi narrowed her eyes at him. "I don't want to say the name—people might be listening."

"How can we evaluate your argument if we don't know who you're talking about?" I asked.

Vi sighed. "Fine. It's a code name for . . ." She lowered her voice even more and glanced over her shoulder. If the rest of the dining room wasn't trying to listen in before, they certainly would now. "Kirk. He's a hunk. And I call him Dory as in hunky-dory. Clever, right? No one will be able to crack my code if my notebook falls into the wrong hands."

Dad snorted and took a swig of wine.

"Clever," I said. Her mind worked in such strange ways. I had given up trying to trace the logic long ago.

Vi sat up straight and stopped whispering now that we were in on the code. "One: newest staff member. Two: strong, so he could hit Clarissa hard enough to knock her out. Three: clearly not equipped to"—here she lowered her voice again—"fix anything. Four: I think he has a thing for that pretty housekeeper. I've seen them talking in the hallway. And Clarissa was not at all nice to her; maybe he was protecting her from Clarissa's bullying." She held up four fingers and went back to her meal.

"That's one of the weakest cases I've ever heard," Seth said.

"Why are you defending him?" Vi said.

"I'm not *defending* him, I'm saying your reasons to suspect him are ridiculous." Seth glanced at Mac and me for backup and we shifted our interest to the conversation at the other end of the table.

Until we realized that Mom and Lucille were talking about tarot cards and the dire messages Mom had been receiving leading up to the weekend.

Dad gave a helpless shrug and tilted his wineglass in my direction. He was caught between Mom and Vi and had no choice but to try to stay out of either conversation.

Mom heard Vi talking about Kirk and leaned across Dad to whisper, "You know my cards say it's a knitter. I doubt 'Dory' is a knitter."

Vi put her fork down and turned toward Mom. "I'd forgotten about that," Vi said. "You're right. This just strengthens my argument that we need more information."

"Hopefully the séance will help," said Lucille. "I haven't been to one in a long time."

Everyone at the table turned to look at Vi, with the exception of Mom, who was examining her napkin on her lap.

"What?" Vi said.

"Séance?" I said.

"Well, we have to do something! You two are just going around talking to everyone." She pointed to Mac and me. "I need some answers."

"Ms. Greer, I really don't think you should do a séance," Mac said. The muscles in his jaw jumped.

"You aren't afraid of a séance, are you?" Lucille said.

"Of course not," Mac said. "I just don't think it will be helpful."

"You never know what you might learn with an open mind," Lucille said, and sipped her water while holding Mac's gaze.

"If some of the suspects are there," Seth said, "you might be able to watch them to see how they react."

"I'll keep the dogs company while you all have your séance," Dad said. He waved his hand at the table.

"Now, Frank, we need some experienced people to keep the energy positive," Mom said. "Please stay." She put her hand over his.

Dad was incapable of saying no to Mom. He nodded and pushed his plate away.

"This is going to be great!" Vi said. "We have several of the knitters lined up, plus you guys."

Mac and I escaped to the hallway as soon as we were able.

"I don't think we should let them have a séance," Mac said.

"It's not going to hurt anything." I hoped this was true.

"It's the idea that she's going to be able to solve a murder by asking ghosts!" Mac said. "It could lead to dangerous and uninformed conjectures. People might begin to suspect just about anyone."

"And that would be different . . . how?"

Mac leveled one of his stony stares at me, but they had lost their effectiveness over the last several months. It was particularly hard to feel intimidated when I was also being stared at by a couple of smiling snowmen. Mac had worn that sweater so much I was starting to think of it as his.

"I hate séances," Mac muttered.

"Think of it as an opportunity to observe all the suspects at one time, like Seth said."

"I could do that if we got them to play charades, and it would be much less creepy. And how am I going to explain to Pete Harris that some of our evidence is based on observations during a séance?"

Mac and I had only made it a few steps away from the entrance to the dining room, so Mavis spotted us immediately when she exited.

She hurried over to us. "Oh, Detective McKenzie," she said, "do you think we will be able to leave tomorrow as scheduled?"

Mac shook his head. "I don't think so. The road hasn't been cleared yet—I think they had trouble with a power line and they've been digging everyone out."

Mavis's smile faded.

"I'm sorry to have to tell you, but Wally said we're expecting more snow this evening," I said. "I think we're stuck here for a little while longer. Do you need to get home tomorrow?"

Mavis turned to look at me as if she just noticed I was standing there.

"No, not really," she said. "I just feel antsy all cooped up like this. I don't mind telling you that seeing a ghost isn't helping me to feel comfortable. And your aunt just keeps asking more questions and speculating about what the ghost wants."

"Don't let Vi scare you," I said. "She's making half of it up anyway."

"Even without a ghost, we're trapped here with a murderer!" Mavis said. "I don't like it one bit. Plus, Vi is talking about trying a séance."

I glanced at Mac. He just sighed and stole a glance at his watch.

"If it bothers you, you don't have to go to the séance," I said.

"Are you kidding? I wouldn't miss it," Mavis said. "It doesn't mean I like the idea. . . ."

Thankfully, Isabel poked her head out of the dining room and asked Mavis to help her organize the workshop room.

Mavis nodded to Isabel and patted Mac's arm before hurrying toward the library.

30

The rest of the dining room cleared out quickly as the knitters went to their rooms to prepare for the séance.

Vi and Mom dragged Wally and Kirk into the lounge to rearrange furniture. They thwarted Dad's attempt at escape out the back door and roped him into the preparations as well. Mac said he needed to spend some time in Jessica's office so he could consult with the police by phone. But I suspected he just wanted to distance himself from the séance and its arrangements.

Seth and I trekked out to the cottage to feed and walk the dogs. He had packed enough dog food for a couple of days in the duffel bags, but we would run out soon if we couldn't dig ourselves out. It was fully dark and windy with large flakes falling again. The beauty was beginning to wear thin as we watched the snow piling up. Baxter had no trouble bounding over the snowdrifts, but Tuffy, as usual, stayed close to Seth and shivered. Seth had to coax him to do his business after shoveling a small area so that Tuffy wouldn't sink into a snowbank.

"Good boy, Tuffy!" Seth said. The little dog looked up at him with adoring eyes and wagged his tail.

Baxter leaped through the drifts to get back to us as we turned toward the cottage. Inside, we grabbed the pile of towels we'd left by the door and began brushing the snow off the dogs. Tuffy shivered and allowed Seth to tend to him. Baxter shook vigorously and sprayed the entire entryway with snow and drool. I grabbed a fresh towel for myself.

"Holly is not going to be happy about this," I said to Seth as we dumped four sopping towels into the tub.

Seth shrugged and ducked his head, unconcerned about the laundry. He placed their food bowls on the floor and both dogs attacked them as if they hadn't been fed in weeks.

"Okay, guys," Seth said, "you be good. I'll be back later."

Baxter had just run into the room with his tug toy. His ears drooped at this news.

Tuffy cast a guilt-inducing pathetic stare at us as we put on our coats again to head back out into the snow. A huge gust hit us as we closed the door and I shut my eyes against the pelting ice crystals. I thought of the scene in *Little House on the Prairie* where Pa has to tie a rope to himself in order to walk to the barn. I was grateful for the lights blazing from the hotel to guide us back and resolved to give Dad a hug the minute I saw him.

An excited buzz of voices greeted us when we opened the door. It sounded like Vi had managed to get several staff members and most of the guests to attend her séance. I had been to a lot of séances in my life and knew that a huge, noisy crowd was not the best arrangement. If I were a spirit, I'd want things to be a little quieter.

They had pushed all the couches to the edges of the room

and had managed to put together several tables from the dining room. Chairs were arranged around the new, large table. Candles cast a warm but jumpy glow around the room. Someone had placed a basket of bread and a glass of wine on the table. The food and dim lighting are thought to attract spirits.

Vi clapped her hands three times to get everyone's attention. No one even flinched. I saw her tug on Mac's sleeve and gesture to the crowd. His shoulders slumped but he put his fingers to his lips and let out a shrill whistle. There was immediate silence. Vi nodded at him and Mac took a step back, separating himself from the proceedings.

I was glad to see him. Even though he complained about the psychic intervention, I knew he wouldn't be able to resist observing everyone.

"Everyone, take a seat around the table," Vi said.

Murmurs and mumblings filled the room as everyone jockeyed for position. Mac and Seth attached themselves to me and we found three seats together. Mac's face was still but his eyes took in everything, Seth grinned and gave off the kind of energy he usually reserves for Christmas morning, or dinner.

Wally sat next to my mother, almost shoving Dad aside to get to her. Fortunately, Dad found a seat on the other side of her and they didn't have to resort to a duel.

Violet clicked the light switch and plunged the room into a candlelit gloom. I had expected to be used to it after our power outage, but it still sent a chill through me to see the shadows dancing on the walls, elongated by the angle of the candles. Holly and Kirk had declined to participate. Linda was still holed up in her room, and Selma said she was worried enough about murderers, she didn't want to mess with ghosts now as well. But the rest of us turned to look at Vi.

The last time we had performed a séance, I had left

wondering if Vi had faked it. I braced myself for a repeat performance. If Mac caught her pretending to make contact with the other side, I would never hear the end of it. Lucille sat across from us and I could feel her watching us. She had taken me aside earlier to thank me for convincing Mac to sit in on this one. She'd been trying for years to get him to attend a séance with no luck. I was pretty sure it had been Seth's suggestion that it would be a good way to observe all the suspects at once that convinced him to join in. But I let Lucille think that I had some sort of influence over Mac—she was so happy to imagine him coming around to her way of viewing the universe that I didn't have the heart to argue.

"Let's all join hands," Vi said. Rustling and shifting noises spread around the table. A gust of wind pelted snow against the window and we all jumped. I heard nervous giggling from the end where Tina, Heather, and Amy sat.

"We ask to be joined by the spirits of Carlisle Castle," Vi intoned in her fortune-teller voice. "Be guided by the light and join us."

The room was silent except for the howling of the wind and people shifting in their seats.

"Did you hear that?" Seth whispered next to me.

I shook my head.

"It sounds like someone walking around upstairs."

"Maybe it's Linda or one of the staff," I said out of the side of my mouth.

Another gust hit the window and then I heard a whistling noise start up—it sounded like a police siren but quiet and continuous. I could tell other people heard it as well—eyes were large and scanned the ceiling and the walls for the source of the noise.

"That's just the window whistling," Jessica said. "It does that when the wind hits it just right."

Mac let out a breath of air.

"Everyone please focus on our intention to commune with the spirits of Carlisle Castle," Vi said.

The quiet was broken only by the occasional gust of wind or snow hitting the windows.

I heard sounds overhead. I glanced at Seth, who stared at the ceiling. The rest of the group must have heard it, too. We all looked upward, the group wearing expressions ranging from excitement to fear. It sounded like someone pacing on creaky floorboards. Creak! Creak! Creak! Silence, then the same sounds going back the other way.

"Is there someone here with us?" Vi asked the ceiling.

A loud thunk and the sound of shattering glass came from the hallway. The candles snuffed out. Several people screamed, chairs fell over, and Lucille said, "Don't break the circle!"

But it was too late. Mac stood and scanned the room. Seth gripped my hand while I tried to make out where everyone was in the dim light from the hallway.

The overhead lights clicked on and I looked to the wall switch where Wally stood. He nodded at Jessica and went out into the hall. I heard voices and then he returned.

He held his hands up to get the group's attention. "It's nothing. It was just an accident. It looks like the cat knocked a vase off a table in the hall."

"Did you see the cat?" Vi asked.

Wally shook his head.

"So, you don't know for sure it was the cat," Vi said.

Wally shook his head. "What else could it be?"

"Exactly," said Vi. "Everyone likes to blame the cat, but they aren't always as mischievous as they seem."

I noticed Amy staring at Vi with her mouth open. I've seen this before; it's a pretty common response before you get to know her.

Mavis cleared her throat and held her hands tightly clasped together. "Do you think we should try again?" She motioned for everyone to sit back down.

Mom shook her head. "It's not likely we'll have any success now."

I sighed in relief. I'd sat through many unsuccessful séances in my time and I still wasn't sure which was worse—one where nothing happened or one where something did.

Seth pulled his hand away finally and acted like I had been the one clutching him. By the way he rubbed his hand, you'd think *I* had crushed *his* fingers.

Isabel took control. "We have an early workshop tomorrow. I hope to get through the instructions for the decreases and bind off of our projects. I had planned to end around two, but if we're stuck here due to the weather, I can give some of you individual instruction on any trouble spots." She made a show of looking at her watch and Mavis backed her up by yawning. It only took about two minutes for the lounge to clear out.

Amy, Tina, and Heather left first, heading for the stairs as quickly as possible. Mavis conferred with Isabel and followed the first group out the door. Jessica and René stood off to the side, in deep conversation. Emmett, grinning and congratulating Vi on a "great show," helped Wally move the tables back to the dining room.

Mac walked me upstairs to my room. I felt a bit like a teenager being dropped off in time for curfew.

"Thanks for coming to the séance," I said.

He pulled me into his arms. "It wasn't that bad. I'm glad you were with me though—that kind of thing gives me the willies."

I chuckled. "The willies?"

He leaned back to look at me. "It's a well-known phrase indicating a sense of the heebie-jeebies."

I laughed. “I *know* what it means. It’s just funny to hear you say it.”

He kissed me then and I forgot all about séances, murders, and black-market intrigue.

“I’ll see you in the morning,” he said.

I shut the door quietly, and got into bed with a grin on my face. I was asleep before Vi returned to the room.

31

I am in a room that is so cold I am shivering. It is plain and white and there is nothing there but a wooden door. I walk to the door and feel the rough texture under my fingertips. There is a cool metal handle and I reach out to pull the door open. A strange scene greets me. Tables adorned with white tablecloths and white plates languish in the grass. The cloths billow gently in the wind and the trees rustle softly. It looks like a summer garden party.

As I take a step forward, Duchess appears and begins to walk next to me. I see Vi sitting at a table. She is wearing a long white gown and her hair is loose around her shoulders. I call to her, but no sound comes out. When I try to approach her, the cat stops me. She blocks my progress and then Vi is gone.

René is there in his white chef's coat and tall white hat. He is looking out over the garden toward the woods. Again, the cat stops me from approaching. But, René comes toward me. He smiles and holds out a silver tray with a ball of white yarn sitting on it. I reach out to take it, but he passes me and approaches Clarissa, who sits in a tall white wicker chair with a wide curved back. She laughs when she takes the yarn and it turns a deep blood red in her hands.

Linda gasps from behind me and I see that she, Jessica, Tina, Isabel, and Mavis are all here at this strange party. They wear white and carry red knitting needles. The cat jumps onto Clarissa's lap and watches me with its gold eyes.

A sudden wind blows the tables over and the napkins and tablecloths flap in the wind and fly up over the castle. I watch them drift away and when one floats up to the turret window, I see a white filmy face in the window. It is trying to speak, but I can't hear it. The wind grows stronger and all I can hear is the howling of the wind as the white table linens form a tornado and pick up all the furniture in its swirling chaos. The tornado heads toward me and just as I think I will be swept up in it, it collapses in front of Duchess, who has placed herself between me and the incoming storm.

My eyes flew open and I was glad for the blue numbers on the electric clock by my bed. The howling wind noise still filled my ears and I realized the blizzard that the weather people had predicted had arrived. I hoped the generator wouldn't fail again and pulled the covers up over my ears to try to go back to sleep.

It was no use. The dream continued to haunt me and every time I closed my eyes, it started up again as if I had merely paused a DVD. I got out of bed and went to the window. It was such a strange dream. Often, the predictive dreams show me events that will happen, but not in the weird, surreal way of this one. I felt like I had been watching a strange art film with symbols and references I didn't understand. But, the underlying feeling was that this dream meant something. I was often frustrated by my own lack of ability to understand these messages, but never more so than when I felt that there was true danger lurking.

Looking down, I saw a small patch of light on the ground below me. I could hardly make it out with all the swirling snow, but because everything was so dark, it stood out. Someone else couldn't sleep and he or she was in the kitchen.

Thinking this was probably a very bad idea, I tossed on my sweatpants and Vi's sweater over my T-shirt and sleep shorts and quietly slipped out of the room. I was thankful for the electricity once again as the hallway was at least dimly lit by the sconces along the wall. I walked quietly down the stairs trying to decide whether to announce myself or sneak up on the person in the kitchen.

I decided stealth would be best and quietly approached the kitchen door once I reached the main floor. Cracking the door open, I wasn't surprised to see Linda there in her pale gray robe again, but this time Emmett joined her. They sat at the small table, sipping something out of mugs and talking quietly.

I hesitated. While I was surprised to see them together, they weren't doing anything wrong and Linda had certainly had a rough enough couple of days. I turned to go back to the staircase and just as I put my foot down, an angry yowl came from the white cat. I threw my hands over my mouth to stifle my reaction. She had snuck up on me and must have been sitting with her tail right where my foot had landed. I bent down to calm her, but she backed away from me with her hair puffed up, hissing and spitting.

"I'm sorry, I didn't mean to step on you," I said to the cat. "You're very sneaky."

"Yes, she is," Emmett said from the door. "I can't keep

track of her. She's always trying to trick her way into the kitchen to steal food. And after the last time, René might lose his mind if he sees her in here again."

I sucked in air and decided to play through—I hadn't planned on revealing myself to these two, but sneaky cat had taken care of that.

"Emmett, I'm sorry to interrupt," I said. "I couldn't sleep and just came down to find a magazine or something to read in the lounge."

"Come in," he said. "Lin—Mrs. Garrett makes the best hot chocolate ever. It will be sure to help you sleep."

After my bizarre dream, I wasn't sure I wanted to sit in a dimly lit castle kitchen in the middle of a stormy night. But I couldn't think of two more unlikely companions for a midnight hot chocolate run and figured I had been handed an opportunity to do some more investigating.

"Who is it, Emmett?" Mrs. Garrett asked.

"It's Clyde Fortune," Emmett said. "A fellow insomniac."

"I can never sleep on a windy night," Linda said. She got up from the small table, poured cocoa into a mug, and placed it in front of me. "I find the warm milk helps."

Emmett picked up a bottle of Baileys and waved it in my direction. "I find this helps even more."

I nodded at the offer and he poured a glug into the cocoa. As he tilted the bottle, I noticed an angry red scratch across the back of his hand. Duchess?

"If I'd known there was hot chocolate and Baileys, I would have roamed the halls earlier," I said.

They both chuckled. "It's mostly on the windy nights that I'm here," Linda said. "Emmett caught me here messing up René's kitchen a while back, so it's become our little secret."

"I guess neither one of you is afraid of the ghost," I said.

They exchanged a quick glance that made me think they wondered if I was joking.

"As long as it stays away from my Baileys, I don't care what that ghost gets up to," Emmett said.

"I'm more afraid of the cat than the ghost," Linda said. "I don't know what we'll do with her now. Ever since Clarissa . . . died, I haven't been able to figure out what she's up to. She used to seek me out for cuddles and now it's like she's gone feral."

"She'll calm down after a while," Emmett said. He put his left hand over the scratch on his right.

"I think once she realizes she's still being fed, she'll adjust," I said. "Was she very close to Clarissa?"

"That's the funny thing," Linda said. "I don't think she was very attached to her. The cat loves the turret room and tolerated Clarissa."

"Who does she belong to?" I asked.

"I suppose she belongs to the castle. She's lived here for about five years. She just showed up one day, we fed her, and she stayed." Linda sipped her chocolate. "If I ever needed to find her, I'd go up to the turret room and there she'd be, sitting in the window seat in a warm patch of sun."

"She was a real friendly little thing," Emmett said.

"Clarissa didn't mind that the cat lived in her room?"

Linda smiled. "No, they seemed to get along just fine. They mostly ignored each other. Sort of like two cats who had been forced to live together."

"Cats are very sensitive," I said. "You should talk to Vi. She'll tell you all about cats and their emotional lives."

"Vi has certainly done well for herself as a pet psychic," Linda said. "Do you really think she can communicate with animals?" She leaned forward and rested her chin on her hand.

That was a tough question. I wasn't sure how much of Vi's success had to do with her treat bag and animal-training knowledge and how much had to do with another kind of connection to the animals. I believed *Seth* could communicate with them—Tuffy and Baxter listened to him and he could get them to do just about anything. But, I didn't want to betray Vi by questioning her abilities to strangers.

"She seems to be very successful in her pet interventions," I hedged. "She must be doing something right."

Linda watched me sip my drink. "Well, I better get back up to bed. It seems we'll have a full house again tomorrow night. I hope Wallace managed to cancel our Sunday-night reservations." She rinsed her mug in the sink and I pushed my chair back as well. Suddenly I was bone tired.

I followed Linda up the main staircase to the second floor. She turned toward the hallway that led to her rooms and stopped.

"Ms. Fortune . . . ," she said. She slowly turned toward me and covered the distance between us. "I didn't want to say anything before . . ."

"Yes?" I said.

"I heard something that night. The night Clarissa died." She stopped and looked away from me. "I didn't say anything before because I wanted to protect my daughter."

"You heard Jessica?"

Linda shook her head. "No, no. I heard René." She hesitated again, and studied the floor. I had the sense she was trying to make me believe she was crafting this story right on the spot.

"You heard René? Where?"

"I went up to talk to Clarissa earlier, before the lights went out." Linda looked up and down the dark and silent hallway and lowered her voice. "We'd had that staff meeting on

Wednesday and there were some disagreements about the management of the inn. Anyway, I wanted to talk to her and maybe calm things down a bit, but before I knocked, I heard loud voices in her room and decided not to interrupt."

"You're sure it was René?"

She took a deep breath and let it out. Frown lines appeared on her forehead as she wavered.

"His accent is . . . distinctive," she said.

"Thank you for telling me," I said. "You should have told us before."

"I didn't want to bring it up in front of Jessica. She can get so jealous of Clarissa. Ever since they were little, Clarissa has always wanted everything Jessica had. If Jess had a new doll, Clarissa had to have one. When they got older, Clarissa went after any boy that Jess was foolish enough to show interest in."

"Do you think there was something going on between René and Clarissa?" I was whispering now as well, even though the whole place was likely asleep.

"Something was up with them, but I don't know what and I don't like to think that René would betray Jessica like that. Truly, I don't know what to think. I just thought you should know."

She patted my arm and turned toward her hallway. I stood for a moment watching her and wondering if she was telling the truth.

32

Sunday morning Mac's four-beat knock sounded on our door at seven thirty. Vi grumbled and pulled the covers over her head. I staggered to the door, pulling on a robe, and stepped into the hall.

I rubbed my eyes and tried not to glare at him for waking me up.

He grinned and pushed my hair out of my eyes. "I have news, are you awake enough to hear it?"

I yawned and nodded.

"I called the police department this morning to see if they got any information back about René Sartin." Mac glanced up and down the hall and lowered his voice. "He's dead."

My stomach dropped and I felt a bit dizzy.

"What? Another murder?" I moved away from the door so Vi wouldn't hear us. "How can he be dead?"

"The only René Sartin they were able to find in their database was from the Upper Peninsula, went to Paris to attend the Cordon Bleu school, and then died in a car accident when he returned home to Michigan. Eight years ago."

"So, who has been cooking all our meals?"

Mac shrugged. "The backstory is all just as our René claimed it would be, except for the fact that the real René is dead. He did, however, have a younger brother."

I met Mac's eyes. "Do you think the younger brother took over René's identity? Why would he do that?"

"He could use his brother's credentials to get a job as a chef." Mac leaned against the wall. "I've asked them to look further into the Sartin family and see what they can dig up. But, it probably has no bearing on the case."

I crossed my arms and burrowed further into the thick terry robe I had taken from the closet. It was one of the things that I disliked about investigating. When a murder occurred, everyone with even the slightest connection to the victim would have their lives and their secrets exposed.

"Let me get dressed and we can go get something to eat," I said. "Are you going to confront him?"

Mac was silent for a moment. "I haven't decided. I don't know whether this is related and I hate to ruin this guy's life. On the other hand, he's been committing fraud and I feel like I have to delve deeper."

I knew he had more to say and waited.

"This isn't my jurisdiction and as far as I know, he hasn't done any harm. If he is faking his identity, then it's likely Jessica doesn't know, which means not only will he lose his job, but potentially his fiancée. I hate to throw a bomb into someone's life like that for no good reason."

"I guess you're right, but it seems suspicious to me," I said.

Mac paced the hallway from the turret entrance to my door. "It may be none of our concern. I'm barely in charge of this murder investigation. I don't have any authority over restaurant licensing."

"If your person was able to find out overnight, it can't be that well hidden," I said.

"The officer who found the information has connections in the Upper Peninsula. When René Sartin popped up as a U.S. citizen, not French, he followed the trail and called his contact," Mac said. "That guy remembered the story—but it's been wiped from any easy search engine—even the local newspaper has deleted all references to the accident."

"Maybe that's how a Cordon Bleu chef ended up at a small bed-and-breakfast in Western Michigan instead of a big city. Maybe he was hoping no one would ever look into his credentials. I think Jessica has a right to know what she's getting herself into before she marries him."

Then I remembered my strange conversation with Linda the night before. I told Mac that she suspected Clarissa and René might have been involved somehow.

"It sounds like René had all sorts of trouble headed his way. Maybe we'll be doing her a favor by letting her know," I said.

"You're right, but we should talk to him first."

I slipped back into my room and quickly got dressed. As I pulled my hair back into a ponytail, it hit me. What if Clarissa had found out about the real René? She didn't strike me as someone who would balk at a little blackmail, especially if it also messed around with her cousin's life. If she was blackmailing René, that gave him a pretty good reason to kill her. Maybe there wasn't an affair, as Linda seemed to think. But Clarissa could have ruined his whole life if Jessica was unaware that he'd been passing himself off as his brother.

I quietly slipped back out into the hall. I opened my mouth to tell Mac when I noticed a new gleam in his eyes.

"What if Clarissa was blackmailing René?" he said.

"Just what I was thinking," I said. "It seems like a pretty good motive for murder."

Mac took my hand. "Let's go have a chat with the chef."

We walked down the stairs, cut through the dining room, and knocked on the kitchen door before entering. René and Emmett were busy cooking eggs, bacon, and pancakes. My stomach growled.

"Mr. Sartin?" Mac said. "Can we speak with you a moment?"

The chef glanced up with a scowl on his face. He rearranged his expression when he saw us. He gestured at Emmett to take over pancake duty, wiped his hands on a towel, and followed us out into the dining room.

"What can I do for you?" he asked after we sat.

Mac took a breath, but I cut in ahead of him.

"One of the hardest parts about a murder investigation is that we have to look at everyone. Unfortunately, many secrets are revealed whether they relate to the crime or not."

René sat back in his chair and crossed his arms. "I told you everything I know. I was busy in the kitchen when Clarissa was killed. I don't know anything." His accent was in full force and I almost felt admiration for his acting skills.

I leaned forward.

"But you do have a secret," I said. "We have to ask you about your past."

He rubbed his arms and glanced toward the kitchen door.

"There's not much to tell." He shrugged and didn't meet my eyes. "I grew up in Paris and went to the Cordon Bleu school—"

He stopped when Mac held up a hand. "Please, don't make this worse by lying."

René's cheeks turned pink. "I don't know what you're talking about."

"I think you do," Mac said. "We have no interest in revealing your secret to anyone unless it relates to Clarissa's murder."

"You think *I* killed Clarissa?"

"We think you aren't who you say you are, which makes us wonder what else you're hiding," Mac said.

Loosening the collar on his chef's tunic, René let out a breath of air.

"I'm not sure what you're getting at. Maybe you should just tell me what you think you know."

I was impressed by the way he stuck to the story. It almost had me thinking Mac's source had made a mistake. That's probably how he'd gotten away with it for so long.

"Okay," I said. "We know that officially René Sartin is dead."

The chef's face went from pink to white almost instantly. He seemed to shrink into his chair.

The door from the kitchen opened and Emmett came through, his arms full of serving platters and food. He grinned in our direction, unaware of the tension around the table.

René lowered his voice.

"How did you find out?" he asked. The accent fell away, and I felt like I was meeting him for the first time.

"We're detectives," Mac said.

"It's not what it looks like," René said. He put his hands up as if to hold us back.

"It never is," Mac said. "Why don't you tell us your story?"

Fake René leaned forward and rested his elbows on his knees.

"René was my brother," he said. "My grandmother raised us all on her own in the Upper Peninsula. She was from Quebec and had come to Michigan when she married my grandfather. She was an incredible cook and taught us all the old recipes from the time we were both young." He stopped and cleared his throat.

"My brother worked three jobs to save enough money to go to France and train there as a chef. I was only nineteen when he left. He went to the Cordon Bleu school and came home with his certificate. About two weeks after he got home, he was in a car accident and died."

"I'm sorry," I said.

He tilted his head at me, and cleared his throat. "My grandmother and I knew that René wouldn't want all that work to go to waste and she said she always thought I was the better cook. We arranged to cover up his death and I would take his name and his credentials so that I could get a job as a chef."

I sat back in my chair and crossed my arms. How did he think he would get away with it?

"Who else knows about this?" Mac asked.

René shook his head. "No one. I took a job in Traverse City and learned everything I could. Then my grandmother died of a stroke."

He passed a hand over his face. "She was so proud that a Sartin was working in a 'fancy' restaurant. After her death, I headed south and ended up here. Linda and Jessica were wonderful to me. They let me have free rein in the kitchen to set the menu and experiment. It was a dream come true."

"They have no idea that your credentials are fake?"

He shook his head. "After a while, I decided I should tell them, but then Jessica and I started spending more time together and she was so impressed that I had grown up in France . . ."

He held his hands out to us. "I just didn't want to disappoint her and by that time, I didn't want to lose her. I was in too deep and felt like I couldn't tell her the truth without her feeling like our whole relationship was a lie. So I kept quiet."

"And no one ever found out?" I said.

"No one until Clarissa," René said to his shoes. "She went through all the employee files when she came here six months ago. I guess Linda had never looked into my credentials, but Clarissa did. She traced my brother's information and found out that he didn't grow up in France, which led her to discover his car accident. She must have put the rest together somehow."

"Was she blackmailing you?" Mac asked.

René nodded, and studied the floor.

"She wanted to renovate the whole hotel and open a fancy spa. She threatened to expose my secret if I didn't take her side. I told her there was no way Jessica would buy it. I've worked for the past five years for our reputation. Jessica knows I wouldn't give it all up to open a spa, but Clarissa wouldn't listen."

"So you tried to convince Jessica to go along with the spa plan?" I asked.

René hung his head. "I didn't know what else to do. I didn't want to lose Jessica even more than I didn't want to lose the restaurant. I think she thought Clarissa and I were having an affair. She got very touchy over the past couple of months and criticized Clarissa every chance she got." His hands went up in a placating gesture and he briefly met my eyes. "Don't get me wrong, I had nothing good to say about Clarissa, either, but it put a strain on our relationship. So, ironically, my plan to go along with Clarissa and buy her silence was backfiring and causing more trouble with Jessica." He leaned forward, elbows on knees, and rested his head in his hands.

"It sounds like Clarissa's death will work out in your favor," Mac said.

René's head snapped up. "I didn't kill her. I may not have liked her, but I didn't kill her."

"So you didn't see her after she left the dining room on Thursday night?"

René shook his head, but wouldn't meet our eyes.

"We have a witness who heard you arguing with Clarissa in her room that evening," I said.

His face drained of color even more and he looked like he might be sick.

He rubbed a hand over his mouth, and closed his eyes briefly. "Okay. I saw her that night—she was agitated over a meeting earlier in the week and wanted me to convince Linda to sell some of the antiques to support the spa."

Mac stared at him and waited.

René looked at me and then sighed. "It was before we served dinner, maybe around six forty-five. I snuck up the back stairs, talked to her, and came back down. I saw her later in the dining room talking to the guests and then I focused on serving dinner."

"You were in the kitchen or dining room the rest of the time?" I asked.

René nodded. "Except for a few minutes when I went to the basement to get the dessert. I did not kill her. I may not have been honest with Jessica and Linda, but I'm not a murderer."

"Okay, Mr. Sartin, we may need to talk to you again," Mac said.

René glanced at the door again and lowered his voice. "Please, don't tell Jessica," he said. "I know she has a right to hear the truth, but I'd rather it come from me."

"We have no reason to tell her anything right now," I said. "But if you had anything to do with Clarissa's death, we can't guarantee your secret will stay safe."

René nodded. "Thanks, I'll tell her . . . soon." He stood and strode back toward the kitchen.

33

“What did you think?” Mac asked.

We walked toward the buffet that Emmett had set out, talking quietly.

“It’s hard to trust someone who has lied to everyone he knows for years, but he lied in order to do something he loves, not to hatch an illegal plot.”

“True, but it makes me wonder if he’s telling us the truth now about his relationship with Clarissa.” Mac took the mug of coffee I handed him and began dumping sugar and cream into it.

“You think they were having an affair?” I asked.

“Not necessarily, just that he seemed very forgiving of a blackmailer.”

“Jessica has been upfront about not liking her cousin; maybe she had a reason to really hate her if she thought Clarissa was seducing René.” I piled my plate with cheesy scrambled eggs and sausage. I needed to stockpile before Seth arrived.

"It doesn't make this case any easier knowing Clarissa ticked off everyone she knew," Mac said.

We walked back to our table and I told Mac the rest of my story about my middle-of-the-night meeting with Emmett and Linda.

"That seems like a strange couple."

"I don't think they were *together* . . . ," I said.

"I just mean, what is the owner of the hotel and the assistant chef doing meeting in the middle of the night?"

I shrugged. "I don't know. I didn't get the impression it was an everyday thing. Besides, Emmett wouldn't normally be staying here overnight."

"I guess." Mac stared into his coffee cup. "Mrs. Garrett just strikes me as a bit snobby and fraternizing with the help doesn't go along with that."

"It is a really small staff . . . but you're right. Jessica seems more down to earth than her mother." I stirred my tea and considered Linda and Jessica.

"Speaking of the Garrett women, we'll need to talk to them again," Mac said. "How many people are likely to know about the tunnel to the cottage, or the secret room?"

"I suppose most of the staff might know. And maybe Isabel as well—she and Jessica have known each other for years. Unless Jessica was sworn to secrecy, a lot of people might know."

"We seem to be adding people to our list instead of crossing them off." Mac slathered grape jelly on his toast.

"Vi is pretty sure it's Kirk, or maybe René . . ."

Mac snorted. "I thought you said the pendulum pointed to a knitter."

"Hey, you're right. I keep forgetting about that. I'll have to ask Vi how she can reconcile the pendulum and the cards being wrong."

"Unless she thinks Kirk likes to knit . . . ," Mac said and smiled.

"He is really good at the yarn bombing," I said. "Apparently, you're a knitter, maybe we should add you to the list."

Just then Tina, Amy, and Heather came into the dining room whispering and giggling. They stopped as soon as they spotted us.

"Hello," I said.

They mumbled hello and headed toward the buffet.

"What are they up to?" Mac asked.

"I'm pretty sure they're plotting ways to get Kirk to climb a ladder."

"What?"

"I heard them talking the other day—they think he's 'dreamy' and they're pooling all their knitting to give them a reason to interact with him."

Mac shook his head. "How did this happen? We should have been on a beach all weekend." Even though we had both said this before, he sounded as though it was finally getting to him.

"Beach? What are you talking about?" Lucille had come up to the table quietly and Mac and I jumped.

"Just bemoaning our fate, Mom," Mac said.

"Well, that never gets anyone anywhere," she said. She sat across the table from us with a mug of tea and a piece of toast. She eyed Mac carefully and pressed her lips together.

"What's on the agenda today in the workshop?" I asked to deflect the tension that seemed to settle over the table.

"I heard Isabel saying she would add a couple of extra classes since no one can leave today," Lucille said. "Are you sure you don't want to give it a try?" She turned to me and smiled. "It looked like you took to the continental method like a duck to water."

"I think I should help Mac with the investigation and Seth needs help with the dogs throughout the day."

"Your mom is going to read everyone's cards today," she said. "I just love your mother's readings. She has a real talent."

I had a sudden upsetting thought. "Did Vi put her up to this?"

"I don't know." Lucille set her teacup gently on its saucer. "Rose said she would do all of the knitters and I heard Vi saying she was going to invite the staff as well."

I groaned to myself. Vi must be trying to track the murderer by having Mom read cards. This was classic Fortune family behavior. They relied heavily on hints and innuendo from the divination technique du jour and then ran with whatever they thought they had discovered. I couldn't decide if this was a good or bad development. If Vi was busy helping Mom interpret cards, she would at least stay out of our way. But, I shuddered to think of what Mac would say. I'd been able to keep the full extent of my family's obsession with solving crimes from him so far.

Mac tilted his head at me. "You okay?"

"Yup. Just thinking about all those tarot readings . . . ," I said.

"When does the tarot extravaganza start?" Mac turned to his mom.

"I think she said it would be around ten—after the first workshop." She smiled. "Are you going to join us? I think you'd really like it, Mac . . ." She stopped when Mac began to shake his head.

"Sorry, no. I just wanted to know what time to make myself scarce."

Lucille sighed.

Fortunately, the rest of the gang arrived and we were all distracted by Seth's stories of Baxter and Tuffy.

I noticed that Isabel sat with the table of younger knitters instead of Mavis and Selma. I would have thought that she was just trying to be a good workshop host except she was completely silent while the young women chatted animatedly next to her. Mavis and Selma cast menacing glances toward the table and it had me wondering if there had been trouble in knitting paradise.

"Mom," I whispered across the table. "What's up with Isabel and Mavis?" I tilted my head in the direction of their table.

Mom swiveled slowly in her chair; she did discreet the way Vi did blatant.

She turned back toward me and shrugged. "I don't know. I guess Isabel wanted to get to know the other knitters."

I watched them for a moment. "She looks miserable. I don't think she's even talking to them, and Mavis is glowering at her."

Mom sighed. "Mavis can be difficult."

I snorted. I thought that was one of her larger understatements. Mac turned to see what had me making strange noises. I shook my head at him to signal that I'd tell him later.

He turned back toward Lucille and I thought about how our table was burdened with its own set of tensions.

The rest of breakfast was a quiet affair. Gone were the giggles and loud exclamations from the young knitters, Mavis and Selma sat off by themselves, and Vi had stopped speculating on the murder in light of our wager. And there was something going on between Mac and his mother. I was glad when Seth asked me to help him with the dogs, and Mac said he needed to go check in with the police again.

34

Seth and I stood by the back door zipping coats and pulling on mittens and I sensed that the heightened tension had permeated the whole building. I caught a glimpse of Jessica's angry face as she shut her office door—René sat inside looking like he was visiting the principal's office.

I sighed.

Seth looked at me and then leaned his shoulder into mine and pushed—his version of a hug. I opened the door and it flew out of my hand as wind struck it full force. I took a deep breath and plunged into the cold. We hurried along the path to the cottage, heads down, holding our hoods up to block the wind.

The dogs wagged tails and barked when we entered the cottage. Baxter pushed his head against my leg and stayed attached to me while I looked for his leash. His tongue lolled out of his mouth as he smiled up at me in adoration. I'm sure he didn't understand why I kept leaving him. I thought that

Seth would be a good replacement, but Baxter and I had bonded last summer and I missed him almost as much as he missed me. After a moment of petting on my part and slobbering on his, I grabbed his leash. Both dogs danced around making it nearly impossible to clip the leather straps to their collars. Finally, they stood ready by the door, tails wagging. Then Seth opened the door and another gust hit us. The dogs hesitated and glanced up at us with an "are you kidding me?" look. With forceful encouragement, they stepped outside and quickly did their business. Tuffy waited for Seth to clear a path for him onto the grass and then rushed back to Seth's legs and cowered. Baxter didn't even seem interested in chasing snowballs.

"I hope we can get out of here soon," I said as we ushered them back into the cottage.

They gratefully allowed us to dry them off and then they raced into the kitchen for a treat.

"It's not so bad," Seth said. "Wally said there's no more snow expected, just this wind and then a couple of days of sunshine."

"It seems like the whole hotel is going stir-crazy," I said as I broke off a piece of chicken jerky for Baxter.

Tuffy, ever alert to possible poisoning by his caretakers, carefully sniffed the entire treat before accepting it from me.

"Have you guys figured out who's been stashing cell phones?"

"Not yet," I said. "Mac talked to the police about it and they've been working the same case from another angle. He didn't tell me any more than that."

"If the murder is connected to the cell phones, it kind of lets the knitters off the hook, doesn't it?"

"Don't tell Vi's pendulum," I said. "She's also stalking the cat to see what she knows. Apparently, the cat is smarter than most of the humans at the castle—she's successfully avoided capture."

"She's probably just scared," Seth said. He sat on the floor near Tuffy and the little dog crawled quickly into his lap. Baxter glanced at me as if he thought maybe he could sit on my lap.

"Not a chance, dude," I said to him. He dropped his head and leaned against Seth.

"Someone would have made a lot of money on those phones," Seth said. "I wonder if he or she has realized that we were there yet."

A cold shiver ran down my spine. I had known there was a murderer among us. Someone who might be sharing a meal, or cleaning a room, or knitting a scarf for a chess queen. But, I hadn't allowed the thought that we might all be in danger to really sink in. I had assumed that Clarissa had been killed because she was unpleasant, but what if she was killed because she knew too much? What if she died because she had discovered the cell phones?

I left Seth with the dogs and braved the weather to get back to the hotel. I thought Mom's tarot reading would be a good time to do some more rummaging in Clarissa's room. Now that we knew she had been blackmailing at least one person, I began to wonder if we had missed something in our earlier searches. We'd been looking for any clues that might have been left by the killer. Maybe there were clues left by Clarissa. She had made enemies since she moved to the castle, but maybe she had also truly threatened someone. If we could find other evidence of blackmail, we might be able to narrow down our suspect list.

I found Mac in the front reception area. He hung up the landline and smiled when he saw me.

"Everything okay?" he said.

"The dogs are happy, if that's what you mean."

"It sounds like they'll get that tree moved today," Mac said. "The power lines have been dealt with and they have a tree removal service working on it. Now that the snow has stopped, they should be able to clear the road so people can get home."

I felt a tightening in my gut. I knew they could pursue the murder investigation after people had left, but I felt very strongly that we needed to wrap this up before the group scattered.

"I think we should check Clarissa's room and her office again," I said.

Mac leaned back against the front desk. "Okay, what do you hope to find?"

"Clarissa came here six months ago and stirred everything up. I wonder if we should be looking into her activities a bit more. It seems everyone had a reason to want her dead, but maybe she had information or plans that were particularly threatening to someone here."

"Your mother seems to be holding the entire hotel in thrall in the lounge right now."

I smiled. "Just what I was thinking."

We quietly approached the door to the lounge and peeked inside. Mac was right; the entire group watched Mom lay out her cards. Emmett, René, Linda, and Jessica were all there, as well as all of the knitters—even Selma. They focused on Mom's hands as she shuffled and cut the cards. We went to the back hall and peered around like a couple of kids skipping out of school.

With most of the hotel staff occupied in the lounge, it seemed a good time to rummage in the office. Mac and I split the room and searched quickly through the small desk and file cabinet. Nothing. It was all bills and invoices for supplies for the inn. A stack of glossy flyers sat on the corner of the desk touting the benefits of deep-tissue massage and regular facials. This must have been Clarissa's promotional campaign. I thought again about the family and their conflicting wishes for the future of Carlisle castle.

With no new information, we climbed the stairs to the second floor and walked toward the turret room stairway. I had climbed this set of stairs enough that I hardly got dizzy anymore as we twisted up and up into the tower.

We entered the room again. This time there were no thumps from Vi, or howling winds from open windows. It was just a silent, still room with a silver wintry light lending a gray cast to the white furniture.

"Let's check the dresser and bedside drawers and see if she kept any papers here in her room," Mac said. He handed me a pair of plastic gloves and donned a pair of his own.

Mac headed to the bedside table that had two shallow drawers.

I took the dresser and started at the top. I swept my hand toward the back of her underwear drawer, feeling for anything that wasn't silky. It was all just as it should be—clothing, scarves, and sweaters. I didn't have that feeling that tells me to keep looking in a particular place. Sometimes it feels like an actual pull toward a certain location, other times I get flashes of an area—often even after I've looked in that spot. It reminds me of a camera flash in the dark and it means I've missed something. It wasn't until I had checked the whole dresser that I decided to pull the drawers out of the dresser and check the backs.

Still nothing. And Mac appeared to have come up empty as well.

"If she hid anything up here, it wasn't anywhere obvious," I said.

If she was a seasoned blackmailer, she probably knew better than to put evidence in a drawer where anyone could find it.

A secret staircase seemed like a good place to stash something unless the people you were blackmailing used that staircase to deliver their payoffs. I reflected that I had been spending too much time with Vi—my own imagination was starting to sound like her. Blackmail, payoffs, and nefarious schemes were more Vi's area than mine.

I wandered to the window and looked out at the snowy view. From this vantage point, the woods were quite beautiful with each branch outlined in white. I sat in the chair by the window and tried to think of any other place she might have hidden her blackmail evidence.

I closed my eyes, and breathed deeply. I tried to relax and clear my mind as Neila had taught me to do. After a few moments I felt a tug. That's the only way to describe it—a gentle pull toward the wardrobe. I opened my eyes and looked across the room.

Mac rummaged in the wardrobe, which seemed to contain a lot of dresses and shoes. The shoes spilled out of it and I began to realize why they always littered her floor—the woman had a serious problem. She even had shoeboxes stacked on top of the wardrobe.

I got up to help Mac sort the shoes out and counted fifteen pairs that had been tossed into the bottom of the freestanding closet under the dresses. She had tossed high-end couture in with drugstore flip-flops.

The tug was stronger here, but didn't seem connected to her shoes. Then I looked up again at the shoeboxes.

"Mac, can you reach those shoeboxes up there?" I pointed.

He caught my eye and grinned. "Good idea—she didn't seem to care about organizing her shoes."

He brought down the three boxes, which didn't rattle like shoes and were heavier than I would expect.

The first two contained journals dating from fifteen years previously going up to about two years ago. The third contained a locked metal box. It was one of those heavy fireproof things that are nearly impossible to break into. And underneath, a worn leather notebook.

Mac picked up the notebook with his gloved hand and flipped to the back. The pages were filled with letters and numbers in what looked like a code. He snapped it shut and slipped it into a large baggie. I examined the metal box.

"Did she have a key on her when she died?" I asked, hoping we wouldn't have to go to the shed and search her body.

"I don't think so. She wasn't wearing a necklace and I did check her pockets."

"Now we're looking for a key," I said. "That's even harder to find."

"Let's check the bathroom."

We took everything out of the medicine cabinet and lined it up on the counter. No key was attached to the shelves or taped to the bottom of her face lotion. I felt another nudge. Something was wrong here, but I couldn't place it. Now that we had taken everything off the shelves, it looked different to me. We put the pain reliever, birth control, bandages, and toothpaste back on the shelf. I still couldn't place it. Mac took the lid off the toilet and checked inside. He ran his hand along the back. He stood and shook his head.

We went back out to the bedroom and I ran my hands along the hems of all her dresses and skirts. Mac checked the pockets of all her jackets. Still nothing.

I was systematically going through each piece of clothing in each drawer when the door to the bedroom slowly eased open.

35

"Oh, it's you guys again," Vi said from the doorway.

"What are you doing here?" I said.

She pulled her hand behind her back and said, "Nothing. Just thought I'd look around while your mother does her card readings."

She'd been quick, but I had spotted the deep purple drawstring bag in her hand.

"What are you going to do with the pendulum?"

"Pendulum?" Mac said.

Vi brought her hand out from behind her back and sighed. "I wanted to see if it would tell me who else had been up here that night."

"You've got to be kidding," Mac said.

Vi drew herself up to her full five feet, two inches. "Detective McKenzie, just because you don't understand it, doesn't mean it won't work."

"You're trying to solve this case using a piece of glass on a string?"

"What are *you* using? Intuition and gut feelings?"

"No, I'm using my experience in solving murder cases," Mac said.

"Well, I'm using my experience in answering questions with a pendulum."

"We're pretty much done here, Mac," I said. "We might as well let Vi swing her crystal around."

Vi pressed her lips together and narrowed her eyes at me. We all stood staring at one another.

"Well, are you going to ask some questions or not?" Mac asked.

"I'd prefer to be alone," Vi sniffed. "The pendulum doesn't respond well when there is negative energy in the room."

I figured she also thought we'd steal her top-secret pendulum information if we hung around.

"Ms. Greer, you have to promise not to move anything or touch anything," Mac said.

"Don't you think the crime scene has been fully contaminated by now, what with cats and ghosts and who knows who else wandering through here—plus what do you think Clyde is doing?" She pointed at the clothing piled on the floor. "I know Clarissa left her shoes everywhere, but I don't remember her storing her clothing on the floor."

Mac rubbed his forehead. He glanced at me for guidance.

"I'll put it all back and then you can ask your questions," I said to Vi. "Just try not to disturb anything."

Vi humphed. "Don't tell *me* not to disturb anything. I know how to act at a crime scene—I've been Googling police procedure for months."

I tidied up Clarissa's clothing without finding a key, and Mac and I went back downstairs, leaving Vi and her pendulum alone in Clarissa's room.

As soon as we exited the stairwell, Mac grabbed my arm and propelled me toward my room.

"We need to talk," he said, "privately."

I pulled out my key and unlocked the door.

Mac ushered me inside, locked the door, and put the chain into the metal slider.

"I need to tell you something that you absolutely cannot share with anyone," he said. He held my gaze and all I saw were his cop eyes.

I nodded. "Of course."

"Not Vi, or your mother, or even Seth. Don't even think about it around that kid—sometimes I think he can read minds." Mac held Clarissa's notebook out and flipped it open.

I stepped toward him to get a better look.

He pointed to the column of numbers and letters.

"I think this is a list of cell phone types and numbers of units." He ran his finger down the column.

I followed his finger and it became clear—IP, BB, NK, SS, for iPhone, BlackBerry, Nokia, Samsung. The numbers looked like they would correlate with what we had found in the storage room. There were way more iPhones listed than BlackBerries.

"Great," I said. "But, what do we do with it?" I didn't think this was any big secret—she kept a list of the inventory—if anything it just proved that she had her nose in everyone's business.

"That's the part you can't tell anyone," he said. "Kirk is an undercover cop working this cell phone case."

"What? How do you know?"

Mac flipped the notebook shut inside the large baggie.

He hesitated. "I recognized him. He worked a case in Saginaw a few years ago. I didn't know him well, but I'm pretty sure he made the connection as well. We talked about it when we took the snowmobiles out to check the road. I need to let him know what we found without exposing him. I don't want to mess up his case, or put him in danger."

"Okay. It's probably better if we don't both go looking for him," I said. "I guess that explains why he's such a terrible maintenance man."

Mac shoved the baggie-wrapped notebook into his waistband and covered it with his snowman. I noticed that his sweater had sprouted buttons. It seemed Mavis was still finishing.

"Let's leave the box here until we find a key or can turn it over to the police," I said. "Who knows if there's even anything in there worth hiding. It could just be legal documents or jewelry."

Mac nodded and looked around for a place to put it. "I don't know about that. You're sharing a room with Vi."

"As far as I know, she can't pick a lock, so she's not likely to take much interest in it. She might try to wave her pendulum over it to see if it contains anything she would consider important . . ."

"Still, we should put it somewhere she's not likely to find it . . ."

I pointed to the closet. The wall safe wasn't big enough, but the top shelf was deep and we could push it to the back. Unless she really was on the hunt, she wouldn't notice it up there.

After we stashed the box and Mac double-checked that the notebook was well hidden behind his sweater, we opened the door and stepped into the hallway.

Mavis was there. She shut her door and clicked the lock with her key.

"Oh, Detective McKenzie," she said. She hurried toward us on her sturdy shoes, her purple pants making that zip-zip sound of polyester rubbing against itself. It was clear she had reapplied her lipstick without benefit of a mirror when she smiled.

Her jaunt down the hall had left her breathless, or maybe it was just Mac's proximity, but she put a hand to her ample chest as she caught her breath.

"I need to speak to you," she said. She glanced at me and added, "Alone."

"Mrs. Poulson, if you have something to tell me about the investigation, you can speak to both of us. Ms. Fortune is a police officer as well."

Mavis sniffed and her mouth pursed as if she'd been given a lemon to suck on. It became clear to me why she bothered Vi so much—they were exactly alike.

"Very well," she said. She turned to me, "I hope your professionalism will override any family loyalty you may have."

Mac gestured toward the stairs, but Mavis balked.

"This needs to be a very private conversation," she said. "Selma is still downstairs; we can go in my room."

She led us to her room and reapplied her key to the lock. Swinging the door wide, she waved us inside.

This room was obviously the pink fantasy room. The curtains were heavy velvet in a deep rose color. The dark wood of the furniture glowed pink in the misty light from the window. Mavis and Selma had evidently been working hard on their yarn-bombing project. Large swaths of knitting draped over the chairs and the couch.

Mavis gestured toward her sitting area, and Mac and I perched on the small loveseat and tried not to upset the rainbow of knitted items. Mavis pressed her lips together and took the wing-back chair.

"I need to confess," she began. "I didn't tell you the whole truth earlier when you asked me about my movements on the night of the . . . of poor Clarissa's death."

Mac leaned forward, resting his elbows on his knees. I noticed he hadn't whipped out his notebook.

"When I came up to get my medicine, I saw Isabel coming back down from the turret room," she said.

Mac and I exchanged a glance—the tilt of his head told me that this had piqued his interest.

Mavis held up her hand. "That's only part of what I want to tell you," she said. "I didn't mention it before because I just know Isabel didn't hurt Clarissa. I've known them both for many years and if anyone was going to turn into a murderer, it would have been Clarissa."

"Did you speak to Isabel when she came back down?" Mac asked.

Mavis shook her head. "She didn't see me. I had just opened my door and I heard someone coming down the stairs. She wasn't very quiet." Mavis took a deep breath and continued. "I popped into my room and cracked the door just enough to see who it was. Isabel came out of the doorway. She was rubbing her head like it really hurt and then she passed by my door and must have gone on to her own room around the corner."

"Why didn't you tell us this before?" I asked, unable to hide my irritation.

Mavis had the decency to look ashamed. "I didn't want to get Isabel in trouble, but now I know who really killed Clarissa." She leaned forward in her chair and looked at each of us in turn. "Violet Greer is your killer, I'm sure of it."

I stifled a snort and turned it into a cough. Mac put his hand on my leg to steady me and probably to keep from laughing himself. It took him a moment to speak.

"Why do you think that Violet is the killer?" Mac asked.

"I know it will be hard for you to hear." She looked at me. "She's your aunt, after all." She turned to Mac. "And a good friend of your mother's. But that woman is not to be trusted." Mavis held her finger up in such a likeness to Vi, I wondered for a moment if these two were punking us.

"Okay, let's stick to the evidence you have against her," Mac said and this time he did pull out his notebook, I assumed for show.

"She's been sneaking around the castle ever since Clarissa died, acting very suspicious if you ask me." Mavis held up one finger. "She didn't like Clarissa because Clarissa had made fun of her pet-psychic business and the knitters in general—which annoyed all of us, but only Vi had a murderous gleam in her eyes."

"So, your evidence is that Vi had a murderous gleam and she's been sneaking around?" Mac asked.

I thought that if that were enough to arrest Vi, we would have been visiting her in prison on a weekly basis.

"And I saw her steal that cable needle." Mavis nodded and sat back in her chair, having given us the clincher.

"Cable needle?" Mac said.

"Jessica told us that Isabel's fancy new cable needle was found at the crime scene—I saw Violet slip it into her bag on Thursday afternoon."

I wondered what Vi would have to say for herself. The sad part is I didn't doubt she had taken the needle. She probably wanted to sneak it up to her room to conduct some sort of knit-swatch experiment. She must have returned it at some point or someone took it from her.

"Tell me about seeing Isabel," Mac said. He casually slipped his notebook back in his pocket as if the Isabel information wasn't worth writing down.

Mavis flapped her hand as if waving away an annoying

bug. "Oh, that was nothing. I talked to Isabel about it." Mavis's mouth pulled into a frown. "She wasn't pleased when I told her I was going to discuss this with you, but you need all the facts, and not telling you was wearing me down. She accused me of being a traitor." Mavis huffed and took a moment to breathe heavily in indignation.

Mac and I waited for her to continue.

"She said she made a mistake and went the wrong way. She never went up to the room—I just saw her coming back out. That's what she told me and I believe her."

"Mrs. Poulson," Mac said, "this has been very helpful and I'm grateful you came forward with your information. I would just like to say, that if you are ever in a position to be questioned by the police in the future, it would be best to tell your whole story up front."

Mavis's face fell from a broad smile to a contrite countenance. She nodded.

"So, will you arrest Violet?" Mavis asked. "It would be really nice if she wasn't snooping around the castle the whole time we're stuck here. Where will you keep her imprisoned while we wait for the police to arrive?"

"Unfortunately, we'll need to gather some more information before we can make an arrest," Mac said. "But you've given us something to think about." He stuck out his hand and Mavis grasped it eagerly.

She showed us to the door and as I passed into the hall, she put a hand on my arm. "I'm so sorry to have to be the bearer of such distressing news. You have certainly shown grace and poise under these difficult circumstances."

"Thank you, Mrs. Poulson," I said. "I try to remain professional in these situations."

36

“I think I should go talk to Kirk about this,” Mac said, and patted the notebook through his sweater.

“I’ll work on finding the key to the lockbox,” I said.

“How are you going to do that?” Mac asked. “Is this another pendulum thing? Are you going to get your aunt involved?”

“No! I’m not even going to tell her about the box,” I said. I didn’t add that I had to keep the information from her or risk losing a bet.

Mac lowered his voice and said, “Are you going to do that finding thing you do?”

I stopped in the middle of the hall. “What are you talking about?”

“I know you can find things.” Mac didn’t meet my eyes. “I’ve seen you do it.”

“You have?” I didn’t remember when I would have told him that I was tapping into that sense to find something.

Ever since we had gotten back together after so many years apart, I had avoided discussing my . . . talents with him. When it came to talking about my psychic abilities I was a coward. Neila's guidance had at least moved me in the direction of not outright denying them. But treating my "finding ability" the same way Mom treated the tarot deck or Vi relied on her messages from animals? I wasn't there yet.

Mac put his hand to my cheek. "Of course I have. I think you're incredible. Even though I don't understand it, I recognize that you have a gift. You should use it."

My heart started pounding. I couldn't believe he was encouraging me to use a psychic method to help solve a case. He didn't even have to write it in a note! Something had shifted between us and the relief I felt at not hiding that part of myself from him had me blinking back tears.

I swallowed hard. "Okay," I said. "I'll see what I can do."

He gave me a quick kiss and turned toward the back door to look for Kirk.

I wandered past the lounge, trying to focus on the key and where it might be. Not knowing exactly what it looked like made the process more difficult.

I glanced in the room and saw Isabel there with a small bundle of yarn in her arms. She smiled when she saw me.

"You caught me," she said. "I'm glad you aren't one of the knitters—I left them working on their projects to sneak down here and do my yarn bombing." She held four or five furry knitted animals. I identified a fox, an elephant, and a monkey. She had already placed a small horse next to the horse statue.

"Wow," I said. "That looks really complicated." I reached out and she handed me the monkey.

"They can be a little fiddly, but it's fun," she said.

I gave the monkey back. "I'm having enough trouble with the scarf."

Isabel looked around the room, presumably searching for a place to exhibit the animals.

I hated to do an interview without Mac, but this seemed like a perfect opportunity to ask her about Mavis's accusation.

"Isabel, I need to ask you again about the night Clarissa was killed."

Her smile faded and she nodded. "Should we sit?" She pointed at the couches by the fireplace.

She set her animals on the coffee table and sat back against the cushions. "How can I help?"

"A . . . witness has come forward reporting that you were seen leaving Clarissa's room on the night she died."

Isabel took a deep breath and let it out. She closed her eyes briefly. "I know who your witness is and I'll tell you the same thing I told her. I did go up to Clarissa's room that night, but I didn't talk to her. She had made a remark about Teresa—that's Mavis's daughter—and how suicide was such a waste, and such a selfish act." Isabel laced her fingers together on her lap and squeezed. "Mavis turned white as a sheet. I was furious, and on my way to my room to get my headache medicine I went to her room. However, halfway up the stairs I came to my senses. There was no reasoning with Clarissa and no way to appeal to her conscience because she didn't have one. I went to my room to calm down and the rest is just as I told you before."

"I'm sorry about your friend," I said.

"Thank you." Isabel relaxed her hands. "Mavis and I got into a bit of a tiff over this whole thing. She told me she had seen me and that she would 'cover' for me. I couldn't believe she thought I had killed Clarissa—and that she would offer to cover it up!" She shook her head. "I'm sorry I didn't say anything earlier, but I just thought it would confuse the issue."

And that she would be a suspect, I thought to myself. It was starting to look like the entire hotel had visited Clarissa that night and they all had a reason to want her dead.

"Thank you for telling me about it now," I said.

Isabel gathered up her animals and I left her in the lounge to continue her surreptitious placement.

Back in the hall, I leaned against the wall for a moment to clear my head. I would have to fill Mac in on Isabel's story, but first I needed to find that key. Usually, I can visualize the item and then "zoom out" and see where it is. Instead, I kept getting a picture of Seth.

Seth couldn't have the key, but I had been down this road enough times to just go with it. If I was seeing Seth, then I should go find Seth. Just like that tug to look in the wardrobe, I had to follow this hint.

I found him rather quickly in the front reception area. He sat on the couch staring out at the snow. I almost hated to disturb him. I was shocked he wasn't already in the dining room since it was close to lunchtime, and it had been at least three hours since he'd last eaten.

As I got closer, I saw that he was petting the demon cat. I heard its purring across the room.

"If you sit down really slow, you won't disturb her," Seth said quietly.

I hated to disturb the crazy cat, so I sat down slowly on the chair across from Seth. The cat opened one eye and stopped purring. Seth scratched her head and she closed her eye and resumed her little motor noises.

"How did you catch her?" I asked. "It seems like everyone in the hotel has been trying to find her."

"I just sat out here to listen to my music and watch the snow and she found me." He smiled at the pile of fur in his lap. She rubbed her head against his hand.

"Maybe there are two cats, because that doesn't look like the streaking, yowling, scratching cat I've seen before."

Seth grinned. "It's the same cat." His smile faded. "She's really scared."

I didn't realize Seth had the same affinity for cats as he did for dogs.

"What's she afraid of?"

Seth shook his head. "It's kind of strange—she's just showing me pictures of things. Yarn, a room with yellow walls and flowers . . . tile with a pool of blood." Seth looked at me.

"It sounds like the turret room—have you been up there?"

He didn't answer right away. "No. Is it really bright during the daytime? She's showing me a big patch of sunlight."

"The windows face east and there are a lot of them, so it probably is bright."

"She likes that room, but she's afraid of it now."

"Seth, did she see who killed Clarissa?"

Seth's big brown eyes took on a faraway look. "She might have, but I'm not sure she realizes it. She keeps showing me yarn, balls of yarn in a basket, and a hand putting food down for her."

He stroked the cat some more.

"I don't know what it means," he said.

I didn't know what it meant, either. Maybe nothing. Maybe Duchess thought about yarn the way Tuffy thought about food—all the time.

Duchess continued to purr with her eyes closed. I continued to not see the key in my mind's eye.

"Are you hungry?" I asked after a few minutes of listening to the purring.

His eyes lit up. He shifted position. Duchess hopped off

his lap and stretched her back legs before jumping onto the windowsill. She sat looking out the window, tail twitching slowly.

"I did find this," Seth said and held out his hand, palm up.

A small silver key glinted in his hand.

"Where did you find it?" I took it from him and looked for numbers or markings on it. It had to be the key to the lockbox.

"It was taped to the inside of her collar," he said. "It was bugging her because it kept pulling her hair."

I glanced at the cat. She kept her gold eyes trained on me while her tail slowly swept back and forth.

I wondered who else knew that she had the key the whole time. And knew what it was for. I tucked it into my pocket.

"Let's go see if this key works," I said.

"What about lunch?"

I grinned at him. "Soon." I slung an arm over his shoulder and we headed upstairs.

37

We entered my room and I was relieved to see that Vi was absent and Seth wasn't going to have to divert her and drag her down the hall. I hadn't seen her since our encounter in the turret room and I didn't want her rummaging in the lockbox. I asked Seth to guard the door and warn me if anyone approached the room.

I took the box down from the shelf by carefully covering it with a T-shirt to protect any fingerprints that might be on it. I doubted it would ever be necessary and recognized that much of our evidence had been tainted at this point. But, just in case.

I set the box on the coffee table, and Seth watched as I inserted the key in the lock. It turned easily and the lid popped up about half an inch. I opened the lid and peered inside. It was filled with cash. Most of it was twenties but there was one thick stack of hundreds. She probably had ten thousand dollars stashed in the box. I took the money out and stacked it next to the box.

"Wow," Seth said from the doorway. He was alternately watching me and peering through the peephole.

A handwritten list of furnishings, statues, paintings, and art sat underneath the money. In the next column were numbers that I assumed were prices or estimates of value. I recognized some of the items as artwork and furniture from the lounge. I glanced at Seth.

"She was keeping track of how much the antiques were worth," I said. "I wonder if this money is from previous sales, or the cell phones, or blackmail."

"Blackmail?" Seth asked.

"She liked to collect secrets," I said.

"It looks like she liked to collect money," Seth said.

"I wonder if she was selling off some of the antiques in the castle?"

I flipped the pages to see if there was a list of "sold" items. There wasn't. Just more numbers and items. I wondered if Jessica and Linda knew that Clarissa had assessed the entire contents of the castle.

"Someone's coming," Seth whispered.

I quickly repacked the box and I set it up on the shelf. I went to the door and listened with Seth. Mavis was talking to someone—probably Selma—and she stopped at her room and unlocked the door.

I went to the closet and pushed the box to the back where it had been.

Something was bothering me about the list and the money but I couldn't quite pin it down. The back of my neck prickled and I struggled to make the connection.

"I think people are going down to lunch," Seth said. He stood with his ear to the door.

"Yeah, let's go," I said. I pushed the key down into my jeans pocket and followed Seth into the hallway and downstairs.

The dining room was in disarray when we arrived. René's hat was askew and he had a wild look in his eyes. He and Wally hastily set the warming pans on the buffet table. They had put out sandwich makings again, a crock of soup, and a large bowl of salad.

Wally brought pitchers of water, and had set up cans of soda on the drinks table.

"What's up with the chef?" Seth muttered to me.

I shrugged and watched as they continued to set up. I glanced at my watch—it was a little after noon. Maybe René got thrown by being a few minutes late? I would be surprised if a couple of minutes made him so anxious. Especially with this group.

I approached him and put a hand on his shoulder.

"Can I help with anything?"

He spun to look at me and I stepped back. He shook his head no.

"I think we have it under control now," he said. "I was meeting with Jessica about the plan for next week if we can't get our deliveries. I thought Emmett would set up the buffet, but he's disappeared." René held his hands out.

"What do you mean disappeared?" Mac said from behind me.

"He's not in the kitchen, or downstairs, or anywhere else he should be," René said. "I haven't seen him since breakfast cleanup."

"Oh, no," Mac said. He grabbed my arm and pulled me out into the hall. "I heard a snowmobile a few minutes ago. I thought it was Kirk and his snowblower, but now I'm worried Emmett may have run away."

I started to ask why Emmett would run away, but Mac held up his hand.

"Kirk told me about his investigation." Mac leaned

forward and dropped his voice. "He thinks Emmett is our cell phone smuggler. I need to go find Kirk and we might have to go after Emmett."

"I'll keep working on the other situation here." I didn't have time to tell him about finding the key and the money in the box before he strode off into the back hall.

As I walked back to the dining room, I wondered again where Vi had gone. If she'd been here, she probably would have tried to tag along on the snowmobiles to keep an eye on her number-one suspect, Kirk. I could hardly wait to tell her she'd been tracking an undercover cop.

Seth was chatting with Lucille and already halfway through his lunch when I entered the dining room. Mom and Dad sat with them. I saw that Wally now manned the buffet table and René had left the dining room. I served up a small bowl of soup and sat with my group.

Lucille complimented Mom on her tarot reading. Mom blushed and waved her comments away.

"Has anyone seen Vi?" I asked.

They shook their heads. "Not recently," Mom said. "She was in the lounge when I started the tarot readings, but she left toward the beginning and I haven't seen her since. Is something wrong?"

"No, I just . . . wondered."

"It's not like her to miss lunch," Lucille said. "I hope she isn't feeling unwell."

"She's not in her room—we were just up there," Seth said.

"Oh?" Mom said, and turned toward me.

I squeezed Mom's hand. "I'll look for her after lunch."

Mom nodded and went back to her meal, but her brows remained furrowed and she only pushed her food around her plate.

"Lucille, didn't you have a yarn-bombing project for Seth?" I asked to deflect attention elsewhere.

"Yes, I do." Lucille turned to Seth. "Maybe we can do that after lunch?"

Seth nodded and continued slurping his soup.

I finished my soup and excused myself. I felt Mom watching me leave the dining room. I didn't want to get the rest of them worried, but I felt edgy and unsettled; something was wrong.

Vi could easily get lost in her pendulum daze for hours. I assumed she was still up in the turret room interrogating her swinging crystal. Or maybe she had finally caught Duchess and was trying to pry some information out of the cat. Either way, I decided to go back to the last place I had seen her.

38

I was out of breath when I reached the top of the steps. I swung the door open and was disappointed to see the empty room. I stepped inside. Everything was essentially as we had left it—the shoes still littered the floor, the open curtains allowed a patch of sunlight to creep into the room. Duchess lay on her side, spread out in the sunshine. She sat up when I moved toward her. Those gold eyes held mine, and she began to purr.

"Have you seen Vi?" I asked the cat. I didn't expect an answer but had to talk to someone.

The bathroom was also just as we had left it, and also no Vi.

I left the cat in her patch of sun and went back downstairs. I stopped at our room, but it was also unoccupied. Where could she be?

Then it came to me—maybe she had gone out to see the dogs. She sometimes liked to sit with Tuffy and Baxter when she was thinking. She said they helped her concentrate. I took the stairs two at a time and headed to the back hallway.

I grabbed Seth's coat, which was by the back door. His coat was way better than mine for this kind of weather. My sister remembered winter here in Michigan, but she must have embellished it in her mind. She'd sent something that could probably keep a person warm at the North Pole—before global warming. I walked to the cottage, thinking about where I would look if Vi weren't there.

I also had a decision to make now. Vi would not win our bet, focused as she was on the undercover cop. But she'd still want to open the detective agency together. I had begun to see it take shape. Maybe it would be the answer to my jobless situation. It felt like I'd be taking over a classroom full of preschoolers, but if Vi was going to do this anyway, I might as well get involved if only to keep her out of trouble. And, I had started to warm to the idea. Working to focus my "gift" over the last couple of months had honed my ability to locate things. At the very least I could be a psychic lost and found. I just hoped I could find Vi, and soon.

Baxter and Tuffy greeted me enthusiastically at the door and bounded out to meet me. Tuffy stopped in mid jump when he realized I wasn't Seth. Before I had a chance to snap a leash on him, Baxter ran through the snow flinging the fluffy stuff over his head. Tuffy stayed much closer to me, did his business and returned to the doorway, where he sat shivering.

I clapped my hands and called to Baxter. I saw him dive into a snowbank, tail wagging.

"Come on, boy! Let's have a treat!"

At the word "treat," he pulled his head out of the snow and whirled in my direction. He had something in his mouth. He ran at me, full force, and I braced myself for impact. I didn't want him racing through the cottage covered in snow, plus I had to get whatever he had found away from him. I just hoped it wasn't anything dead.

Rather than run into me, he stopped just in front of the door and dropped his prize at my feet. I bent to pick it up, my brain not willing to believe what my eyes were telling me and not wanting to make the connections it was making.

Vi's bright pink and purple striped mitten sat on the ground. Vi adored these mittens; they were the first pair she had managed to make that fit humans and not some alien life form and she had been wildly proud of them. She'd made others over the years that were much better than this pair, but she always returned to these. She'd used yarn that had belonged to my grandmother and said they reminded her of her mother's love of bright colors and winter walks.

I knew I wouldn't find Vi in the cottage. Alarm bells sounded in my brain. I had to find her, and fast. The snow fell in big heavy flakes and the temperature had been dropping throughout the afternoon. I had worried about Mac and Kirk venturing out in this new storm and now Vi was out in it as well.

Thinking about Vi's love of these mittens had my brain spinning in other directions. Sometimes the things we work so hard to make or to preserve take on a life of their own. Protecting the past can become a mission, or an obsession. I wondered what a person would do to protect his or her heritage, even from one's own family. I thought about the list we had found in the box.

I gave the dogs their promised treat and shut them back in the cottage. I followed Baxter's paw prints to the place where he had found the mitten, dreading what I might find. But there was nothing. Just a trampled snowdrift.

I pulled the hood up against the wind and realized Seth

had stuffed his ridiculous fur-lined deerstalker hat in the hood. I put it on and rethought my position on the hat. It was soft and warm and my ears thanked me. I put Vi's glove on my left hand and stuffed my other hand in the coat pocket. I felt Seth's penknife and a pack of gum.

I surveyed the landscape, looking for footprints, but the snow and the wind had smoothed everything except the area Baxter had just stepped on. Some slight depressions headed into the woods. Clutching the knife in my pocket, I followed the only lead I had.

I was fairly certain they were footprints and as I got to the edge of the trees, the prints became more clear. There was more than one set. They walked into the woods where the land sloped down and away from the castle. The shed where Clarissa's body was stored sat at the top of the slope and the prints curved around behind it. I knew I was now lost to view from the hotel.

I called Vi's name every few steps but there was no response. Finally, I heard a weak "help" off to my left. I turned and followed the sound. I spotted the mate to the mitten in another snowdrift, but this one moved when I approached.

39

I rushed to Vi's side and brushed the snow off of her.

"Vi! Are you hurt?"

Her whole body was covered with snow like someone buried in sand on the beach.

She didn't answer and I slid my arm under her head to try to get her to sit up. I heard a muffled *snap* behind me and turned just in time to see a large tree branch swing toward my head.

I ducked and the branch glanced off my left temple. If I hadn't been wearing Seth's hat and hood, I would certainly have been seeing stars. As it was, I fell on top of Vi.

I quickly got up and moved away from Vi. If there was a branch-wielding lunatic in the woods, I didn't want Vi caught in the cross swings. I dodged to the left and turned just in time to see the branch swing again. I spun toward it and grabbed it as it whistled past. The person at the other end was thrown off balance and we both fell to the ground. The assailant was bundled up like a Michelin man and wore a ski mask.

I rolled onto the branch to keep my attacker from using it again, but before I could turn, he or she was on top of me, trying to bury my face in the snow. I tried to fight but I couldn't get a grip on the slippery coat.

The snow burned my face, it was so cold. I felt her—and I knew it was a woman now—pushing my head into the ground and pulling on my scarf at the same time. She thought she could strangle me with my own scarf. I reached over my head and tried to grab any body part I could. I came away with the ski mask but didn't slow the efforts of the maniac trying to choke me.

I remembered Seth's knife and fought to get my hand into the pocket. I momentarily felt the scarf tighten as I only held it with one hand. I barely felt the coldness on my face anymore and it was hard to breathe. The snow was thick—a moment of fear flashed through me. Could a person suffocate in snow? I didn't want to find out. Flicking the knife open, I reached behind and jammed it into what I hoped was a leg. The blade was too short to penetrate very far past a heavy coat, but it would go through the thin pants I had felt while grappling with my attacker.

A satisfying howl resulted when I made contact. I felt her grip loosen and she rolled off of me. Even before I turned I was certain I would see Linda.

She scrabbled away from me, clutching her thigh where I had stabbed her. I was still worried about getting Vi to safety and trying to figure out how to subdue Linda *and* drag Vi to the hotel when I heard huffing and snow-crunching noises.

"What's going on back here?" Wally rounded the corner

of the shed. His eyes grew large when he took in the scene of me holding a short Boy Scout knife and looming over a moaning Linda.

"Wally, thank goodness," I said.

He stood straighter and looked at me warily. "What's going on?" He took a step back.

"Linda just tried to kill me and Vi." I tilted my head toward where she lay under the snow. "Vi needs to get back to the hotel."

"She's lying, Wallace!" Linda said. "She's the one with the knife."

Wally hesitated and looked at me. I showed him the Boy Scout knife, folded it, and tossed it to him. "Vi really needs help, Wally." I pointed to where she lay, still and silent.

Wally rushed to Vi's side and finished brushing her off. "She's really cold," he said. "Did she pass out?"

"I'm not sure how Linda got her out here, but we need to move Vi inside quickly," I said.

"Right, of course," Wally said.

He turned to Vi and picked her up. Since she couldn't weigh more than one hundred pounds, I figured he staggered under the weight of her coat and all those sweaters. He took a few unstable steps and then put her feet down in the snow. He put his hands under her arms and dragged her backward toward the hotel.

Linda whimpered quietly as I hauled her to her feet. I kept a firm hand on Linda as she hobbled toward the hotel, making a much bigger show of her injured leg than I thought necessary.

It was a noisy procession with Wally huffing and puffing and Linda gasping each time she took a step.

"How did you know we were out here?" I asked Wally.

"I was looking out the window from one of the upstairs

hallways to see how much snow was piling up." He stopped dragging Vi so he could catch his breath and talk. "I saw Mrs. Garrett heading in this direction. She never ventures into the woods in the winter if she can help it, so I came out to see what was going on."

"I'm so glad you did." I smiled gratefully at him.

That seemed to galvanize him and we quickly made it to the inn.

I opened the back door and swung it wide so Wally could get inside with Vi. Then I shoved Linda in before closing it against the cold.

René met us in the hall. He stopped short, taking in the scene.

"I thought you might be Emmett," he said. "I heard from Holly that Emmett took the snowmobile and Kirk went after him," he said. "What's going on?"

"Vi might be hypothermic," I said. "Please find Heather. She's the blond one and she's a nurse."

"I know where she is," Wally said. "I'll go get her."

René took Vi's limp form from Wally and rushed her to the lounge.

Linda's head hung and her hair covered her face. It looked like she had given up on the idea of escaping, but I didn't trust her.

Dad and Seth rushed toward us as we stood in the back hall.

"We heard Vi was hurt," Dad said. "Where is she?" Dad was breathing hard and his shock of white hair seemed to stand even taller than usual.

"Wally went to find Heather," I said. "René took Vi to the lounge."

Seth ran down the hall to check on Vi.

"Clyde, are you okay?" Dad asked. He searched my face and squeezed me into a bear hug.

"I need to go call the police," I said to Dad. "I've got our murderer."

Linda slumped against the wall and held her hand on her leg wound.

"She's been hurt," Dad said.

I looked at Linda, who had now begun to moan in light of Dad's sympathy.

"She'll be fine," I said. "Keep an eye on her until I get back. I hope Wally knows a place we can put her until the police get here."

I rushed to the front desk and called 911 from the landline. I reported the need for an ambulance if they could get through and asked her to get a message to Pete Harris that we had a suspect in custody. I then ran back to Dad and Linda.

Just as I arrived at the back hall again, Wally and Seth approached. Seth's eyes were big and he said, "They took Aunt Vi into the lounge by the fire." He swallowed and looked from me to Dad and back. "She's not waking up."

"Dad, we need to secure Mrs. Garrett somewhere," I said. "Wally, I don't trust her—do you have a place that can be locked?"

Wally shook his head. "Not really." He glared at Linda. "But I know where Kirk keeps the zip ties."

Jessica ran toward us down the hall. She was out of breath.

"Mom! I just talked to René. What's going on? Are you okay?" She moved to examine Linda's leg.

I stepped between her and Linda. "Your mother is under arrest."

"What? What for?" Jessica stepped back, her hand to her chest.

"Reckless endangerment, attempted murder, and probably the murder of Clarissa."

Jessica's hands shook as she covered her mouth. Her eyes were huge and she stared at her mother.

"I don't believe it," she said. Linda dropped her head. "You've made a mistake. Mom, tell them." Jessica stepped toward her mother again and I steered her back down the hall.

René must have heard the noise and came out of the lounge. He approached Jessica and turned her toward the reception area.

Linda remained silent, but scrubbed at her eyes as Jessica walked away.

40

Thirty long minutes later, Vi groggily sipped the hot tea with brandy that René had prepared. She made a face and pushed it away.

"What's in that tea? Is it that healthy green stuff?" she said. "It's horrible!"

I grinned at Mom. Vi would be okay.

Heather had done a quick check of Vi's extremities to be sure frostbite hadn't set in. I was worried about Vi's left hand since she'd lost her mitten and I had no idea how long she'd been outside.

Heather gave a thumbs-up and said it looked like Vi would be just fine. She quietly told me it would be better if we could get her to a hospital just to be safe.

I was mulling this over and wondering if it was worth trying to get the hospital helicopter to fly in and take her, when we heard boots stomping in the front reception area. Wally's eyes got big and he scurried off to take up his post.

I thought it might be Mac and Kirk finally returning. My spirits lifted and I followed Wally out of the room.

I rushed to the front entrance and stopped short when I saw police uniforms. Even though I had called them, my gut clenched as I thought they might come bearing horrible news about Mac.

As the sky began to turn deep purple, I knew the wind would pick up again and the temperatures would plummet. Were they stuck in the woods? Did they crash into a tree? Did Emmett have a weapon? I crossed my arms to keep my hands from shaking and stepped forward to meet the police.

"I'm Detective Harris." The plainclothes officer with salt-and-pepper hair and the weather-beaten face of an outdoorsman addressed Wally. "Someone called emergency dispatch and said there was a suspect in custody?"

"I'm Wallace Prescott." Wally stepped forward and shook hands with the officers. "We have her . . . detained in the office."

Wally saw the officers' attention had shifted to me, and he turned to see who had come into the room.

"Detective Harris, this is Clyde Fortune," Wally said. "She's the one who caught our suspect. She and Detective McKenzie have been trying to identify the murderer."

I was amused at Wally's use of the word "our." I supposed he deserved it after coming to my rescue.

Detective Harris stuck out his hand and we shook.

"I've known Mac for a long time. He told me you were here as well when we spoke on the phone. From Ann Arbor, right?"

"Formerly Ann Arbor. I live in Crystal Haven now." I felt a calm settle over me as I said it. It felt right.

"We finally cleared the road down below," he said. "It sounds like we got here just in time to miss all the excitement." He turned to Wally. "Maybe you should show me where you're keeping our suspect."

The three officers trooped after Wally and me. We briefly filled them in on the afternoon's events as we made our way to the small supply closet where Wally had incarcerated Linda. I summarized the situation for Detective Harris and he asked for a few minutes to talk to Linda.

I returned to the lounge to check on Vi.

She sat with a bright afghan over her lap and sipped a different cup of tea. René had provided a tray of sandwiches and cookies, which Seth eyed carefully. I saw the wheels turning in his brain, trying to figure out how to get some of Vi's food without appearing insensitive.

Vi wasn't paying any attention to the food; she was too busy telling her tale.

"I just *knew* there was something going on with her," Vi said.

I bit my lip to keep from interrupting and reminding her that her main suspect had been Kirk.

"But she was a tricky one," Vi continued. "She invited me to her room for coffee and cookies." Vi looked around to be sure she had everyone's attention. "I wanted to see their apartment and thought I could pump her for information about . . . her staff."

Vi glanced at me and I smiled. I wasn't going to ruin her story by telling the young swooning knitters that Vi had suspected their yarn-bombing beefcake.

"She must have put something in the coffee," Vi said. "I started to feel funny, but she insisted she'd just seen someone sneaking around out near the shed where Clarissa's body was." Vi adjusted her afghan, and Tina stepped forward to assist.

I finally remembered what was missing from Clarissa's

medicine cabinet—Valium. Linda must have used that on Vi to relax her enough that she would pass out in the snow.

"She hustled me outside after I grabbed my coat and we walked through the snowbanks to the far side of the shed."

Vi stopped and took another sip of tea.

"I don't remember a whole lot after that. I felt really dizzy and she told me to sit down. The next thing I knew, I was freezing and I heard Clyde calling me."

Everyone turned to look at me and I filled them in on my side of the story. By the time I finished, the police had found us again and said they'd take Linda with them. They asked me to show them where Clarissa's body was stored.

I put Seth's coat on again and prepared to venture back outside. Wally produced the key and handed it to me. He evidently didn't want to join us for this part of the process.

It had gotten even colder in just the last hour or so since we'd come in. More worried than ever, my ears strained to hear the sound of snowmobiles but, except for the wind, all was silent.

I showed the officers the shed and gave them the key. I agreed with Wally's sentiments—I had no desire to look at Clarissa again. I watched as they carried her plastic-wrapped body out of the small building and up to the crime-scene van.

I followed them back to the inn. Each step crunching through two feet of snow, I began to spin more and more dire scenarios in my mind. Where could Mac and Kirk be?

"I'm going to check on something here in the cottage," I said and gestured at the cottage door as we passed by.

Pete Harris nodded and followed his officers as the men with Clarissa's body veered off to the parking lot and opened the back of the van. I still hadn't heard snowmobiles and dejectedly opened the cottage door to go inside.

I needed a moment to myself, but was greeted exuberantly by Baxter. He calmed down quickly when he sensed my mood. He sat and leaned into my leg. Tuffy's ears drooped and he also sat and regarded me carefully. I leaned against the wall and then sank to the floor.

Baxter put his head on my knees and sighed. The tears came then and I didn't try to stop them. I had been so worried about Vi, it was partly in relief that I cried. But Mac had been gone far too long and I was very worried. I didn't know what I would do if anything happened to him. Tuffy walked over to me and put his head under my hand. His way of providing comfort was to demand some petting.

I resolved to be more forthcoming with Mac about my plans for the future. I knew that I wanted him in it and we wouldn't make it if I kept trying to hide who I was.

I allowed myself five minutes. I knew I would be missed if I stayed any longer and didn't want to be found with a red nose and swollen eyes. I went into the bathroom to splash water on my face. The dogs trailed after me and watched quietly.

"Okay, guys," I said at the door. "I'll be back soon—you be good." Both dogs wore the forlorn expression of being left behind.

A loud swell of voices greeted me as I walked in. I was only able to distinguish two sounds: Mac's deep rumble and Vi's "I knew it!"

I rushed to the lounge and straight toward Mac. I had to touch him to be sure he was really there; my imagination had run so wild. His face was bleeding and he was developing a black eye, but he was safe. My vision became blurry and I turned away from the watching crowd to hug Mac and get control of myself. Mac seemed surprised at my tearful greeting but held me close until I was ready to face the rest of the gang.

Kirk stood to the side, clutching Emmett's arm and glowering. He also looked like he'd been in a brawl, with scrapes on his face and a split lip.

Emmett appeared worst of all. His nose was bent at an odd angle and dripped blood onto his coat. He held his right arm carefully cradled in his left and kept his eyes on the ground.

Officer Harris had followed me into the room and quickly took control of Emmett. He handed him off to one of the other officers and went out into the hallway with Kirk and Mac.

"What are they talking about out there?" Vi said. She sat up and stretched her neck to see over her admirers. "Mac was just getting to the good part, where Emmett crashed into a tree and they had to chase him through the woods."

"That must be why I didn't hear them return," I said.

Mom nodded. "They had to walk back through all that snow and Emmett tried to get away twice!"

"Emmett was the one stashing the cell phones," Seth mumbled through a mouthful of cookie. He sat with Vi's plate on his lap.

"I can't believe we've been staying here right under the nose of a thief and a murderer!" Mavis said. She sat down next to Selma, who nodded and patted Mavis on the back.

Holly rushed into the room. "I heard they're back, where are they?"

"They're talking to the police in the front room," Isabel said.

"Is he all right?" Holly said.

"Who? Emmett?" Mom said.

"No, Kirk!" she said.

Heather and Tina narrowed their eyes at her.

"He's fine," Dad said. "A little beat up, but Emmett looks worse."

Wally stepped forward and talked quietly to Holly. She sat in a chair by the door and mangled her apron in her lap.

She jumped up as Mac and Kirk came back into the room. She gasped when she saw his cuts and bruises and he quietly reassured her that he was fine.

He put his arm around her and they stepped out into the hallway.

Vi waved Mac over to the couch and imperiously patted the spot next to her. He glanced at me and sheepishly sat with her.

"Now tell us the story," Vi demanded.

Mom nodded, and the rest of the crowd murmured agreement.

Mac wasn't used to reporting to civilians on his cases, but he did an admirable job of reassuring them that everything was wrapped up without giving away too much.

"Emmett and Linda were involved in a stolen cell phone ring," Mac began.

"Linda?" Mom asked.

"Rose! Let the man tell his story," Vi said.

"Yes, Linda. She needed money to keep the inn going," Mac said. "Apparently there were a lot of necessary repairs and they don't have the kind of steady business to support costly renovations."

I remembered how proud Linda was of the antiques and artwork. She must have been desperate to save it all.

"When Clarissa moved here after her father died, it became clear that she had the majority stake in ownership and that her vision for the future of the castle was very different from Linda's."

Isabel shook her head and her mouth pulled down into a frown.

"Her father, David, had loaned some money to Linda

back when they first opened and that gave him the majority ownership. He had promised to keep it as a handshake deal, but Clarissa got wind of it and made him formalize the agreement."

Mac nodded thanks to Wally, who handed him a mug of hot coffee.

"Emmett told us he thought Linda may have killed Clarissa because that fight they had on Wednesday was about selling off some of the art work and antiques to fund Clarissa's spa project." Mac turned to where I stood next to Mom and Dad. "He didn't tell us the whole story—he knew what the meeting was about because Linda told him they would have to get a good price for the cell phones so she could buy Clarissa off."

"Linda found me in the turret room with Duchess." Vi interrupted Mac's story. "She thought I was trying to get information from the cat, but I wasn't. Duchess had just come in the room and I was petting her, but not trying to interview her."

Vi made sure we were all listening.

"I think she tried to kill me because she thought I knew she had killed Clarissa. The cat must have been in the room at the time." Vi turned to Mac. "She did tell me she was shocked when she came downstairs and found a police officer staying for the weekend. She didn't tell me she was shocked in a bad way. But she must have seen the whole thing unraveling when you and Clyde identified yourselves as police."

41

The next couple of hours were filled with activity. The snowplow arrived and cleared the road and the parking lot. The police van took Clarissa's body away. Mac and I spent an hour with Pete Harris sharing all of our evidence and he took Linda into custody.

By early evening, the inn had cleared out. The knitters couldn't wait to load up their bags of yarn and knitting goodies. Lucille had won the yarn-bombing award for her piano cozy. She and Seth had spent well over an hour that afternoon covering the baby grand piano in a neon-colored knitted monstrosity. Lucille said she had called ahead to get the measurements and the piece fit the piano perfectly. I secretly thought the woman needed to get out more and resolved to be sure Mom and Vi invited her over more often. Tiny scarves for chess pieces were one thing, but this was truly impressive.

We had decided to stay one more night to give Vi a little

more rest before packing and driving back home. Of course, we all had to pretend that it had nothing to do with her near-death experience.

The big surprise of the afternoon was Tina. She finally admitted to being in Clarissa's room the night she died—the presence of actual police and a suspect in custody must have convinced her to tell her story. No one was more shocked than Jessica to learn that Tina was Clarissa's half-sister. David Carlisle, Clarissa's father, had had a relationship after his divorce but never claimed the child until he found out he had terminal cancer. He located Tina and promised he would leave her half his estate in his will. When he died, the will left everything to Clarissa. Tina suspected Clarissa had managed to destroy the new will. Tina had joined the knitter's workshop to continue to put pressure on Clarissa to do the right thing and to get closer to Linda and Jessica in case she needed their help in obtaining her inheritance.

René and Jessica had gone to the police station to help Linda procure a lawyer. Unfortunately for her lawyer, she'd admitted that Clarissa taunted her about selling her favorite paintings to pay for the spa, and Linda hit her over the head with the Maglite. A good attorney might be able to get her a reduced sentence for that, arguing temporary insanity. But the calculated strangling and then the attempted murder of Vi would be harder to talk her way through.

Mac had warned René that he needed to tell Jessica the truth about his past, but agreed that maybe he should wait until Jessica felt less blindsided by her mother's criminal activities and the news of a new cousin. Wally had taken over management duties until Jessica was ready to return to work.

"I don't understand how the cable needle ended up in Clarissa's room," Mom said.

I shrugged. "Linda may have put it there to cast suspicion on the knitters, or even specifically Isabel, knowing that Isabel and Clarissa hated each other."

Putting all the reports together, it sounded like Clarissa had had a busy evening before Linda hit her in the head. René had been there, Tina had been there, and I suspected Emmett had also paid a visit. Probably only Duchess knew how many visitors Clarissa had received. It was up to the Kalamazoo Police Department to sort out all the stories.

I had just rested my head on Mac's shoulder and closed my eyes for a moment when I heard *thump, thump, rattle, thump* down the stairs. I sat forward, as did everyone else, and we watched the door.

"It's the ghost," Vi breathed.

"Good grief, Vi," Dad said. "There's no ghost."

We heard *rattle*, *smack*, and *shhh*-ing noises. Mac stood up and took a step toward the door. A small box rolled into view. Duchess followed right behind and batted it into the room like a kitty hockey player. It didn't slide as well on the carpet as it must have on the wood floor of the hallway. She turned her golden eyes toward Seth. Abandoning her toy, she prowled toward him, leaped into his lap, and settled in, purring.

Mac's eyes had gotten big and he strode to the box, picked it up, and stuffed it into his jeans pocket.

Lucille cleared her throat and gave Mac a little nod. Mac humphed, grabbed my hand, and pulled me into the hallway. He held a finger to his lips as he led me toward the back of the hotel and the now vacant library.

"Mac, what are you doing?"

I thought I heard footsteps behind us.

He dragged me into the library and softly shut the door. He pulled out the little box. My palms broke out in a sweat and the roar in my ears made me dizzy. I wasn't ready for a proposal. Mac took my hand and dropped the box into it.

"What's this?" I said.

"Open it." Mac stepped back to watch.

I eased the ribbon off the box and peered inside. My whole body relaxed when I saw what it contained. A beautiful pair of knitted seashell earrings nestled on blue tissue paper. There was a little pearl bead right in the center of each one.

"They're gorgeous," I breathed. "Where did you get them?"

"I had some help from Isabel. Apparently, she knits jewelry and I asked her for something with a beach theme."

"Beach . . ."

I looked up, and Mac now held a printed airline ticket.

"Oh, Mac, you didn't," I said.

"I did."

"You got another flight? How—cell service has been down for days. And the Wi-Fi is still not working."

"I know it's a shock, but some things can still be done without the Internet." His eyes crinkled at the corners as he smiled. "Also, I had some help from Pete."

"When do we leave?" I asked.

He checked his watch. "In about an hour if you want to make the flight."

I threw my arms around him and thanked him enthusiastically.

"You missed something," he said. "There's still something in the box."

I pulled the tissue paper out of the box and saw a key sitting in the bottom. I met Mac's eyes. "Is this to your house?"

"Clytemnestra Fortune," he said, "I love you."

"Wait! Stop," I said. I remembered the look his mother

had given him and the grumpy way he snatched the ring box off the floor.

"What?"

"Did your mother put you up to this?"

He pulled me closer. "Of course not."

"It's just, I know you've been arguing about something. And I saw her nod at you when you picked up the box . . ."

"Clyde." He put his hand on my chin and tilted my head up so I had to look in his eyes. "I've been waiting for months to go away with you. And I want to spend as much time as possible with you when we get back. Nothing has changed."

"Even if I don't go back to the police force? Even if I use my psychic abilities?"

"What? Of course. The only reason I was arguing with my mother was because I wanted to wait to ask you to move in with me until I could do it the way I had planned." He turned away from me. "I wanted it to be romantic. On the beach, with the moon shining on the ocean, in a place far away from here."

"That sounds nice," I said.

"But, we aren't there. We're here and it doesn't matter because we're together."

"Well, then, yes. But I think I'll need to give you a key to my place instead."

He smiled and kissed me and from the other side of the door I heard, "I knew it!"